Aileen,
Thank you for everything!
Emma

Wings to Fly

Emma Mooney

Design: Bukovero.com
Editor: Sue Barnard

Wings to Fly: 978-1-911381-40-2

First Green Line Edition
Crooked Cat Publishing Ltd. 2016

To David, Andrew and Laura

Never let anyone clip your wings

Acknowledgements

My first thanks go to my family. It takes a lot of patience to put up with a writer in the house, yet you always stop and listen when I have a question, whether it's about a character, a scene I'm stuck on or if I want your opinion on the artwork for the cover. This book belongs to you guys too.

Thanks also to the amazing team behind Crooked Cat. In particular, I'd like to thank Steph and Laurence for their continued support and advice, and Sue Bernard for her input and her eagle-eyed editing skills.

The opening chapter in the book was written after listening to a friend recall a terrifying encounter with a snake in a stream when she was a young girl. Thank you, Lesley, for giving me permission to write about this. Along the way, I received support and encouragement, but mostly inspiration from fellow writers, Ellie, Grace, Sylvia and Mary. Thanks also to Liz, Carole, Laura and Lesley for taking the time to read the first draft. The story has come a long way since then, and I think you'll be as pleased with the end result as I am.

The idea behind *Wings To Fly* came from a project run by Glasgow Women's Library, which explored the issue of sectarianism in our society, and its impact on women. I'd like to take this opportunity to thank all of the women involved in the project. Whilst this book is a work of fiction, many of the scenes are based on events I experienced and witnessed growing up in Scotland in the 1980s. My hope is that women and men from all backgrounds read this book, and start a conversation.

It's important, when writing a novel, that as far as possible all facts are correct, and I'd like to thank Aileen and Hazel for answering my never-ending questions. Thanks also to all of my friends on social media who shared their memories of the 1980s, including their favourite pick 'n' mix sweet. My personal favourite is the fizzy cola bottle!

I'd also like to thank all of the readers who took the time after reading my debut novel, *A Beautiful Game*, to leave a review. It takes courage to release a second novel after such an overwhelmingly positive response, so please be gentle with me, and I hope you enjoy getting to know the characters in this book too.

And finally to all of my childhood friends who shared in the adventures growing up – I'd like to thank you for the laughter, the tears, and for keeping a whole bunch of secrets. It was fun!

Emma Mooney

About the Author

Emma Mooney grew up in Scotland in the 1980s and spent her Saturday afternoons in the record department, and the pick 'n' mix aisle of Woolworths. She's happy to admit she was once a Madonna fan, and owned a pair of black lace gloves and several oversized crucifixes.

Emma has completed courses in creative writing at both Glasgow and Edinburgh University, and this year she joins the MLitt Creative Writing programme at the University of Stirling.

This is her second novel and she hopes you enjoy reliving the 1980s as much as she did.

Find Emma at www.emmamooney.co.uk!

Also by Emma Mooney:

A Beautiful Game

Wings to Fly

There are
two gifts
we should give
our children.
One of these is roots,
the other,
wings.

~ *Hodding Carter (1953)*

Part One

1980

Stick to your own kind.

The Tunnel

Cathy feels her welly boots fill with water. Freezing cold water.

She stares in to the gaping mouth of the concrete tunnel, and thinks of the lion snarling and baring its teeth on the circus posters stuck up around town. She takes a deep breath, imagines she's the lion tamer, and steps inside.

The tunnel is some sort of large pipe, and she prays it's not a sewage pipe. Within a few metres it narrows and she has to stoop before she can go any further. It's cold inside. And dark. Her back scrapes along the concrete ceiling as she squeezes forward, and she's beginning to wish she's stayed at home and played with her Pippa dolls. She pauses and waits for her eyes to adjust, but very little sunlight reaches this far in.

The air in the tunnel smells bad, and she remembers last summer when her dad found the dead rat in the box of old *Reader's Digests* at the back of the garage. It'd been dead so long that maggots were crawling out of its eye sockets. Or at least that's what Jimmy told her. She hadn't been brave enough to look.

There's a flicker of movement ahead and she freezes. Any rats in here are still very much alive. She holds her breath and stares into the darkness.

The ball is lying a few metres away and she calculates she should be able to reach it within two or three more steps. Nearly got it, she tells herself, and slides one foot closer. The water ripples – but that's okay, it's just the movement of her foot. She lifts her other foot ready to step forward and grab the ball, but stops. Something is moving in the water in front of her. She's not alone.

Her screams bounce off the curved walls of the tunnel,

sending the creature into a frenzy as it whips its body towards her. She screams again and tries to turn around, but the pipe is too narrow. Thrusting her hands against the cold damp walls, she pushes backwards, but doesn't notice the rock on the ground behind her until it's too late and she tumbles down. Dirty water covers her, and she splutters and spits to try and clear her mouth. She grabs a corner of her t-shirt to wipe her face, and stops. There it is. In front of her. Two black eyes stare back at her out of the darkness. She needs to do something quick, something to scare it away before it swims towards her. Before it bites her, paralysing her.

She splashes the water with both hands but the snake doesn't move. She's trapped. The cold water wraps itself around her body, grips her tight and squeezes.

Keeping her thoughts focused on reaching the outside world, she scrambles backwards, barely noticing the tiny shards of gravel cutting into the heels of her hands. A glint of sunlight flashes on the ceiling, and she keeps pushing, kicking at the muddy water in front of her. She needs to get out of here before the creature makes its move.

'What the fuck are you doing? Where's my ball?'

Jimmy is behind her, shouting, but she doesn't take her eyes off the opening in front of her. The snake might appear any moment. A hand lifts her gently to her feet and leads her away, back to the piles of jumpers that are this afternoon's makeshift goalposts. She pulls her eyes away from the tunnel entrance and looks up to see her rescuer rummaging through one of the piles until he finds her blue hooded top.

Thomas.

'Here,' he says, and wraps it around her shoulders.

Jimmy appears back with the ball, and Thomas moves away. 'Got it,' Jimmy says, holding the ball up for everyone to see. 'Wasn't so fucking hard, was it? What's up with you?'

'There's a snake.'

The gang of boys all burst out laughing.

'A snake?' mimics Jimmy. 'In Scotland?'

'I saw it. It was in the tunnel.'

'You don't get snakes in Scotland. You're making it up.'

'Am not,' she shouts. Tears sting at the corners of her eyes and she squeezes them back in. There's no way Jimmy's friends are going to see her cry. They'll laugh at her and call her a sissy. But she's different. She'll show them that girls can be as brave as boys.

Jimmy's waving his hand about in front of her face. 'Och aye, I'm a Scottish snake.'

'Leave me alone,' she shouts. 'I know what I saw.'

But her brother's not going to give up so easily. He's enjoying the game.

'Or maybe it escaped from the circus. Maybe it disappeared through the sewer tunnels and swam all the way here. Oh, wait a minute though; snakes can't swim.'

A voice speaks up from the back of the group. 'Actually, you do get snakes in Scotland.'

Cathy turns to see who is brave enough to disagree with her brother. She's surprised to see it's her rescuer, Thomas O'Donnell.

'And snakes *can* swim.'

She could hug him right now. If he wasn't a boy.

Jimmy picks up a stick from the ground and steps towards Thomas.

'What would you know? All they teach you in that school is a load of mumbo jumbo. You know fuck-all.' He presses the stick into Thomas's chest and pushes him backwards. 'You're only here cos my mum said we had to bring you.'

Cathy watches Thomas walk away and wishes she could run after him, take his hand like he took hers and stand up to her brother. Thomas says there are snakes in Scotland, and she believes him. She doesn't think all the kids who go to that school are as stupid as Jimmy says.

The Blue Lady

Thomas lives in the house next door; the one with the neatly-clipped lawn and the pretty flowers. Cathy's dad says Mr O'Donnell spends all of his time in the garden so that he doesn't have to speak to his wife, but Cathy thinks Dad's just jealous because the O'Donnells have the best grass in the whole street. 'Don't know how he does it,' Dad says, 'but there's never a dandelion or daisy.' Cathy likes daisies, and thinks her next door neighbours are missing out. How do they ever make a daisy chain on a sunny day? Cathy loves making daisy chains.

She stands at her bedroom window and watches Mrs O'Donnell get into her car. She waits until she sees the car reverse out of the drive and disappear out of view, and then she races downstairs and slips into her wellies – they're quicker than her trainers.

'Cathy?' Her mum is in the kitchen.

'Back in a minute, Mum.'

She throws open the front door and runs across the lawn and up the path to Thomas's house. She bangs on the door and wishes he'd hurry up and let her in before any of the neighbours see her standing here. Thomas's mum doesn't approve of Cathy, and Cathy knows this. The children go to different schools and in Mrs O'Donnell's eyes that means they shouldn't be friends. Cathy thinks this is silly. Her heart is thumping so loudly she's sure everyone in the street can hear it.

She knocks again, louder this time. She's never been inside Thomas's house before, although she's often tried to imagine what it's like. Jimmy says Catholics own most of the world's treasures, and she wonders if the O'Donnells' house is filled with gold. Not that she thinks their television is gold (everyone knows the Queen is the only person in the world to have a gold television set) but she imagines the rooms are filled with lamps, ornaments and candlesticks all made of pure gold. She's tried going to his door a few times to ask him out to play, but she never gets to see inside and the answer is always no. *He's doing his homework. He's having his dinner. He's just about to have a bath.* At five o'clock? Who has a bath at five o'clock?

The front door opens a little way and his eye peers through the thin crack.

'It's me. Quick, let me in before everyone sees me standing here.'

'You? What are you doing here?'

'I saw your mum drive away.'

'And…?'

'And you promised I could see your Atari.' She sees him look past her and down the hill, double-checking his mum has gone. 'It'll only take a minute,' she says, but he still doesn't move. 'Are you going to keep me standing here all day where everyone can see me?'

This jolts him into action. 'Quick, go to the back door and I'll let you in that way.'

Cathy does as she's told and follows the path round the side of the house and into the back garden. Thomas is already waiting for her at the back door. She slips out of her wellies and enters the kitchen, knowing the cooker will be on her left next to the stainless steel sink which sits directly below the small square window that looks out onto the drying green. All of the houses in the street are laid out identically to her own.

She looks around at the bare walls feeling a wave of disappointment. There's not a speck of gold to be seen.

An alcove tucked into the right-hand side of the room is just wide enough to fit in a table and chairs, and in her own house everyone squeezes around a small pine table at meal times. Being the children, she and Jimmy have to sit in the seats next to the wall, even though he's now taller than

Mum and his head touches the ceiling.

She stares at the empty space. 'Where's your table?'

Thomas looks at her.

'Where do you eat?'

'In the dining room.'

She's not sure whether he's pulling her leg or not. Sure, they have a dining room too, but they only use it on Christmas Day. The rest of the year it's stacked high with all kinds of stuff: piles of papers waiting to be filed, old books and toys waiting to go to the charity shop, and, well, just stuff. The last time she looked there was a half-empty box of Christmas crackers that had missed the trip up to the attic in January, and a Scalextric set Mum had picked up in the sales. Too good a price to miss!

Cathy looks at Thomas. 'But where do you eat your breakfast?'

'In the dining room.'

She looks around at the rest of the kitchen but there's not much to see. There are no postcards, leaflets or pictures on the fridge door, no recipe books or Tupperware dishes cluttering the counter top.

'Can we go through to the living room?' She's guessing all of the gold will be in there.

'The living room? I thought you wanted to see my Atari.'

'Well, don't we have to go through the living room to get upstairs?'

'You know we do, your house is the same as ours.'

'Well,' she says, 'what are we waiting for? Let's go.'

Despite the warm sunshine outside, the living room is cold, and she shivers as she looks around her, inhaling the reek of furniture polish. Heavy velvet curtains hang at the window and several large pieces of dark furniture fill the room. Crocheted doilies cover the arm-rests of the sofa and chairs, and a team of shire horses stand proud on the mantelpiece. A framed photograph sits on the coffee table.

She picks it up and looks at the man and woman in the picture. They're standing in a church doorway, dressed for a special occasion, hands clasped neatly in front of them.

'Is this your grandparents?'

'Yeah.'

'Are they still alive?'

'Of course they're still alive.'

Her stomach squirms. 'Do you see them often?'

'Every Sunday in church. And then we go back to their house for lunch.'

'Every week?'

Thomas nods. 'And all my aunts and uncles come too, and my cousins.'

'Is there enough space for you all around the table?'

'Gran has a special table with sides that lift up to make it bigger.'

'How many of you are there?'

Thomas lifts up his fingers, loses count and starts again. 'Twelve.' He stares at his fingers as if to make sure.

Cathy tries to imagine what it must be like having twelve people eating all at once, and thinks it sounds fun. 'I wish I had cousins.'

A simple wooden crucifix is centred above the doorway, and above the mantelpiece hangs a painting of Christ unlike any she's ever seen before. His shirt is open to his waist, and his exposed heart is wrapped in thorns and is dripping blood. She can see the holes in his palms from the crucifixion.

'Why have you got that horrible picture in here?'

'It's an heirloom. It was my great-great-grandmother's.'

She steps forward to take a closer look, but Thomas interrupts her. 'We'd better hurry up before my mum comes home.'

Cathy could swear the eyes in the picture follow her as she leaves the room.

The hallway is even darker, and the wallpaper is a ghastly diarrhoea colour with so many swirls and loops that she feels sick just looking at it. A ceramic bowl filled with water is hanging on the wall by the front door, but before she can ask Thomas what it's for she sees that he's already making his way upstairs. Halfway up, the stairs turn and she stops to look out of the window that faces onto her own back garden. She blushes as she sees her white training bra hanging on the washing line. She must remember to ask her mum to dry her underwear in the airing cupboard.

She points to the porcelain figurine sitting on the windowsill.

'Who's this?'

The young woman is wearing a long robe with a flowing blue sash tied around her waist, and she has the most beautiful face Cathy's ever seen. Her eyes match the colour of the sash, and her skin is perfectly white with just a hint of pink on her cheeks.

'That's Our Lady.'

'Mrs O'Donnell?'

'No,' says Thomas impatiently. 'Mary.'

Cathy's not sure but she thinks Thomas's mother's first name is Theresa. 'Who's Mary?'

Thomas scowls at her. 'She's Christ's mother, the Virgin Mary.'

'Oh.' Cathy picks up the delicate figurine and a yellowed stain on the painted windowsill marks her place. She looks more closely at her face. 'Why does she look so sad?'

'How should I know? She always looks like that.' He snatches the figure from her hands and puts it back on the windowsill. 'Mum brought it back from Lourdes.'

'Lourdes?'

'It's a town in France.'

She waits for him to tell her more.

'Mary appeared there and spoke to a young girl in a cave.'

'And what's so special about that? I bet she spoke to lots of people.'

'She'd been dead for almost two thousand years.'

'You mean she was a ghost? Is the story true?'

'So they say.'

'But people can't come back from the dead and talk.'

'That's why everyone goes to visit it. Because it's a miracle.'

'A miracle?'

'Jeez, you really don't know anything. Now, are you coming or not?' He marches upstairs, but before Cathy follows she takes a moment to turn the figure around so that she's facing outside. Maybe now she'll smile.

Thomas's room isn't much different from her own. Her curtains are pink, his are blue. Her bedcovers have butterflies, his have footballs. Her room has a shelf filled with cuddly bears, his has a unit covered with Lego models. She slumps on to his bed and a glimmer of something sparkling catches her eye, and she sees a small gold cross pinned to the top of one curtain. It's the only gold she's seen so far. Other than the tiny decoration, this room is like Jimmy's was before he went to the academy. She's hardly ever allowed in Jimmy's room any more, but she knows his football posters have all gone and been replaced with giant pictures of Debbie Harry above his bed. She wonders if he kisses them. She thinks he does.

She turns around and there it is. Tucked in the corner of his room is the TV set. Thomas is the only person in the whole world she knows who has a television in his room. He's even got a special cabinet for it to sit on. Wait till she tells Jimmy she got a shot on an Atari. He'll be so impressed.

'Can we play a game?' she asks.

'It takes too long to set up. And my mum might be back any minute. She's just nipped out to the butcher's.'

'Please.' She's been practising batting her eyelids like Mrs Henderson does in front of the school minister, and she gives it a go.

'What's wrong? Have you got something in your eye?'

'I promise I'll disappear out of the back door as soon as we hear her car coming up the hill.'

He doesn't look convinced.

'I'll be over the fence before she even pulls into the drive.'

Jimmy won't be impressed unless she can tell him she got a shot. Batting her eyelids might not have worked, but she can think of something that will. She smiles at him.

'I'll let you kiss me.'

He leans forward and pulls out a box from beneath his bed.

'It takes a minute to set it up.' He slides the console out of the box and connects a cable to the small portable television. 'And it doesn't always work first time.' He pushes the knob on the front of the TV set, and they sit side by side on the edge of his bed watching the image on the screen slowly expand as the television set warms up.

'Our picture appears straight away,' she brags.

'Do you want to play or not?'

She sits quietly, waiting for the game to appear, and wonders when he'll make his move. She's never kissed a boy yet, but her best friend, Linda, says it tastes even better than Hubba Bubba. White lines appear on the screen building up the word *Pong* and Thomas turns a dial on the console and chooses *One Player*. A small square moves across the screen and, using the dial, he knocks it back to the other side of the screen where it then bounces back to his side again.

'Squash is the easiest game.'

She watches him play, mesmerised at how quickly he moves the racquet, and for now she forgets about the kiss. The square moves back and forth across the screen, beeping every time he intercepts it. It looks so easy.

'Can I get a shot?'

Thomas grins. 'Go for it.'

She nudges him out of the way and sits as close to the TV screen as she can. He hands her the console, but the 'ball' goes out of the screen before she can hit it back.

'That's not fair; you need to start a new game for me.'

He leans closer to flick a switch and she can smell his coal tar soap.

'Ready?' he asks. But she's struggling to concentrate. The game starts but she can't seem to turn the dial at the right time and keeps missing the ball.

Thomas laughs at her. 'Here,' he says, 'let's change it to

tennis. That way we can both play, and I've got a feeling I'm going to win.' He puts his hands on her shoulders and pushes her gently. Playfully. 'Budge over.' He laughs.

'Make me,' she squeals, and now he's tickling her and they're both laughing.

The bedroom door bursts open and Mrs O'Donnell stands in the doorway. Cathy doesn't remember her ever being so tall or so wide before. Her figure fills the whole frame and her face looks like it's about to erupt.

'You,' screams Theresa O'Donnell. 'Get out.'

These three words are all Cathy needs to hear, and she pushes herself to her feet and runs towards the door. At the last second Mrs O'Donnell steps aside to let her past, and Cathy bolts down the stairs two at a time and then stops. The Blue Lady has been turned back around to face indoors.

'No wonder you look so bloody miserable,' Cathy murmurs.

Behind her she can hear Mrs O'Donnell's screams. *Bringing a girl into your bedroom is a sin. And not just any girl but a Protestant girl.* She hears the slap and Thomas begins to cry. She knows there's nothing she can do and she should get out of here before he finds out she heard him crying, but she takes a moment to pick up the Blue Lady and slip her under her t-shirt. At least one of them can get out of this place.

Minnows

The key to the basement hangs by the back door, and Cathy has to stretch up on her tiptoes to reach it. The metal feels cold in her hand and she grips it tightly. It's another sweltering day and already she's feeling hot and sticky in her shorts and t-shirt. When she woke this morning a summer dress with pink and yellow flowers was laid out across the bottom of her bed, but Cathy ignored her mother's usual subtlety and chose a plain, navy blue t-shirt to go with her denim shorts. The dress is back in the wardrobe.

She stands frozen to the spot and waits for the sound of the hoover to start up again. When it does, she makes her move. She wants to be long gone before her mum notices she's missing. As usual, the lock to the basement sticks. Cathy jiggles the key from side to side, but it doesn't budge.

'Bloody hell,' she mutters. It's the strongest swear word she dares say, and she remembers the day she used it when she dropped a plate on her foot and her mum launched into a big lecture about why swearing isn't suitable for young ladies. She hadn't even bothered to ask Cathy if her toe was okay. But then her dad had interrupted, arguing that the word bloody wasn't really a bad word. She scribbled down the little rhyme he used so she could repeat it the next time she got into trouble for swearing:

Bloody's in the Bible, bloody's in the book.
If you don't believe me take a bloody look.

She's imagined using it in school, and has pictured Mrs Henderson's face a hundred times. Her head teacher is always getting them to recite the names of the books of the Old Testament in order.

Then the key turns with a jolt and she pushes open the heavy door to the basement. As she sneaks downstairs she tells herself there's no such thing as the bogeyman, but she still looks back over her shoulder. Just in case.

The glass jars are stored in a cupboard below the stairs, washed out and waiting, ready to be filled with this summer's homemade jam. Fresh labels are on the clean jars and a pile of carefully-cut waxed paper circles are stacked in preparation for a new batch. She ignores the niggle of guilt as she takes four jars, and promises herself she'll wash them out before returning them.

'I'm not stealing,' she whispers. 'I'm borrowing them.' She balances the jars carefully in her arms and closes the cupboard door after rearranging the other jars to conceal the fact some are missing.

Upstairs the hoover stops.

Cathy doesn't hang around. She disappears through the back door and climbs over the fence at the bottom of the garden before her mum can track her down and force her to wear a dress. She runs through the long grass, ignoring the thistles and barbs that scratch at her bare legs. They've arranged to meet at the tarzie swing at ten o'clock. She's already late, but Thomas is going to be proud of her when he sees she managed to get four jars. She runs over the last hill, her heart racing with excitement as she sees him leaning against the old horse chestnut tree.

'Told you I could get them,' she says, holding up the jars.

'I wasn't sure if you'd be on your own.'

'Jimmy's got a game on'

'I thought maybe some of the others might tag along.'

'None of them are my friends, they just put up with me cos I'm his wee sister. They probably can't even remember my name.' She hands him two jam jars. 'Here, you can help me carry these.'

He does as he's told and juggles the glass jars along with two fishing nets as they walk towards the burn. Cathy's practised what she's going to say next several times in front of the bathroom mirror, but now she's here it feels like someone's tied a knot in her tongue.

'I, erm…' she begins.

Thomas looks at her and her face burns scarlet.

'Erm, I…'

He's waiting for her to speak.

'I wanted to say thanks for sticking up for me the other day. You know, with the snake and everything, when everyone was laughing at me and thinking I was a baby for screaming over a snake and then they didn't believe me, and Jimmy was saying there's no such things as snakes in Scotland and then you told him there is and…' Oh God, she's prattling on. 'And well, anyway, I just wanted to say thanks.'

'Is that it?' Thomas asks.

She nods her head. She's already said more than enough.

'Okay, now let's get into the water and see what we can catch.'

She watches him strip off his shoes and socks and roll his jeans up past his knees, and she copies him. Next he strides out into the middle of the burn, but as her big toe touches the water she pulls it back.

'It's freezing,' she squeals, but Thomas ignores her. Sod it, if she wants to be treated like a boy then it's time she stopped crying just because the water's cold. She bites down on her lip and plunges her foot into the water. Unlike the gritty floor of the tunnel, the bottom of the burn is lined with soft mud. It feels like velvet against her skin.

She lifts her other foot and steps in. This time the cold water no longer takes her by surprise and she wriggles her toes deeper into the thick, oozy mud and imagines this is what stepping into melted chocolate would feel like.

'Keep still,' Thomas shouts. 'You're scaring all the minnows away.'

She does as he says and he passes her a net.

'The trick,' he tells her, 'is to keep the net side on and don't move a muscle. Then all you have to do is wait till the minnows swim to you.'

Again, she does what he tells her, but soon her arms are aching and she's struggling to keep the net still. She spies a large shoal of tiny fish out of the corner of her eye. She can easily catch them, there are hundreds of them. She waits until they swim a little closer and then… swoosh… she sweeps the net through the water and scoops it into the air in one clean move.

'Got some,' she yells and Thomas wades through the water to see her catch. She did it, she caught some baggies, and she's a girl. That'll show all the boys and she can't wait to tell them she caught them first. And she did it like a proper fisherman, not standing about waiting for the fish to come to her.

Thomas lifts her net up to the sun. 'It's empty,' he says, and walks back to his place upstream.

'It can't be,' she cries. 'There were hundreds of them, there's no way they all got away.'

'I told you, you've gotta wait till they swim to you.'

She wants to splash and kick her feet in protest. But Thomas is a statue again, staring at the net underneath the water, and she knows he might not invite her along again if she makes any more fuss.

The sun is directly above them now and she can see his bag of Maltesers on the bank, melting in the heat. Her feet are numb and she's not sure how much longer she can stand still like this. It must be nearly lunchtime and she's starving. She wishes he would hurry up and admit defeat, but the boy is unstoppable. He barely blinks. Maybe she should pretend to catch something again so she can move and then make some sort of excuse to get out of the water and back on dry land.

It turns out she doesn't need to do any of these things, because Thomas has landed a catch.

'Baggies,' he shouts. 'Hundreds of them. Quick, quick, grab the jars.' Cathy doesn't know which way to move. Her feet are stuck in the thick mud and she has to pull at her knees to lift them out of the water. 'Quick,' he shouts again, 'before they die in this heat.'

She splashes awkwardly to the edge of the burn and grabs a jam jar.

'I'll need them all,' he shouts. 'I'm telling you, I've caught hundreds.'

She grabs two jars and carries them to him.

'Fill them with water,' he shouts at her, and she wishes he'd stop being so bossy. She holds a jar under the water until it's half full, and then holds it out in front of her.

'Keep still,' he says, as if she doesn't know that already. Carefully he tips the net up at an angle and a ribbon of minnows flip and twist themselves downwards into their new home.

'Fill another,' he shouts, and she does as she's told, now caught up in the excitement of saving the fish before they dry up.

It takes all four jars before his net is finally empty. Cathy places them carefully on a flat patch of grass next to the burn and watches the tiny fish swim round in circles.

Thomas plonks himself on the ground beside her and puts his hand on her shoulder.

'They're ours,' he says, and she likes the way he says 'ours'. She can feel him staring at her but she can't take her eyes off the fish going round and round inside the jam jars. There's nowhere for them to hide from the bright sun so she lifts her hand to make a shadow.

'Do you think we should keep them?' she asks.

'Keep them? Of course we're going to keep them. We didn't stand in a bloody burn all morning just to throw them back in the water.'

She can't remember ever hearing Thomas swear before. 'I thought Catholics weren't allowed to swear.'

'Says who?'

'Well, won't you go straight to hell?'

'I'm still here, aren't I?'

'I didn't mean you'd go right this second, I mean when you die.'

'But I can go to Confession anytime I need to.'

‘Confession?’ She doesn’t know what he means.

‘Yeah, to absolve me of my sins.’

She looks at him, confused.

‘Never mind. Anyway my dad says bloody’s not a proper swear word.’ Thomas jumps up. ‘*Bloody’s in the Bible, bloody’s in the book. If you don’t believe me take a bloody look.*’ He finishes and throws himself back down beside her again. ‘There,’ he says. ‘That’s what my dad says.’

‘Mine too,’ she says, but Thomas isn’t listening.

‘Fancy a sweet?’ he asks.

‘They’re probably all melted.’

‘Won’t matter where they’re going,’ he says, and grabs the packet. He rips it open and they dip their fingers in the delicious, gooey mess.

They walk home together across the fields, fishing nets balanced over their shoulders, a jam jar in each hand.

‘Can you keep them at your house?’ Thomas asks her. She doesn’t need to ask why. If his mum finds out he’s been down the burn with Cathy he’ll be grounded for ever.

‘I could put them in the shed where there’s shade.’

He nods. ‘Good idea.’

The hay in the fields reaches above their waists and Cathy imagines they’re miles away from everything. ‘Why don’t we play at pirates?’ she suggests. She wants today to last forever.

‘Don’t be stupid, we’re miles away from the sea.’

‘Well, cowboys then.’

‘I need to get home before Mum gets suspicious. I told her I was at Declan’s house.’

‘Oh. Okay.’

They carry on in silence for a few minutes and Cathy wishes she could pluck up the courage to ask him about his mum. She wants to know why Mrs O’Donnell doesn’t let Thomas play with the other kids in the street, and she’s trying to think of a way to ask him when he grabs her arm and puts a finger to his lips. She understands immediately, and this time she has no problem keeping still. She looks at Thomas, but he’s staring straight ahead to where the tall grass is waving back and forth in the wind. Except there's no wind today.

'Someone's in there,' he whispers.

The grass shakes violently and this time she hears a girl cry out.

They put down their jars, and together they make their way forwards. The hayfield no longer feels like a playground.

A girl's scream fills the air and disturbs a group of crows on a tree in a nearby field. Cathy watches the birds circle overhead and remembers the word for a group of crows is a murder. *Murder*. A shiver runs down her spine. Why did she think of that word?

Another scream fills the air and Thomas leaps into action. Cathy watches as he lunges forward. All she can see is a flash of his red t-shirt as he disappears amongst the long grass, roaring like a Zulu warrior, with his spear, the blue fishing net, waving ferociously above his head.

The girl screams again, only this time Cathy recognises the cry of surprise, and the next thing she sees is Thomas running back out of the long grass.

'Pick up the minnows and run,' he shouts. She doesn't need to be told twice and she follows him back in the direction of the burn. As she looks back over her shoulder she sees a teenage boy standing on the flattened grass yelling and punching his fist in the air, his pants around his ankles. It's the first time she's seen a boy's willy since sharing a bath with her brother when they were both little, and it's not at all like she remembered. Jimmy's willy hung down, and was floppy. But this boy's is pointing upwards to the sky as though angry about something. She imagines the crows swooping down and pecking it off, and suddenly she's laughing and she can't keep running.

'Stop,' she shouts to Thomas. 'It's okay, he's not chasing us.'

'He might and he's bigger than us. He could catch us easy.'

'Not with his pants round his ankles,' she says, and bursts

out laughing.

Thomas starts to laugh too, and soon they're clutching each other in hysterics.

'Are the minnows okay?' Thomas asks once they get their breath back.

'They're fine.'

They flop down onto the grass and sit side by side in silence for a few moments before she dares to ask him what he saw.

Thomas blushes. 'I think they were at it.'

'It?'

'You know,' Thomas won't look at her. 'Having sex.'

'Oh.' Cathy doesn't really know about sex.

Silence.

'What were they actually doing?'

Thomas shrugs his shoulders. 'Not sure.'

'Were they kissing?'

'I suppose so.'

She thinks about the girl's screams. 'Do you think it hurts?'

'What?'

'Sex.' She pictures the boy's large, angry-looking willy.

'I don't know,' says Thomas.

Cathy watches the minnows swimming around inside the jam jar. 'I don't think I ever want to have sex.'

Thomas picks up his fishing net. 'The priest says you should only ever have sex to make a baby, otherwise it's a sin.'

'Couldn't you just go to Confession?'

He doesn't say anything.

'Can you have a baby by kissing?' she asks. Her best friend, Linda, kissed Richard Wilson behind the huts last week.

Thomas laughs, 'Of course not. My big cousin, Jeffrey, says a girl can't get pregnant as long as you do it standing up.'

Cathy looks back towards the field of hay. 'Were *they* standing up?'

Thomas shakes his head.

'Oh.'

Silence.

'Have you ever kissed a girl before?' she asks. Her heart is thumping so loudly she's sure he'll be able to hear it.

Thomas shakes his head again.

'Would you like to?'

This time he doesn't move.

'I'll let you kiss me if you want.'

Without a sound he moves around in front of her and rises up on his knees until they're almost touching. He leans forward a little and she does the same. Then he closes his eyes and she does the same. And then his wet mouth is touching hers and she thinks this is what it would be like if she kissed one of the minnows.

They pull apart and she opens her eyes and catches him wiping his lips on his t-shirt.

Jumping up, she picks up the jars of minnows and starts walking towards home. She looks back over her shoulder and sees Thomas is following a few paces behind.

'If you dare tell anyone about that, Thomas O'Donnell, I swear to God I'll kill you.'

Death on a Sunday Morning

Cathy closes her book and looks up at her bedroom window.

'You can't scare me, Jimmy. I know it's you.'

Her brother's been reading *Salem's Lot* and keeps teasing her about dead children coming and knocking on her window in the middle of the night when she's asleep. But it's not the middle of the night. It's half past eight in the morning and the sun streaming through her pink curtains gives her bedroom a warm, rosy glow. Surely dead children don't come to visit when the sun is shining.

The rattling on the glass comes again and she jumps out of bed and pulls her jeans and a jumper on over the top of her nightdress, and without stopping to think about it she marches across her bedroom floor and pulls open the curtains.

Thomas is standing on the path below with a handful of pebbles and when he sees her at the window his face erupts into a grin. She's surprised to discover this pleases her. She holds up a finger, indicating to him to wait a minute.

In fact, she makes him wait five minutes; enough time for her to change into clean clothes, fix her hair in the mirror and brush her teeth.

She sneaks out through the back door and meets him beside the clothes line.

'You look fancy,' she says. He's dressed in a dark blue suit with a white shirt and a red tie. 'Is it somebody's birthday?'

'I've got church in half an hour, but I wanted to check on the minnows before I go.'

'Isn't it a bit early for church?'

'I always go at this time,' he says. 'You just don't see me

because you're still in bed.'

She looks along the row of back gardens and sees Mrs Prentice from number thirty is hanging out the washing, and the twins from number thirty-two are already fighting over who gets next shot on the swing.

'How do you know I'm still in bed?'

'Because your curtains are shut. Now can we hurry up before my mum realises I'm missing and comes looking for me?'

'They're in the shed.' She runs ahead, eyes darting to check no one is watching them. The only window in his house overlooking her back garden is the one halfway up the stairs where the china figure used to stand. Has Mrs O'Donnell noticed it's gone yet?

'Come on,' she says, 'you can pass me down the key.' The key to the shed is tucked into a crevice above the door and Thomas stretches up on to his tiptoes to reach it. Cathy takes the rusted key from him and unlocks the door. She reaches in and pulls the cord. A bare bulb flickers but its light barely reaches the cobwebs in the corners.

'Dad put them in his big red bucket,' she says. 'The one he uses for washing the car.'

Mum had been furious when she saw the tiny fish in her precious jam jars, but Dad had stepped in and removed Cathy from the firing range of her mother's tongue. Like a magician he'd produced the big red bucket out of nowhere, and within minutes the minnows were in their new home, complete with some stones from the garden. He'd then turned to Cathy and held out the four jam jars, saying 'I think it's your job to wash these out.' But before she could take them from him, her mother had them cradled in her arms. 'You're kidding,' she'd snapped. 'I think Catherine has done enough damage for one day, don't you?' Her mother only ever calls her Catherine when she's angry with her. 'These will need to be boil-washed. Twice.'

'But what about the pond weed?' Thomas asks.

'Stop worrying,' Cathy says. 'I used the pond weed and the water from the jars to fill the bucket.'

Thomas laughs. 'And did you give them names too?'

She ignores his teasing and leads the way inside into the musty-smelling shed.

'They're over here under the window so they'll get some daylight.' She pushes her way past an old wheelbarrow and stacks of forgotten plant pots, and there, standing in a thin beam of early morning light, is the red bucket. Cathy looks down and lets out a strangled mewing sound. Her head swims and she reaches out for Thomas. The minnows are lying belly-up in the water, blood oozing out from their bloated bodies. Each one is dead.

Tears come and there's nothing she can do to stop them. She waits for Thomas to tease her, but he slips his arm around her shoulders and holds her tight.

He bows his head and begins to whisper something under his breath. Cathy recognises it from the end of term visits to the local church. She wishes she could join in, but she doesn't know the words so she waits till the very end and mumbles *Amen.*

'We killed them,' she says.

He doesn't disagree.

The window in the small kitchen is open wide in the hope of catching a breeze, but the net curtain hangs motionless in the thick, heavy air. Cathy can't remember a summer like it, but her mum and dad keep talking about the summer of '76 when, according to them, it got so hot the tar in the streets melted and stuck to your shoes. Cathy thinks they're exaggerating.

She grabs another handful of strawberries from the punnets stacked on the counter top next to the sink. Making jam is her mum's way of distracting her from thinking about the dead minnows, and Cathy's grateful to her. The fruit is warm and soft in her hands, and pink juice trickles between her fingers and down her arm. She laps up the sticky sweetness and imagines this is what Heaven must taste like. She drops the fruit into the strainer and pummels it with water from the cold tap. But today even the water from the cold tap is warm.

Mum passes her an ice cube from the freezer. 'Suck it,' she tells her. 'It's the only way to cool down in this weather.'

Cathy closes her eyes and sucks the ice cube but it soon melts, leaving her feeling hotter than ever. So she goes back to work, using her thumb nail to scoop out the stalks. 'Better that than using a knife,' Mum has told her. 'If you use a knife you'll lose half the fruit.'

Cathy waits till her mum's not looking and sneaks a strawberry.

'Here, pass me one,' Mum says.

Cathy grins and pops the largest one she can find into her mum's mouth. She giggles as strawberry juice dribbles down her chin.

A big, fat bee buzzes in through the open window and lands on the top punnet. Cathy shouts, 'Shoo!' and bats it with the tea towel, but the bee refuses to move. Mum picks up a small strawberry, squeezes it gently and places it on the windowsill. Cathy watches as the bee finds the fruit.

'Now let's get this fruit ready and into the pan before we melt.'

'Who taught you how to make jam?' Cathy asks. 'Was it your mum?'

The room suddenly feels too big for just the two of them and she wishes she'd kept her mouth shut. *The Golden Hour* continues playing from the transistor in the corner but the music fails to fill the empty space around them. Without saying a word they stand side by side and continue to rinse and chop the swollen pounds of fruit.

Living Doll comes on the radio and Mum dashes across the room and cranks the volume up. Cathy watches her pick up the wooden spatula, pretending it's a microphone.

'My granny had the biggest crush on Cliff Richard and always said he wrote this song for her.'

Cathy's never heard her mum talk about her granny before.

The song finishes and the fruit is finally ready. Mum

scrapes the strawberries into the giant pan with the wooden spatula.

Cathy dares to ask another question. 'Was it your granny who taught you to make jam?'

Mum smiles. 'She made jam out of every fruit imaginable: strawberries, raspberries, gooseberries, and when it was the end of summer we'd go gathering brambles.' She points at Cathy's red thumb. 'By the time we arrived home we'd have bright red hands and sore tummies from eating the fruit along the way.' She taps the side of the pan with the wooden spatula.

'This jam pan right here belonged to Granny.'

Cathy looks at the enormous silver pot sitting on the hob. She never knew there were things in the house that belonged to her mum's family. She looks around the kitchen. Does anything else in here belong to Granny? She pictures an old woman standing beside her at the sink in a yellow and blue apron and, when she closes her eyes to help conjure up the image, she can almost feel the weight of Granny's hands on her shoulders as she scoops out the green stalks. *Better that than using a knife.*

At last it's time to add the sugar. This is Cathy's favourite bit.

'This room is about to get a whole lot hotter,' Mum says as the strawberries in the pan start to boil. 'Maybe not the best day for making jam.'

'Imagine it on bread, Mum.'

'Or scones,' Mum adds.

'Or on a teaspoon straight from the jar.'

'Hungry?' Mum asks.

'Starving!'

They stand over the pan and watch as the perfectly white granules of sugar turn candy-floss pink.

'Can I stir it?' Cathy asks, but she knows the answer will be no. Mum never lets her stir the jam because it's too dangerous. If any spills it'll scald her.

'Why not?' Mum says. 'As long as you're careful.'

Cathy grips the long wooden handle tightly.

'You're fine,' Mum says and gently guides her hand as she stirs the giant pot of bubbling sweetness. The smell clings to her clothes and her hair and she can almost taste the air.

'Is it nearly ready?' she asks.

Mum laughs gently. 'You know it won't be ready for hours yet.'

Lunch is a plain cheese sandwich, no crusts, no butter. Just the way she likes it. Sometimes she has to eat it with the crusts on, but today the sun is shining and Mum's in a good mood. They take their plates of sandwiches outside and sit on the back step. Cathy watches her mum take a bite of her cheese sandwich then lean back and close her eyes.

'Mum, what was your granny like?'

Mum opens her eyes and stares off into the distance. Maybe she shouldn't have asked.

'Wait here,' Mum says and disappears indoors.

She reappears a few minutes later clutching an old black-and-white photograph. 'Here,' she says. 'This is a picture of me as a baby in Granny's arms.'

Cathy looks at the woman in the photograph. She's wearing a floral dress and looks dressed for a special occasion. 'Do you remember her?'

'Like it was yesterday.

'She looks nice. I like her smile.'

Mum smiles and Cathy thinks she sees the family resemblance.

'She was nice,' Mum says. 'Every Sunday afternoon she'd make a big meal for everyone, and the children would always have to eat first because there wasn't enough space for everyone round the kitchen table. She'd make us mince and tatties because that was our favourite, and it was the one day of the week I didn't have to eat my veg. Granny would tell Mum that we'd been good all week and therefore we could miss out on eating our greens on a Sunday.'

Cathy stares at her mum. She always makes her eat her veg. No excuses.

'We'd all sit round the table and Granny would chat to us about our week while she whisked the Yorkshire puddings to go with the roast. She was the only one who stayed in the kitchen and talked to us while we ate our dinner. All the other grown-ups would disappear into the living room.'

'Did I ever meet her?'

Her mum shakes her head. 'She died before you were born.'

'Oh.' She looks at the woman in the photo with the nice smile and wishes she'd had the chance to meet her. Just once. 'So she never knew I was born.'

'Of course she did.'

'How?'

'Because she watches over you from Heaven.'

'But Dad says there's no such thing as Heaven. We all turn back to molecules of carbon after we die.'

'Well, maybe your body does, but what about your soul?'

Her soul? Nobody has ever spoken to her about her soul before. 'Do animals go to Heaven?'

'I don't see why God wouldn't welcome all of his creatures.'

Cathy smiles as she pictures the minnows swimming in a crystal clear pond in Heaven, the sun sparkling on the surface. Mum has gone quiet, and Cathy's worried she's going to take the photograph away before she gets to find out more. She points to the blurred image of a young girl in the background.

'Who's that?'

'That's my big sister.'

Cathy's confused. Her mum has never mentioned she has a big sister before. 'What's her name?'

'She was called Catherine.'

Butterflies dance around in her tummy. She didn't know she was named after someone and it makes her feel special.

'Have I ever met her?'

She can feel her mum tense beside her.

'She died before you were born. They all did.'

The Circus

Thomas is already at the lamp post on the corner by the time she arrives. 'Thought I'd better leave the house at least ten minutes before you, so my mum wasn't suspicious.'

'Where does she think you are?'

'I've told her I'm going over to Declan's. His mum works and is never in so I know Mum can't go asking her any questions.' He looks proud of himself.

'You got my note?'

'I'm here, aren't I?'

Cathy punches him on the arm. 'No need to be smart.'

'So what's your big plan this time?'

'Thought you'd have worked it out if you're so smart.'

He looks offended and she grabs him by the arm.

'Follow me.' They start walking towards the park on the edge of town, and the flag on the top of the red and white striped tent is soon visible.

Thomas stops and looks at a poster on a lamp post. 'Is this where we're going?'

Cathy nods.

'But I've not got any money on me. And besides the show doesn't start till seven o'clock and it's only half past five just now.'

'Linda says there's a gap in the fence around the back, and she and Rachel Jones sneaked through it last night and went to see all of the animals in their cages. She said nobody's around at this time because they're all getting ready in their caravans, putting on their costumes and make-up and stuff.'

There are posters all over town, but this one shows a lady in a fancy sequinned costume doing a handstand on the back of a white horse.

'Who cares about seeing some stupid horses?' says Thomas.

'Linda says they've got elephants.'

This grabs his attention. 'Elephants?'

'And a lion.'

'From Africa?'

'Wanna see it?'

Thomas clearly can't resist the chance of seeing the exotic animals, because they're soon walking around the outside of the chain-link fence looking for the gap Linda told Cathy about.

'Are you sure she wasn't winding you up?' he asks.

Cathy gives him a dirty look. Linda White has been her best friend since their first day at primary school.

There's no one hanging about inside the fence, but she still doesn't want to be here much longer. She's sure someone will spot them and call the police.

And then she sees it. A small break in the fence at ground level. She reaches down and pulls back the twisted wire, but it doesn't give easily and cuts in to the palm of her hand. She bites down on her bottom lip to distract herself from the pain and pulls harder until the gap opens enough for her to squeeze through.

She bends down and wriggles through the tiny space. She's almost through when something catches and she can't go any further.

'Wait,' hisses Thomas. 'Your jacket's caught on the wire.'

'Hurry up! Someone will be along any minute and I'm stuck.' A dog barks somewhere nearby.

'If you'd stay still.'

'I *am* staying still. That's the problem, I can't move.' Her hand is bleeding now and she sucks it hard to try and get it to stop. She feels him pulling at her jacket and then, suddenly, she's released like the cork from Jimmy's old pop gun and comes out on the other side of the fence.

'Come on,' she urges. 'As quick as you can before

someone finds us.'

Thomas climbs through the gap with ease and Cathy watches in disbelief. How does he manage to do everything so easily? Why couldn't it have been her who caught the minnows, and why did she have to be such a girl and cry in front of him when they found them dead in the bucket?

Life's not fair when you're a girl.

She jumps up before he can take the lead and he follows her through a maze of generators, trailers and caravans to the back of the site where the animal cages are kept.

'What do we say if someone finds us?' he asks.

'Say?'

'Yeah, do we pretend we're looking for the ticket office, or do we say we're here for the next show?' He looks at his watch. 'Although I'm not sure they'd believe that one, it's still another hour until people will start arriving.'

'We don't stop to say anything. We run as fast as we can back to the hole in the fence.' She points behind her, but she's no longer sure where the way out is.

The trailer in front of them has a picture of a lion on the side, painted inside a ring of fire with its mouth stretched wide open like the lion in the MGM films they go to see at the matinees on Saturday mornings. Thomas nudges her in the ribs.

'I'm guessing the lion's inside there.'

Cathy looks at the trailer. It seems too small to keep a lion in, especially a lion that's come all the way from Africa.

'Look,' he whispers, 'the side panel lifts up. But it's locked.' He points to a row of padlocks running along the bottom of the trailer. The excitement she was feeling earlier is slipping, and a knot tightens in her stomach as she imagines the lion kept inside. In the dark.

'Over here. I've found the elephants.'

In the furthest corner of the park is a giant tent. The once-white tarpaulin is now dirty grey, and heavy-duty metal poles hold the enormous guy ropes in place. Thomas is already there, standing guard at the entrance, waiting for her to catch up with him.

'Wait till you see inside,' he says.

She steps towards him, but the smell of urine forces her to stop and cover her mouth with her sleeve.

Thomas laughs. 'Stinks, doesn't it?'

She nods. She doesn't want to open her mouth and let the smell in.

He gestures with one hand for her to join him, and she's unsure now she wants to see what's kept hidden within this giant tent. Thomas slips inside leaving her standing outside by herself, feeling exposed.

She edges her way towards the tent, all the time listening carefully for any sound that will let her know someone is coming. But the place is deserted. When she watched the vans roll into town a few days ago, she'd pictured the circus as one giant happy family with jugglers practising non-stop and clowns showing off their tricks to the children in the group. But this place is like a ghost town, and the animal enclosures are eerily quiet.

'Hurry up.' Thomas reappears at the tent's entrance.

The stench inside hits the back of her throat and she pinches her nose to stop herself from vomiting. Straw and sawdust are scattered sparsely across the bare earth and her eyes are drawn to a large, metal ring which has been hammered into the ground. Attached to the ring are three separate chains, each one leading to an elephant.

'There's three of them,' she says.

'Big, aren't they?'

'Big? They're enormous. No, bigger than that, they're gigantic.'

'Humongous,' says Thomas.

'Humongous,' she repeats. She's forgotten about the smell as she stares at the magnificent creatures standing in front of her. Each elephant is tethered by an individual chain connected to the central ring. 'Can't they just pull that out of the ground?'

'Don't be daft,' says Thomas. 'Look. Their legs are chained up too.'

Cathy looks more closely and sees that around the ankles of each elephant are a series of linked chains that prevent the animal from moving more than a couple of steps, and she's reminded of the links Jacob Marley forged for himself in *A Christmas Carol*. She looks into the eyes of the nearest elephant.

'But what have you ever done wrong in life, eh?'

The elephant looks back at her with heavy eyes. Her mum said that God would welcome all of his creatures into Heaven, but if that's true, then what kind of God would let them suffer like this?

'Let's get out of here,' she tells Thomas, and he looks at her in bewilderment.

'But we've only just got here.'

'I think I can hear dogs. Someone's coming.' She doesn't wait for him to say anything else but turns on her heels and leaves the tent. She rushes past the other enclosures, barely noticing the pictures on the side of the trailers.

Thomas runs after her. 'Are you okay?'

'Just didn't want to put up with that disgusting smell a second longer.'

'Yeah, I know what you mean,' Thomas says. 'But it was worth it. Tomorrow you can tell Linda you saw the elephants.'

Cathy doesn't answer. But she knows she'll never speak to anyone about what she saw inside that tent.

Tupperware Party

In the safety of her bedroom, Cathy pushes a box of old toys in front of the door before reaching in to the back of her wardrobe and bringing out the small package wrapped in newspaper. She hasn't dared to take her out before now, and her fingers tremble as she lifts the fragile china figurine and holds her in her hands. She's even more beautiful up close, and Cathy absorbs every detail, from the intricate gold edging around her robe to the waves of brown hair, swept back from her face. The wide sash around her waist is a shade of blue that reminds Cathy of the bluebells which grow beneath the horse chestnut tree each spring. The figurine holds her hands together in prayer, and Cathy wonders what she might be praying for.

She places the statue on her desk and takes out her sketch pad from the drawer. She sharpens her pencil, removes a clean sheet of paper from the pad and begins to draw faint lines, starting with the robe and slowly adding in detail.

'Thomas says you're the Virgin Mary, but if it's okay with you I'll call you Mary.'

The figurine doesn't answer.

'I guess you're shy. That's okay because I'm shy too. My mum says everyone's shy inside but I don't think I believe her. My best friend Linda's never shy. She talks to all the boys.'

Cathy stops and thinks for a second before continuing…

'Can you keep a secret, Mary?'

No answer.

'Good. Last week Linda told me she kissed a boy. Properly. Richard Wilson. Well, sometimes we play Kiss, Cuddle, Torture in the playground at lunchtime, but nobody's ever admitted they've kissed before, not properly. If a boy catches you, you have to choose kiss, cuddle or torture, and all the girls pick torture because they know the boys don't ever really hurt you. When it's our turn to chase the boys we always run away when they choose kiss. But last week Linda disappeared behind the huts with Richard Wilson, and when they came back out they were both red in the face. Linda told all the girls that it was a proper kiss cos he'd put his tongue in her mouth.' Cathy looks away. 'I don't think I ever want a boy to put his tongue in my mouth.'

Mary remains silent in her spot on the desk.

'So if you're Jesus's mother, does that mean I can give Confession to you? I've thought about going to the chapel, but the priest would know I'm not Catholic and would have me thrown out. But you look nice; you've got a kind face. I don't think you care whether I'm Catholic or Protestant. That's what Mrs O'Donnell called me. A Protestant girl. That's what they call those of us who don't go to the Catholic school.

'Anyway, because I can't go to the chapel I thought I could confess my sins to you. I hope you don't mind. And I'm new to it, so you'll have to be patient with me because I've probably got a lot of catching up to do.'

She puts down her pencil and stares at the china figurine, not sure where to start. Should she tell her about the time she took an Opal Fruit out of the big bag of sweets her neighbour, Mrs Prentice, brought with her the last time she came to babysit? Mrs Prentice is the street gossip and she loves nothing more than sharing a juicy bit of scandal, and Cathy's worried that she's just waiting for the right time to tell her mum about the stealing. Every time Mrs Prentice comes over, Cathy sits in her bedroom waiting for her mum to give her a row for being a thief. Although technically she wasn't stealing, as the sweets were for her anyway. Well, her and Jimmy. Still, she should have waited until she'd been offered, and she remembers the look on her neighbour's face when she caught her with her hand in the bag.

Cathy decides the story of the Opal Fruits can wait till another day. If she dies in her sleep tonight she doesn't think God will stop her getting into Heaven just because she stole a sweet. No, it's important to deal with the more serious sins first. She clears her throat before beginning, and tries to remember what Thomas told her about Confession.

'Dear Mary, please forgive me for my sins. I am guilty of murder.'

She looks up at the ceiling, half-expecting a bolt of lightning to come crashing down from above. But it doesn't appear. The sun goes on shining and the world keeps spinning. She waits until she's sure nothing's about to happen before continuing. She thinks of telling Mary about how she and Thomas were fishing for minnows, but it occurs to her that God might keep a record and if Thomas hasn't confessed yet then she might be getting him into trouble. She decides to play it safe and keep him out of it. Just in case.

'I murdered some fish. Caught them in a net but instead of letting them go back into the river I carried them home in jam jars.' Should she confess to taking the jam jars without her mum's permission? But her mum has already punished her for that one, so it probably doesn't count. Done the crime, done the time. She decides to ask Thomas next time she sees him. 'I put them in a big red bucket and when I came down the next day the water had turned to blood.' She looks out of the window. 'They were dead.'

What happens now? Is she forgiven?

And then she hears the answer. The Virgin Mary is talking to her, like she did with the girl in the cave, and it becomes clear. The Blue Lady is showing her the way to Heaven.

The doorbell rings. Cathy runs downstairs and opens the door to find Thomas standing on the doorstep, holding both hands behind his back. 'Guess what I've got?'

She glances sideways and sees that Mrs O'Donnell's car

isn't parked in the driveway next door. 'No idea.'

'I said guess.'

'Just tell me.'

'But you're supposed to guess.'

She's not in the mood for childish games. 'A bus.'

Thomas looks annoyed. 'A bus? How can I possibly hold a bus behind my back? That's a stupid answer. Guess again.'

'A tarantula?'

'You're being silly on purpose. Now last guess, and make it a good one.'

'I give up.'

Thomas flaps two pieces of paper above his head. 'I've got two tickets for the circus. Now we can go for real and see the elephants without having to crawl through a gap in the fence. And this time we'll get to see the lion too.'

Cathy pictures the three elephants tethered to the bolt in the centre of the hard ground. She remembers the expression in their eyes, and has to fight to stop herself from crying again. How can it possibly be right to keep such beautiful creatures in chains?

'I can't go,' she says.

'What? But why not? They leave town tomorrow and you've been desperate to go.'

Cathy's glad they're leaving tomorrow. She feels sick every time she thinks about those poor animals locked up. The cut on her palm has turned a deep shade of purple, but she refuses to clean it. If the elephants have to put up with the pain from being kept in shackles and chains, then she, Catherine Munro, can put up with the pain from a tiny scratch. She read somewhere that some priests inflict pain on themselves to remind them of the pain Jesus suffered on the cross, and now she thinks she understands why they do it.

'My mum's having a Tupperware party tonight, and I promised her I'd help out.' This is actually the truth, and she's relieved she doesn't have to lie to Thomas. If she lied to him she'd have to tell the Blue Lady, and she's already got a long list of things to confess to.

Thomas isn't giving in that easily. 'If you tell your mum you've got tickets to the circus then I'm sure she'll let you out of it. She knows how much you want to go. Think about it, Cathy. A real live lion jumping through fire. In front of you. And you'd be able to tell Linda you'd been. Picture her face.'

'I've told you, I can't go. Now stop asking me.'

He looks hurt, and she wishes she could tell him the truth. Tell him how she can't stop thinking about those big, sad eyes. But if she tells him this he'll think she's like all the other girls. Soft. So instead, she watches him turn away and walk down her garden path clutching two tickets to the cruellest show on Earth.

'Was that Thomas?' Her mum appears behind her with a yellow duster in her hand, and Cathy nods. 'What did he want?'

'Nothing much.'

Her mum hands her the duster. 'You can make a start in the living room.'

By seven-thirty, everything is set up and ready for their guests' arrival: chairs are lined up around the edge of the living room wall, and the kitchen table has been carried through and placed in the middle of the room. A red and white checked tablecloth covers the scorch mark from Jimmy's chemistry set, and in the centre of the table, in pride of place, sits a peculiar hedgehog-like creation. As usual, Mum got the idea from one of her magazines. This time a giant baking potato wrapped in kitchen foil has been skewered with dozens of cocktail sticks, each displaying a bland pattern of pickled onions and cheese cubes. It looks ridiculous, but her mum seems pleased with it. Peanuts and mini-sausages are laid out at various points around the room. All in Tupperware tubs – of course!

The Blue Lady is hidden away at the back of Cathy's wardrobe again, and she'll probably not get a chance to take her out until after everyone's gone home. Knowing her mum's Tupperware parties, that might be very late. She's tempted to have a quick look now, but what if her mum was to come into her room? She could never explain how she came to have a stolen china figure of Jesus's mother tucked away at the back of her wardrobe. She could say she found it, but her mum would never believe that. She wonders if it's worth a lot of money, not that she plans to sell it. She didn't steal it for the money. She never intended to steal it in the first place, and maybe she should take it back before Mrs O'Donnell notices it's missing. But how can she do that? She thought about waiting for Thomas coming home from school and slipping it into his satchel while he's not looking. That might work – but what would he think if he finds the Virgin Mary in his bag? And, worse, what if she got broken?

Like a bizarre game of Ker-Plunk, she pulls a cocktail stick from one side of the hedgehog and slides the pickled onion from the bottom of the stick. She doesn't like cheese.

'I'm telling mum.'

She nearly chokes on the onion as it goes down her throat in one piece. Jimmy is standing in the doorway watching her as she forces the cocktail stick (now only containing a single lump of cheddar) back into the silver foil body.

'You can't do that,' he says.

'Watch me.'

'Mum will kill you if she finds out.'

'If you grass on me then I'll tell Mum what really happened to her crystal vase.'

'You wouldn't dare.'

'Don't think she'll be too happy when she hears you've been playing football in the living room.'

'You were there too.'

'Only cos you made me go in goals.'

Jimmy shoves his hands deep into his pockets, and she knows that this time she's won.

'Pass me a sausage then,' he says.

'I can't.'

'What do you mean you can't? If you had a pickled onion

then I can have a sausage.'

'Help yourself.'

'Pass me one.'

'I've already told you. I can't.'

'What do you mean you can't? They're right there in front of you.'

'I'm vegetarian.'

'Vegetarian? Since when?'

'Since I decided that I don't want to be responsible for the death of any more innocent animals.'

'Holy shit, you're nuts! Does Mum know about this?'

'Not yet.'

'And what do you think she's going to say when she finds out?'

'It's my decision. There's nothing she can do about it.'

Jimmy shakes his head and grabs a handful of sausages from the Tupperware tub on the table.

'Anyway, where is she?' he asks. 'Shouldn't she be ready by now?'

But before Cathy can answer, the doorbell rings. They stand in the middle of the living room, staring at each other.

The bell rings again, twice this time.

'Quick, you run upstairs and let Mum know that the first guest has arrived and I'll answer the door.' Cathy knows the routine off by heart: offer to take the jacket, show them into the living room, and get them a drink and a 'nibble'. Coats will go upstairs on the bed in her mum and dad's room, and paper plates are laid out in the kitchen, napkins to the side.

She watches Jimmy run upstairs, and feels a twist of resentment tighten in her chest. It's not fair; just because he's a boy he doesn't have to help out. He gets to sit in his room all night and listen to his music, as long as he doesn't play it too loud. Dad's already disappeared for the night and won't be seen again until everyone's gone home. And yet she has to hang around, filling up everyone's wine glasses and offering salted peanuts from a Tupperware bowl. Like she says, not fair!

Cathy knows who is on the other side of the door before

she even opens it. Mrs Prentice from number thirty is always the first to arrive. Mum says she's just trying to catch them out. Cathy opens the door and stares at the fur jacket, trying to work out how many poor rabbits died to make it.

'Aren't you going to offer to take my coat?' asks Mrs Prentice, and Cathy holds out her hand. The fur coat is heavy in her arms, and she wonders if rabbits have souls.

'Make sure you look after it,' snaps Mrs Prentice, and looks around in the hope that someone is listening. 'It cost me a small fortune, you know.'

Cathy gets the impression she's supposed to say something at this point, but she doesn't care. She struggles to open the door to the living room with the fur coat in her arms, and she wishes her mum would hurry up.

'I'm not early, am I?' Mrs Prentice makes an exaggerated show of looking at her watch. 'Isn't your mother ready for us yet?'

Cathy has no idea what's taking her mum so long, she's usually ready early, hopping nervously around the door waiting for people to arrive.

The doorbell rings again, saving Cathy from having to answer Mrs Prentice's question. She throws the fur coat over the banister and opens the door to a young woman she's never met before. If she had, she'd remember. This woman is younger than her mum and is possibly the most beautiful woman she's ever seen in real life. She's not beautiful in the way the Blue Lady is beautiful. No, this woman is beautiful in a Farrah Fawcett kind of way. Her blonde hair is flicked backwards to reveal her shimmering face. Cathy looks closely and is sure she sees glitter on her skin. Even her lips are sparkling, and she wonders if Linda's got any lip gloss like it. She decides to ask her next time she sees her.

The shimmering lady isn't wearing a coat, so Cathy shows her straight through to the living room and seats her beside Mrs Prentice, who stabs the newcomer with a look that's definitely not friendly. Mrs Prentice turns to Cathy.

‘Does your mother know we’re here?’

‘I’ll go check.’

She leaves the two women together in the living room and runs up to her mum’s room, two stairs at a time. She wants to get back downstairs quickly, so she can offer the shimmering lady a drink of Babycham and some cheese cubes. Maybe she should sit beside her and keep her company; after all she’s probably closer in age to her than any of the other women that’ll be coming tonight. She wonders what her name is, and guesses it’s something exotic. After all, she looks like a model.

Upstairs, Jimmy has already retreated to his room and the bass notes of *Heart of Glass* are reverberating through the walls. She bets if he knew there was a model downstairs he’d be falling over himself to help, and she can’t wait to see his face when she tells him in the morning. She smirks as she walks past his shut door and makes her way to her mother’s room. Mum’s been in there for over an hour, and Cathy’s beginning to get worried, but just as she reaches out for the handle the door is thrown open and her mum rushes out of the room and collides with her. She’s tried her best to hide it with make-up, but her eyes are puffy and red and she’s missed a streak of blue mascara that’s still smudged in one corner. Cathy doesn’t know what to say.

‘Everything ready?’ Mum asks in a chirpy voice that’s so fake it’s embarrassing. Thankfully, she isn’t expecting an answer, and instead turns on her heels and heads downstairs in a cloud of perfume. Cathy looks back and reaches out to close the door, but something catches her eye. The photograph of her mum as a baby in her grandmother’s arms is tucked in to the edge of the mirror that stands on her mum’s bedside table.

Cathy gets a queasy feeling in her stomach. Could the picture have something to do with why her mum is so upset?

Before she can give it any more thought, the doorbell rings again. She’s kept busy for the rest of the evening – collecting coats, pouring drinks, serving nibbles, refilling drinks, serving more nibbles. She watches through the kitchen hatch as her mum delivers her spiel on the many different ways the range of Tupperware can be used. 'Versatile' is the word she uses to describe it, and Cathy likes that word. Her mum has performed the routine many times before and she knows how to work her audience. Tonight, many of the women will go home with more tubs and containers than they can possibly need, and, hopefully, her mum will make enough money for the new pair of trainers that she's been pestering her for. Watching her now, Cathy wonders if she imagined the flustered, puffy-faced woman who came crashing out of the bedroom earlier.

'Trust me,' her mum whispers, and everyone is hanging on her every word. From her vantage point, Cathy can see the women gazing at her mother with a sense of wonder. It's as though a spell has been cast on everyone in the room. Everyone, that is, except Mrs Prentice, who is sitting bolt upright on a dining room chair, arms folded across her chest, and lips pursed tightly together in a way that reminds Cathy of a dog's bum.

'Once you've bought this milk container for your fridge you'll wonder how you ever managed to live without it.'

'A milk container,' Mrs Prentice repeats loudly. 'Huh, who needs a milk container?'

Cathy watches her mum and sees the corner of her mouth twitch ever so slightly, and then it's gone, and she carries on as if Mrs Prentice hadn't said a word.

'We all know how important it is to clean the door of our fridge; I know it's a job I have to do at least once a week.'

The other women all nod in agreement. Cathy knows her mother hardly ever cleans the fridge door, but she sees what she's doing. If any of the women admit that they never clean their fridge door then that would be like admitting you don't wash your hands after you've been to the toilet. And nobody's going to admit that, although Cathy secretly doubts grown-ups wash their hands as often as they say they do.

'And why does the door get so filthy?' She produces a

bag from under the table and pulls out a pint of milk like a magician revealing a rabbit from a top hat. Ta-da! 'Look at the bottom of this milk bottle.' She holds the bottle on one side for inspection. 'The dirt from your doorstep will be transferred directly to your fridge if you're not careful. And think of the germs and bacteria.' She shudders for effect and then quietly adds, 'On the other hand, it doesn't bear thinking about.' She pauses. 'Does it?'

A silence fills the room and Cathy can almost see the women's minds filled with pictures of evil bacteria and killer germs. Her mum is a genius. She too is watching the women in the room, and Cathy knows she's about to play her trump card. Luckily for them, the milk container is on offer for tonight only. No sick kiddies in their street.

Just as Mum's about to seal the pitch, Mrs Prentice speaks up.

'Never heard such nonsense.'

'We don't all have time on our hands to spend cleaning out our fridge door every week,' Mum says.

'I don't clean my fridge door.'

'But what about the germs?'

'Simple,' says Mrs Prentice. 'I take a cloth and wipe the bottom of my milk bottle.'

The women in the room turn and face Cathy's mum, waiting for further explanation, but she doesn't even tell them about the fantastic one-night-only offer. Instead, she goes straight on to the next product – the Tupperware butter dish.

When the routine is over it's the time of the evening when the ladies open their purses to buy that container they just can't live without. This is the time of the night Cathy hates most. Her job is to make sure everyone's glass is full while she answers polite questions about school. Small talk, her mum calls it. *Just smile and make small talk, and if they ask about the products send them over to me.* She looks around the room and figures everyone looks happy enough, so she leaves the empty glasses for now and stands next to the young model.

Mrs Prentice is sitting with her back to the young woman, and Cathy decides to be brave. 'Hi,' she tries.

The young woman smiles, and again Cathy notices the sparkling lip-gloss. She catches the other neighbours watching them before quickly looking away, pretending to be discussing Tupperware. Nobody seems to be very welcoming to the newcomer, and Cathy can't understand why.

'Can I get you another drink?'

The young woman holds her glass up and shows Cathy it's still full.

'You haven't touched it,' says Cathy. 'Would you like something else? We've got Martini.'

'Don't want to mess up my lipstick.'

'It's beautiful,' Cathy gushes. Great. Now she sounds like a wee girl. But the woman doesn't seem to mind. 'What's your name?'

'Sandra.'

Is Sandra a model's name? It doesn't sound like it.

'Would you like a cocktail sausage?' She lifts the bowl from the coffee table and offers it to the beautiful Sandra.

Sandra scrunches up her nose and waves her hand in disgust. 'I'm vegetarian.'

'Me too.' Cathy can't believe it. It must be a sign from the Blue Lady.

'How long have you been vegetarian?' asks Sandra.

And it's at this point Cathy realises she might not always stick to telling the truth.

'Years,' she says.

Sandra looks at her. 'Really? You must have been very young.'

'It's so upsetting when you think of all the poor animals dying just so they can feed us. Don't you agree?'

'Never really thought about it,' laughs Sandra. 'I'm just on a diet.' She flicks her hair, sticks out her chest and pouts. 'So does anybody actually buy any of this crap? I mean, I'm just here because your mum invited me along and I couldn't think of an excuse to get out of it.'

‘You’ve moved into Mr Smith’s house?’ Cathy asks. But Sandra just shrugs; her mother clearly never taught her about the importance of small talk. ‘Nobody liked him,’ says Cathy. ‘Used to shoot at cats with an air rifle. And one time when my brother’s ball rolled into his front garden, he took it and burst it with a pair of scissors.’ She doesn’t tell Sandra the bit about the ball crushing Mr Smith’s best roses. ‘Mum said she wasn’t surprised he had a heart attack because he always got so wound up about everything.’

‘A heart attack?’ Sandra repeats. ‘Was he okay?’

‘Course not,’ says Cathy. ‘Or else you wouldn’t be living in that house, would you?’

‘Oh.’

‘He dropped dead in the front room. Mum says he was probably watching through the window for a passing cat or football.’

‘He died in the house?’ Sandra asks.

‘Like I said. Heart attack.’

Sandra looks like she’s about to throw up, and Cathy notices the glitter on her cheeks doesn’t look so good against green skin. She supposes she’ll need to confess to the Blue Lady again tonight, but she thinks even the Virgin Mary will see the funny side of this one.

She’s thinking about asking Sandra if she believes in ghosts when there’s a loud knocking at the front door. Everyone turns to look at her mother. The hammering starts again. Someone is impatient.

Her mum goes to answer the door and everyone in the room stops talking, hoping to hear whatever conversation is about to take place. Cathy gets up and moves across the room on the pretence of fetching a bowl of nibbles, but nobody seems to be watching her, so she leaves the bowl where it is and leans against the bookcase – just in time to see her mum opening the door. She obviously isn’t expecting to see whoever is on the other side of the threshold.

Cathy can’t hear what the visitor says, but her mum looks angry.

'Don't be ridiculous. Why would anybody want to steal a statue of the Virgin Mary?'

Cathy grips the edge of the bookcase and looks to the heavens, to the wardrobe above her head where the Blue Lady is hidden.

Mum raises her voice. 'My daughter is not a thief.'

If the ladies in the room weren't looking at Cathy a minute ago, they are now. She clamps her hand to her mouth. Why now? Mrs O'Donnell knows Mum is hosting a Tupperware party tonight. Cathy looks round the room, desperately hoping no one else can hear the conversation going on out in the hallway, but it's obvious they can hear every word, and Mrs Prentice is looking at her the way she did when she caught her with her hand in the bag of Opal Fruits.

Cathy can't help it; she laughs. But the sound comes out all wrong, and she's sure everyone knows it's a guilty laugh.

The party finishes early, and Cathy helps her mum tidy the house in silence. Dishes are washed and put back in the cupboard, and the chairs are placed back round the kitchen table. When they're done, the only evidence of the party is the lingering smell of Mrs Prentice's talcum powder.

Upstairs in bed, Cathy can still hear Mrs O'Donnell's words ringing in her ears. *Your daughter's a thief. A thief. Thief, thief, thief.* The words repeat over and over again like a scratched record. She slips out of bed and takes the Blue Lady from her hiding place and sneaks her under the covers.

'Mrs O'Donnell turned up on my doorstep tonight and called me a thief in front of all the neighbours.' She switches on her torch and a red glow fills the small space. 'Am I a thief? And if I am, well, does that make me a sinner?'

A voice comes to her softly and she has to listen very carefully to hear it.

You didn't steal me, Cathy. You rescued me.

'But I took you and you weren't mine to take. Doesn't that mean I'll go to hell?' She stares at the Blue Lady. 'I'm scared of hell. The Reverend Small says that's where all the bad people go. He says it's a burning pit of screaming sinners. Please tell me what I must do so I don't go there.'

She clutches the Blue Lady tightly. And this time her voice comes through more clearly, telling Cathy what to do.

Redemption

Cathy pulls the duvet over her head and tries to hold onto her dream, but the details fizzle out like popping candy on her tongue. Angry voices rise up above the sound of her brother's music, but she can't make out what's being said so she climbs out of bed and goes through to his room.

'Get out.' Jimmy throws a pillow at her.

'I'm not even in.'

'You're not allowed to come in here.'

She stamps her foot on the carpet outside his bedroom door. 'I'm not in.'

'Well, you're not allowed to open my door.'

If they keep arguing she'll miss the conversation downstairs. So she storms into his room and lifts the needle from the record.

'Careful! You'll scratch it.'

'Shhh!' She puts a finger to her lips. 'They're arguing.'

'Who cares?'

'Sounds like it's important.'

'What's it about this time?'

'That's what I'm trying to find out.'

They creep out onto the landing at the top of the stairs and Dad's voice can be heard coming from the kitchen.

'You've obviously been putting ideas into her head.'

'Don't be ridiculous.'

'Well, why else would she steal a statue of the Virgin Mary?'

Cathy glances over her shoulder to her bedroom, to where the Blue Lady is hidden. Mum is shouting louder now.

'Our daughter is not a thief.'

Jimmy looks at Cathy. 'What the fuck have you been up to?'

She doesn't like it when her brother uses that word. He's pretending to be a grown-up just like he's doing by shaving. Last week, she caught him using their dad's Old Spice, and he made her promise not to tell. She doesn't want her brother to become an adult; it means she'll have to grow up too one day, and she can't imagine that happening. No, Cathy has decided to stay a child forever.

Jimmy is still waiting for an answer. 'Have you been stealing?'

'Of course not.'

'Then what have you done?'

'Nothing.' Cathy blushes. She never could lie to Jimmy.

The kitchen door slams shut and footsteps can be heard on the stairs. They dash back to their own rooms, and Cathy picks up her book and throws herself on to the bed just as Mum appears in the doorway.

'I suppose you heard all of that?' she asks.

Cathy shakes her head and pretends to be focussing on her book, but she knows her mum doesn't give up that easily.

'Your dad wants to know why Mrs O'Donnell is accusing you of stealing a china ornament from her house.'

Cathy prays she doesn't ask her if it's true, because she's told enough lies lately.

'Of course I told her my daughter's no thief. What a cheek,' she mutters to herself, 'coming over here in the middle of my party and accusing my girl of stealing a statue of the Virgin Mary.' Mum laughs nervously. 'I mean, what does an eleven-year-old girl want with the Virgin Mary?' Her face turns serious. 'But what I do believe, and what I think she really wanted me to know, is that you were in her house.'

Cathy looks away.

'We've been over this a million times, Cathy. Mrs O'Donnell has told you to stay away.'

'Sorry.'

'Just promise me you won't do it again.'

Cathy is sorry. But she's not sorry for going into Mrs O'Donnell's house, and she's not sorry for taking the Blue Lady. She's sorry her mum believes she's a good girl.

As soon as Mum disappears back downstairs Jimmy comes through to her room. 'What the fuck made you steal from the freaks next door?'

'Stop swearing!'

'You steal a china ornament, and yet you're giving me a row for swearing. Did you think they weren't going to notice?'

'I didn't take it,' she says, but Jimmy just stares at her and she knows there's no point in arguing.

'Where is it?'

She tilts her head towards the wardrobe. 'Should I take it back?'

'Of course not. Then they'll know for definite it was you. Best get rid of it.'

She nods her head, but she knows she'll never part with it.

'Jimmy,' she asks, 'what's a virgin?'

'Jesus Christ, what are you asking me that for?'

'That's what Mum called the Blue Lady. She called her the Virgin Mary, and I wondered what it meant.'

Jimmy doesn't give her an answer. 'Don't suppose you fancy kicking a ball about?' he asks instead. 'Just out in the street.'

She jumps up and pulls on her trainers.

'Great,' Jimmy says. 'You can go in goals.'

Cathy groans. Some things never change.

Out in the street they throw down their jumpers to make the goal posts and Jimmy throws his old goalie gloves at her. 'Here,' he shouts, 'these should help.'

Cathy never gets a shot at taking penalties. She's a girl. And when girls play football they go in goals. It's the law. She stands between the jumpers, but she can't see Thomas's bedroom window from this side of the street. She lifts her hand to her eyes and pretends to block out the early morning sun.

'Can we swap ends?' she shouts. 'The sun's so low I can't see a thing.'

'Does Kenny Dalglish ask to swap ends because he's got the sun in his eyes?' Jimmy boots the ball as hard as he can and it goes straight past her, between the posts and into Mr O'Donnell's flower beds. And here's another thing. Girls aren't just goalkeepers; they also have to fetch the ball.

Keeping one foot on the pavement, she places the other carefully amongst Mr O'Donnell's pansies and stretches forward. She reaches as far as she can but she still can't quite get her fingers on the ball.

'Nearly got it,' she shouts to Jimmy. She looks up and her heart quickens. Thomas is watching her from his bedroom window. She gives him a quick wave, taking care to keep her balance, but he looks away.

Back in goal she can't concentrate and keeps letting the ball in.

'What's up with you?' Jimmy asks.

'I'm trying my best.'

'Yeah, well, try harder.'

The ball flies past her face and she scowls at him.

Mum and Dad leave to go to the garden centre and she decides to make her move. She makes the excuse of going to the toilet and sneaks in through the back door of the garage and takes what she needs. Jimmy is playing keepy-uppy when she comes back round.

'I remembered I had something to do today,' she tells him.

He stops and holds the ball in both hands. 'Mum and Dad will kill me if you're not here when they return.'

'I'll be back in half an hour.' She doesn't look up at Thomas's bedroom window. This is something she must do by herself and she doesn't want to have to explain anything to him. It's better if he knows nothing about it.

'You'd better be, because I'm not lying for you. Where are you going anyway?'

'I can't tell you.'

‘Meeting up with your little boyfriend from next door, aren’t you? Well, if I were you I’d stay away from him for a while.’

‘Why should I?’

‘You only ever seem to get in trouble when he’s around.’

‘Not true.’

‘I’m just saying it’s probably best if you stick to your own kind.’

She storms away from her brother’s words. *Stick to your own kind.* She runs and runs and doesn’t stop until she reaches the local park. Already the big top is being taken down. Is she too late? She rushes round to the gap in the link fencing and squeezes through without waiting to hear if someone’s coming. There’s no time to hang about. She weaves her way between caravans and generators towards the animal enclosures. This time, she ignores the large truck with the painting of a lion on the side, and makes her way forward until she’s outside the tent of elephants. Without stopping to think, she slips inside and comes face to face with the three gentle giants. The smallest of the three turns its head towards her, and she looks down at the shackles around its ankles.

‘I’m sorry,’ she says. ‘There’s nothing I can do to help you.’

No one’s spotted her yet, but she knows it won’t be long until she’s found, so she’d better act fast. After a couple of dead ends, she finds the horses tied to a metal post outside a large camper van, and she immediately recognises the white stallion from the poster she and Thomas saw on their first visit. She’s relieved to see each horse is secured only by a length of rope, and she takes the gardening scissors out of her pocket and begins cutting through the rope holding the white stallion. But the rusted blades have no impact. The horse to her left starts snorting and blowing, and she knows she must hurry.

She gives up on the scissors and grabs hold of the knot with both hands and works furiously. From behind her she can hear men’s voices shouting out across the park. It’s time to leave, but the knot is nearly free. The white stallion stamps at the ground furiously.

'Nearly done,' she whispers and places her hand gently on the horse's neck. Her touch panics the beast and it bucks and rears up on its hind legs.

'Something's upsetting the horses.' The voice catches her by surprise and she looks up to see two men appear round the corner just as the rope slips free from the pole.

'Who the fuck are you?'

'She's stealing the horses.'

Cathy panics. Which way to the gap in the fence? She has no idea and no time to stop and think about it, so she turns and runs in the opposite direction from the men, grinning as she sees she's not the only one who is escaping.

'Run free,' she shouts to the stallion. 'Run free.'

She daren't look over her shoulder again but runs as fast as she can towards the perimeter, hoping she'll find the gap in the fence before she's caught. Behind her, the escaped horse seems to be causing havoc. She looks up to the sky and prays it'll get away from here and make it to the freedom of the fields and hills.

And then she sees her way out. She squeezes through the small gap in the fence and runs the whole way home. She needs to speak to the Blue Lady, tell her that she's done what she had told her to do. She's freed the stallion – and by doing so has surely earned her place in Heaven.

She arrives home to find an assortment of bedding plants laid out on the drive and her dad lifting a bag of compost out of the boot of his car.

'Ah, there you are.' Mum appears from the garage carrying some trowels and a pair of gardening gloves. 'Didn't you hear me calling you?' Looks like Cathy's going to have to wait until she can tell the Blue Lady her news. 'Well, you're here now. So pop these on and let's get started.' Mum tosses the gloves to Cathy and flashes a look at next door's garden. 'Let's show the O'Donnells they're not the only ones who can have pretty flowers.'

Cathy sees her dad roll his eyes. So that's what all this is about. She pulls on the gardening gloves and listens to her mother's planting instructions.

'Has anyone seen my gardening scissors?' Dad asks.

Cathy reaches into her pocket but it's empty. The scissors have gone. She must have dropped them at the circus.

'I'm sure I left them on the shelf in the garage. Someone must have stolen them.'

Mum laughs. 'Why on earth would anyone take your gardening scissors?'

Cathy gets down on her knees and starts to dig with her green trowel. How could she have been so stupid? What will happen if the horse's owner finds them? Will the police be able to get her fingerprints?

Her thoughts are interrupted by Sandra's loud voice. 'Thanks for inviting me last night. I had a great time.'

Cathy can see her mum's grin without looking up. Mum loves throwing a party, and loves it even more when people tell her how wonderful she is as a host.

'You're welcome,' Mum says. 'I'm glad you had such a lovely time.'

'If I'm honest I was a bit bored to start with, I mean who cares about plastic boxes?'

Cathy stops digging and stands up next to her mum. Her neighbour is wearing a pair of white pedal pushers, a white boob tube and white sandals. She looks like an angel in heat.

'But then that crazy woman from next door turned up and things really got lively. And from the look on your poor daughter's face I'd say she's definitely guilty of something.' Sandra winks at Cathy. 'But imagine having the nerve to wait until you had a house full before turning up and accusing her. What a cow.' She looks up at the O'Donnells' house as she says this last word. 'And old Mrs Prentice looked like she might actually die on the spot. It was fantastic; better than watching *Coronation Street*. And then I've heard this morning's news.' She throws her head back and laughs, exposing a painfully thin neck. 'I mean, who'd have thought living in a small town could be so much fun?'

Mum looks like she might put her hands around that neck and squeeze. Hard.

'What happened this morning?' Cathy asks.

'Oh, haven't you heard?'

Cathy thinks she might strangle Sandra before her mum gets the chance, but then she remembers the Blue Lady upstairs in her wardrobe and knows she'll never make it into Heaven if she strangles one of the neighbours to death. Mum puts her hand on Cathy's shoulder and gently presses.

'Please tell us,' Mum says.

Sandra puts her hands on her skinny hips and laughs again. 'Some poor horse from the circus escaped.'

Escaped. She did it. She managed to release one of those poor wretched animals and now it can live its life in the wild. Maybe she should go back and release the other one.

'Stupid beast got caught up in some guy ropes and broke its leg.'

Cathy stops breathing.

'Oh, the poor thing; is it alright?' Mum asks.

Sandra stops smiling and shakes her head. 'Had to be put down. Shot right there and then by one of the circus owners. Apparently, the poor guy is distraught.'

Cathy can't stop it coming. She folds at the waist, and bright yellow vomit splatters her neighbour's white sandals. A beautiful creature has been shot dead. She pictures a trail of scarlet blood running through the white hair of the stallion's mane and retches again, barely aware of Sandra's screams. It's her fault. All her fault. She's to blame. If she hadn't run away when she did. If she hadn't been a coward. If she'd been brave enough to see it through to the end, to guide the horse away from the circus ground. But instead she left it to die.

She lets her mum take her indoors and strip the clothes from her shaking body. She's dressed in clean clothes, a damp facecloth is held to her forehead, and she's led through to her bedroom and tucked into bed.

Images of hooves trapped in wire fences and the sound of a gunshot fill her head as she tries to get some sleep. Maybe, when she wakes up, it will all have been a bad dream.

There's a knock on her bedroom door and she pulls herself up to sitting. The door opens and Thomas walks in. Why is he here? She pulls the covers up to her neck and smooths down her hair.

'Does your mother know you're here?'

He shakes his head. 'I heard about her visit last night,' he says. 'Sorry about that. I'm surprised your mum let me come in to see you.' He hovers in the doorway, unsure what to do or say next.

'Well, you're here now, so you might as well come in.'

He walks across the room and sits down on the bedcovers beside her. She loves her mum for cleaning her up and changing her into fresh clothes.

'Your mum said you heard the news about the circus horse.'

Cathy reaches for her pillow and hugs it close to her chest. There's no way she's about to cry in front of a boy, even if it is Thomas.

'It's not fair,' she says. 'How could God let an innocent animal die like that?'

'It wasn't God's fault. He didn't have anything to do with it. It was an accident.'

'It wasn't the horse's fault.' She knows she's shouting but she can't control herself. 'What kind of God lets an innocent animal get shot?'

'But it was hurt. Its leg was caught in barbed wire and it was in pain. The best thing for it was to put it out of its misery.'

'It's not fair. God should never have let the horse get its leg caught.'

'I don't think God is able to watch every animal every second of the day.'

'But why does He let animals be chained up like that in the first place?'

'I don't know.'

'But you should know.'

'Why should I have the answers?'

'Because He's your God. You go to church every Sunday. You speak to Him.'

'And you think He tells me His plans? Why He chooses to do things? Nobody knows that.'

'Well, then God's stupid.'

'Don't say that.'

'But it's true.'

'It's not true.'

'I don't think I want to know Him if He doesn't care. If He thinks it's okay to let animals suffer like that.'

'Cathy, you're not listening. God can't be there every time someone or something needs help. Instead, He tries to teach us to be good and kind, and I guess His plan is that we all look out for one another. He didn't shoot the horse. And the man who shot the horse did it for the horse's own good. Don't you understand?'

'So, you're saying the person to blame is the person that let the horse free in the first place?'

Thomas looks at her. 'What do you mean? The horse got tangled up in some wire.'

'But say that only happened because someone let the horse free.'

'Who would do that?'

'Maybe someone who thought it was cruel to keep it tied up in the first place. So if that person was trying to help, does that make them evil? Or would God see they were trying to do good?'

Thomas rubs his head. 'I don't think I can keep up with you half the time, Cathy Munro.'

'Would the person who let the horse free go to hell?'

'Nobody goes to hell if they repent for what they did.'

Cathy listens carefully as Thomas explains what happens in Confession, and she has an idea.

'Tell me what the chapel looks like. And I want every detail.'

'Why don't I do better than that?'

'What do you mean?'

'It's my Confirmation next Saturday. Why don't you come along?'

'But I'm not Catholic.'

'You wouldn't be able to sit up front but you could sneak in to the back row. No one would know you were there except me.'

'Are you mad? Have you forgotten what happened when your mum found me in your bedroom? She'll go mental if she spots me. She hates Protestants.'

'No, she doesn't.'

'Then why did she throw me out of your house?'

'Because you're a girl. She thinks if I have a girl in my room then she must be my girlfriend.'

Cathy can't see him properly in the dim light, but she's pretty sure he's blushing.

'So will you come, you know, to my Confirmation?'

She'd love to see the inside of the chapel. 'Of course I'll be there,' she says. 'Wouldn't miss it for the world. But how will I get in?'

'If you can sneak into the circus and untie the reins of a horse, then I'm sure you can sneak into the back row of the chapel.'

'You know?'

'I guessed.'

'But how?'

'I saw how upset you were when we saw the elephants, and then you refused to take the tickets, so when you told me just now that someone had set the horse free then I figured it had to be you. You're the only person I know that's crazy enough to do it. And the only person I know that's brave enough.'

'But I wasn't brave. I ran away when the men came. And then the horse must have tried to escape and got caught in some wire and then...' She stops. She can't bear to finish the sentence.

'Cathy Munro, you're braver than anyone I know.'

Confirmation

Cathy watches all the comings and goings from her bedroom window. Today is Thomas's big day, and although she can't be by his side she hopes he'll seek her out at the back of the chapel. She's picked out the dress with the pink and yellow flowers to wear. She hates dresses.

His mum has bought a Polaroid camera for the occasion, and Cathy watches as she fusses around all the guests in the front garden like a bee flitting from flower to flower. First she sorts Thomas's collar, and then straightens his father's tie. Then she holds up the camera but stops to squeeze everyone in closer together for the shot. She squints through the viewfinder again, but clearly still can't fit everyone in because she takes a step back and tries again. And again. And Cathy's hoping she's going to keep stepping back until she lands in the flower bed. But she doesn't. She gets the group to shout *cheese* and then presses the button. Everyone's laughing, and the adults keep ruffling Thomas's hair.

Cathy feels a sharp pain grip her chest. She remembers reading somewhere that when you have a heart attack you can't move your left arm. Or is it your right? She's not sure. She wiggles her fingers and feels a tingle in her left hand. Laughter floats up and in through her open window from next door's garden and she goes back for another look. Thomas is getting his photo taken with a girl in a turquoise dress with matching sandals.

The pain returns and she crumples, clutching her chest with both arms. She bangs on the wall and Jimmy appears.

'What's going on?'

'Help me,' she says, but he doesn't look worried. 'I think

I'm dying.'

'What from this time?'

'I'm having a heart attack.'

'Don't be daft, you're only ten.'

'Eleven.'

'Huh?'

'I'm not ten, I'm eleven. I had a birthday, remember?'

'Of course,' Jimmy says but he's looking out of the window, and she knows he's not really listening. 'What's going on next door?'

'Thomas has his Confirmation today.'

'What's that mean?'

'He's got a special service at the chapel.' Thomas had tried explaining to her what happens during the service, but it was all very confusing.

'Are you not invited?'

'Kind of,' she says.

'What do you mean, kind of?'

'Well, he's asked me to come to the chapel and sneak in at the back.'

'So that's what's wrong with you. You're not having a heart attack, you're just jealous.'

'Am not,' she snaps.

'You're jealous because your boyfriend's having a party and you're not invited.'

'Stop saying he's my boyfriend.'

'Why? He is, isn't he?' She ignores him and he goes back to looking out of the window. 'So what's he all dressed up like a poof for?'

'He's going to be sealed with the Holy Spirit.'

'So, he is a poof.' Jimmy laughs. 'Is that a Polaroid camera his mum's got? Do you think she'd let me see it if I went and asked?'

Cathy lets go of her chest and leans against her brother to watch what's going on outside. Everyone's getting into the cars and Thomas is getting to sit in the front next to his dad. She keeps her eye on him, hoping he'll look up. But he doesn't. The cars drive away from the house and she turns to Jimmy.

'Fancy coming with me?'

'What are you going on about now?'

'I'm going to the chapel. Are you coming with me or not?'

'No chance.'

'Please.'

'Are you kidding? We'll get thrown out.'

'I'm not planning to get seen, I'm going to sneak in and watch from the back.'

'My friends will kill me if they find out I was inside a chapel.'

'It's not much different from a church,' Cathy says.

'It's a whole lot different.'

'How?' she asks, but Jimmy doesn't answer. So she changes tack. 'I promise not to tell if you don't.'

'No way.'

'I'll pay you.' She goes to her piggy bank and pulls out a pound note. 'Besides, what else are you going to do today?'

He takes the money and pockets the Mars bar that's sitting on her desk. 'Alright, then. But if we get caught, you're taking the blame.'

From the outside, the chapel doesn't look much different from any of the other churches in town.

'Now what?' Jimmy asks as they watch everyone gathering outside for more photographs.

'We wait until they've gone inside.'

They don't have long to wait as the guests make their way through the large double doors. Jimmy starts to cross the road.

'Shouldn't we wait a bit longer?'

'What for?'

She's no longer sure this is a good idea, but he's on the other side of the road now so she crosses over to join him. 'Maybe we should go home.'

He laughs as he throws her own words back at her: 'What else are you going to do today?'

They enter the grounds through the black iron gates and she hears an organ churn out the same melancholic notes it does when she visits the High Church with school at the end of term. An old man appears from around the corner. 'Hurry up,' he says, ushering them inside. 'The service has already started.'

They do as they're told and shuffle into a pew at the very back. The people in the row in front turn and stare at them as they sit down. Cathy ignores them and looks around the enormous whitewashed room. It's even more beautiful than she'd imagined. Elaborate lamps hang from the ceiling; a ceiling so high it must surely touch Heaven itself. Paintings hang on every wall, and at the front of the church a mosaic of Jesus fills an enormous arch. It looks like it's painted in pure gold, and she can't believe nobody's told her about this before. The church her school makes her attend on the last day of every term is grey and drab in comparison, and the only decor is the faded, moth-eaten tapestries that hang on the cold, stone walls. She looks at the gold candlesticks displayed on the long table beside the priest. How is it possible that her small town can be so rich? Surely all this gold should be in Egypt or Rome, not here in Scotland.

Every pew is filled, and everyone seems to have dressed up for the occasion. The family in front of her has a young boy with them, but he won't sit still or stop fussing. Cathy pulls a funny face and he rewards her with a big grin, but then a hymn starts and he returns to face the front and mime along.

She takes the opportunity when everyone's standing up to shuffle along the bench and peer between the rows of people, but it's too busy and she can't find Thomas.

Jimmy leans over and whispers in her ear, 'Have you seen enough yet? This place gives me the creeps.' Then an elderly woman slides in to the pew beside them, blocking their escape route. 'Fantastic.' Jimmy sits back down and peels open the wrapper of the Mars bar. 'Now we're fucking stuck here.'

Cathy glances up at the tall ceiling, praying it won't fall

down on them. 'You're not supposed to swear in church.'

Jimmy nudges her. 'Stand up,' he whispers, and she sees everyone around her is standing again. She jumps up from the hard wooden pew and stands to attention.

Everyone sits back down and Cathy feels like she's caught in some well-rehearsed dance where everyone knows the next move except her. She takes her seat and hopes no one notices she's the last one down. The priest holds his hands out and speaks to the room and everyone repeats his words back to him. 'What are they doing?' she asks, but Jimmy's too busy eating the Mars bar. She looks around the room for Thomas.

'This is boring,' says Jimmy, his mouth full of chocolate. 'Let's go.'

'But we haven't seen him yet.'

The congregation sit back down and the hall falls silent. Even the young boy in the row in front sits still. Pathways of light create a magical effect as they cut across the room at every angle, tinged with different colours as they pass through the stained glass windows. Is this what being inside a rainbow is like?

The priest introduces the bishop and calls out the name of the first child to be confirmed. Cathy's stomach does a full somersault. She crosses her fingers and desperately hopes Thomas will see she's here for him.

At the front of the chapel a young girl steps forward with an older woman at her side. They walk up to the altar, and Cathy's surprised to see the girl is wearing a white, lace veil. Do the girls in the Protestant Church wear veils?

Her stomach tightens and she clutches the back of the pew in front. Jimmy looks at her,

'Are you okay?'

Another cramp grips her, forcing her to bend over. And then it happens. A pulsing warmth spreads between her legs and she slips her hand down to check. She feels dizzy. And sick. She pulls her hand away and finds it's covered in blood.

Bloody's in the Bible, bloody's in the book.

Is it going to pour from her onto the floor?

If you don't believe me take a bloody look.

She looks at the wooden crucifix to the left of the altar, and sees the blood running from Christ's hands and his feet where the nails hold him to the cross. Was there that much blood earlier? A droplet of blood trickles down Christ's foot, and the pain in her stomach tightens its grip. It's her fault this is happening. She's the one who blamed God for the death of the stallion, and this is her price.

She pushes herself up from the pew, aware of the dark, sticky patch she's leaving behind, squeezes past the old woman sitting beside her, and runs for the doors at the back of the room. She needs air. Quickly. She reaches the entrance but the doors to the outside world are shut. She pushes them with both hands, but they don't budge and she feels herself sliding downwards on to the floor. The air around her is thick with the smell of the lilies that stand on the pedestals at either side. To her left a bright beam of sunlight streams in, and she sees the old man from earlier holding a side door open for her. She forces herself back up on to her feet and runs all the way home.

No one is home and she rushes upstairs to the bathroom and strips off her dress and pants. She throws them into the bath and soaks a handful of toilet paper under the tap and washes herself. The toilet paper clumps in the new hair that has recently started to grow 'down there' but she keeps rubbing until the wet paper no longer shows any signs of blood. She then folds a handful of toilet roll and holds it between her legs, and takes yesterday's pants and jeans out of the laundry basket and pulls them on. It'll do. Right now she needs to wash her dress before her mum gets home.

She turns on both taps and watches as the swirling water turns pink.

The front door slams shut.

'Cathy, where are you?'

Holding on to the sink with one hand, she reaches across the small bathroom and locks the door just in time as her brother tries the handle.

'Leave me alone,' she shouts through the locked door.

'Are you okay?'

'Go away and leave me alone.'

Silence. Then *Heart of Glass* starts to play, and she knows he's given up and gone to his room.

She takes the dress and folds it around the bar of soap and rubs and rubs until a lather forms. She washes the dress under the tap until the water runs clear.

Cars can be heard pulling up outside the house next door. She opens the bathroom window a few inches and listens to the shouts of excited chatter ringing out across the whole street. The sun is shining and the heat seeps through the narrow gap. It must be one of the hottest days yet, and she's trapped indoors. She can't remember feeling so alone before.

Thomas has changed out of his stuffy suit and is back in his shorts and a t-shirt, and she watches him bounce up and down on the pavement outside on his space hopper. Every time he passes the front of her house he slows down. Is he hoping she'll go out and join him? How can she tell him she might never be able to bounce on a space hopper again? Or ride her bike? How can you possibly ride a bike when you're bleeding? She watches him hopping up and down the street with envy. Why hadn't she been born a boy?

Thomas sees her watching and stops and waves up at the window, but she doesn't wave back. She goes through to her bedroom and kneels in front of the Blue Lady.

'My mum told me women bleed so they can have babies. She said not to be scared, that it's a good thing when my periods start because it means I can have a baby when I'm older. But what if I don't want one?' Her stomach cramps and she feels a rush of blood soak into the toilet paper between her legs. She feels dirty. 'The teacher said you got pregnant after an angel visited you, but Linda said that a man and a woman have to *do it* to make a baby.' She blushes. 'You know, have sex.' She's confused and wishes the Blue Lady would talk to her. 'I hope an angel never visits me.'

She gets up from the floor and looks out of the window. The sun is still shining, and all of the guests next door are now eating from paper plates outside in the garden. It's a picnic for grown-ups.

'I think God must be a man. I overheard Mum saying giving birth was the worst pain she's ever felt in her life. If God was a woman she wouldn't make us go through all of that. No. I've decided I'm never having a baby and that's that. In fact I've decided I'm never going to have sex.'

New Shoes

Her friends all buy their shoes from a stall at the market, but there's no way her mum would ever let Cathy buy hers there. No, the shop she's being dragged to is tucked in between the bank and the wool shop, and the shoes in the window are displayed behind strips of orange cellophane and look like they've been there since the shop opened. Even the name, Bayne & Duckett, is old-fashioned. Cathy checks to see no one is watching as they go inside.

A bell above the door jingles and the shop assistant looks up from the sales desk, visibly unhappy at the interruption. She, too, looks like she's been here since the shop began business. They are the only customers, and Cathy sits down on the bench and prises her feet out of her old trainers, showing off the pair of pristine white socks her mum insisted she put on before they left the house. The narrow store is dimly lit and she gazes round at the towers of shoe boxes that stretch all the way from the floor to the ceiling. The air is filled with a pungent mix of sweaty feet and new leather.

Her feet are measured, boxes are brought down, and soon the floor around her is littered with sheets of tissue paper. She's secretly hoping to get a pair of trainers like her brother's: black Adidas Sambas with three white stripes up the side. Maybe then she'll be taken seriously by the boys. But, without a doubt, the assistant believes girls should wear 'pretty shoes' and tries to persuade Mum that the cerise pink ones are the latest in fashion. In the end, Mum and Cathy compromise and agree on a pair of white trainers with a neon-green stripe along the edge. The shop assistant is disappointed, but Mum's pleased because this pair is cheaper.

'Do you want to wear them now?'

'Can I wait until I get home? I want to keep them as clean and new looking for as long as possible.' This lie is so small she's sure she won't need to tell the Blue Lady about it. The real reason she doesn't want to wear them now has nothing to do with the shoes and everything to do with the box.

They don't go home straight away, and she has to follow her mum to the post office, the butcher's and then down to Woolworths for some picture hooks. It takes forever, and she's desperate to get home and get started.

When they finally make it home, Mum pops the kettle on and Cathy disappears upstairs. She waits until she hears the television going on before she gets to work. She's been collecting the gold and silver foil from sweet wrappers for over a week, and in case her mum walks in she has a story prepared about a school project. She takes out the craft box she was given for Christmas last year and lays everything out on the desk in front of her. She's managed to save two ice lolly sticks, and she tucks them up her sleeve and sneaks through to the bathroom to wash them. She scrapes them back and forwards across the bar of Imperial Leather soap and rinses them under the tap, but the smell of Strawberry Mivvi still lingers.

She lays the two sticks on the desk in front of her in the shape of a cross, tears some sellotape from the roll and wraps it around the centre several times. The tape doesn't stick very well because the wood is still wet, but it'll do. She remembers the simple, wooden cross above the door in Thomas's living room, but she wants this one to be special. She carefully wraps the sticks in the gold paper from the inside of a packet of Rolos. The paper's not quite big enough and she has to use another sweet wrapper for the arms of the cross, but it looks perfect. Almost.

She puts her new trainers on the floor and lifts the shoe box onto the desk, placing it on its long edge. She glues the gold cross to the inside back of the box and then digs deep into the pocket of her jeans and brings out her last stick of juicy fruit gum. She unfolds the silver foil and pops the warm gum into her mouth. Her mouth waters and she chews slowly, knowing the sweetness will quickly fade until all she's left with is a tasteless piece of gum and a sore jaw. She takes the strip of silver foil and scrunches and twists it into a shape that loosely resembles a candlestick. Using the rest of the foil that she's been saving up she makes several more candlesticks and sticks them in a row in front of the gold cross. She then draws some cross shapes with glue around the inside of the box and sprinkles red glitter over them. She smiles. It looks amazing. All sparkly and special, just what the Blue Lady deserves. The job is nearly finished, but there's still one thing missing.

Thomas called it the font, and it stands at the front of the altar. She goes over to her bedside cabinet, slides open the top drawer and takes out the gold lid from the Lucozade bottle that she's been keeping specially. She sticks it down in the very centre of the box.

Now all she needs to do is make sure no one will look inside. She fetches her pencil case from her school bag and writes her name on the lid in bubble writing, but she doesn't think that'll be enough. She picks up the red pen.

KEEP OUT!
PRIVATE!

She goes to the bedroom door and checks the TV is still on downstairs, then collects the Blue Lady from the back of the wardrobe. It feels good to hold her in her hands, and she looks even more beautiful than Cathy remembered. She has a kind face.

'I bet you'd let your daughter get Adidas Sambas.' She carries her over to the miniature chapel. 'Wait till you see it. I've made it especially for you.'

But the Blue Lady doesn't fit. She's too tall.

Cathy can't believe it. Why hadn't she checked first? She turns the box upright. That way the Blue Lady fits, but now the cross is in the wrong place and the candlesticks are all on their side. Carefully, she peels off the candlesticks and the font and puts her hand inside the box to remove the cross, but the gold foil tears as the two lollipop sticks come apart in her hand. She throws them down in a fury, and from somewhere deep inside a memory resurfaces…

She's a little girl playing dress-up in her mum's room, and she's wearing one of her mum's dresses and a black hat with a pink feather sticking out of the top. She's swishing her skirt from side to side as she parades back and forwards in front of the mirror, but something's missing. She needs a pair of Mum's high heels to finish the outfit. She opens the wardrobe door and looks at all of the fancy shoes, but something in the corner of the wardrobe attracts her attention: a box tied shut with a baby blue ribbon.

She forgets all about the shoes and lifts out the box. It's heavier than she expects and she kneels on the floor with the box in front of her. She pulls one end of the ribbon and lifts up the lid. The box is full, but her eyes are drawn to a green velvet pouch. A pouch for keeping jewellery in. The silver cross inside is studded with jewels and she lifts it up to the light, spreading an arc of colour across the bedroom wall. The chain slips over her head and she lets the pendant fall over the top of her mother's dress. She's nearly ready. She sits at the dressing table and opens the floral make-up bag. By the time her mum finds her, she's painted the full works over her face: lipstick, blusher, and bright blue eye liner.

A shadow creeps into the corner of her memory.

Her mum is furious when she spots the cross and tears it from Cathy's neck, leaving a burn mark that doesn't fade for days. The hat is returned to the shelf, the dress is put back on its hanger, and she makes Cathy scrub the make-up off with a cold, damp face cloth until her cheeks are red raw.

Cathy can't remember what happened to the cross, but she guesses it was returned to the green velvet pouch. It would be perfect for the Blue Lady's chapel.

She slips through to her mum and dad's bedroom and looks inside the wardrobe. The hat is still in its place on the shelf but the jumble that littered the floor has been tidied and the box is no longer there. She looks around the room and tries to picture where her mum would hide it. The photograph of her great-grandmother is still tucked in to the mirror on her mother's dressing table, and Cathy slides it out and searches the woman's face for any similarities to her own, desperate to find a connection that links them. She doesn't have much time and puts it back exactly as she found it and continues her search. She checks the chest of drawers and rummages through an odd assortment of old towels, pillow cases and brightly-coloured, knitted scarves, but it's not in there either.

Maybe her mum threw it out.

She turns to leave the room but stops. There's one last hiding place. In a last-ditch attempt she throws herself down on to the floor and lifts up the valance that goes all the way round the base of the double bed – and there, in the centre of the floor under the bed, is a box tied with a blue ribbon. She wriggles forwards and reaches her arm out as far as she can. She wriggles a little more until her fingers manage to brush the side of the box. The telephone rings downstairs and she can hear footsteps in the hallway. She stretches as far as she can, ignoring the pain as the base of the bed digs into her shoulder. Nearly there…

And then she's got it. Her fingers curl around one corner, just enough to allow her to work it towards her. Mum's voice rises through the floorboards as she answers the telephone, and Cathy grabs the box and pulls one end of the ribbon. Everything inside is arranged in neat piles, and the green pouch is tucked into a corner under a pair of baby bootees.

She lifts the pouch and discovers a pile of old black-and-white photographs underneath. The picture on top captures a family all dressed up for a special occasion. She scans the faces searching for anyone she might recognise, but the image is too faded to see clearly. The next photograph was taken at the seaside: two girls sit proudly in front of a giant sandcastle, waving their spades in the air and grinning for the camera. The girls in the picture look almost identical; they both have the same dimple on their chins and the same twinkle in their eyes. She's sure the girls in the picture are her mum and her big sister, but hadn't her mum said there weren't any other pictures of her sister? She must have been mistaken.

Cathy leans up on her knees and looks in the mirror. Does she have the same dimple on her chin? She thinks maybe she does.

The next photograph is of Mum and Dad on their wedding day. Dad's got this enormous, bushy moustache and Mum's wearing a simple dress and holding a large spray of carnations. There's a similar picture downstairs in the dining room, and she's always imagined the flowers to be pink but she can't tell for sure.

Beneath the photographs she finds a small white Bible, and she lifts it out carefully. The edge of each page is painted gold, and she thumbs through the book, watching flickers of gold rush past.

The telephone conversation ends and she can hear footsteps on the stairs. She quickly ties the blue ribbon around the box and slides it back under the bed. Clutching the velvet pouch in her hand, she bolts towards her room and runs straight into her mum.

'What are you up to?'

Her mum is going to spot the pouch in her hand any second now.

'Just playing.'

'Well, go and play somewhere else,' Mum says and walks past her into her own bedroom, shutting the door behind her. Whatever that phone call was about, it seems to have upset her. Cathy stares at the closed door to Jimmy's room, the full-length poster of Debbie Harry pouting at her, mocking her for being a little girl. Her brother is becoming a man and she can't stand it. She wants to burst into his room and tell him that Mum's upset, tell him she's worried about these phone calls Mum keeps getting, tell him something important is going on behind their backs.

Debbie Harry looks down with her tousled hair, painted lips and provocative stance, and dares her to enter. Cathy leaves the door closed and heads back to her room to tell the Blue Lady everything.

The Minister

Cathy usually loves a Thursday afternoon; silent reading followed by art. She loves art! And when the bell rings at the end of the day it means there's only one day left to go before it's the weekend.

But this Thursday afternoon is different. Miss Turner went home sick at playtime, and already the rumours are spreading. 'She's on her dabs,' says Linda, and nobody dares to disagree. 'You could tell.'

Cathy wonders how Linda can tell, but she's too scared to ask. Asking would mean admitting you don't know. Her own bleeding had stopped as quickly as it started, and if it wasn't for the dark stain on her dress she'd believe the whole thing had been a bad dream. She'd searched inside the special toiletry bag her mum keeps in the bathroom, but isn't any the wiser. She'd found cotton wool shaped like mini space rockets, but she doesn't dare to imagine what her mum does with them. When she buys them in the supermarket she always tucks them away at the bottom of the trolley underneath the rest of the shopping. She remembers when she was little she'd asked her what they were, but her mum had turned scarlet and muttered, 'Plenty of time yet, plenty of time.' From that day Cathy knew they were something never to be spoken about.

Linda was the first girl in their class to start her periods, and Cathy's not sure about the others. Billy Weir told all the boys that Jennifer Robertson had started, but Jennifer's mum came marching up to school to see Mrs Henderson, the headmistress, and Billy had been made to apologise. He's always getting into trouble. Cathy's mum says it's because he doesn't have a mum. Everyone in school knows his mum killed herself. Richard Wilson said she was found dead in the bath with the toaster, but Linda said she heard that she hung herself from the living room ceiling. Miss Turner caught them talking and gave them a row for gossiping. She said they should all try and be nice to Billy, but he smells of wee and looks like he hasn't had a bath in weeks.

Cathy can't imagine her mum not being there.

Anyway, this Thursday afternoon Miss Turner isn't in class, Mrs Henderson is, and so everyone is behaving themselves and sitting quietly. Even Billy Weir.

'This afternoon,' begins Mrs Henderson, 'I've organised a treat for you all.'

Cathy sneaks a look across her desk at Linda and Linda rolls her eyes. Everyone knows Mrs Henderson's treats are never any fun.

'I've arranged for a special visitor to come in.'

Bang goes the art. Cathy crosses her fingers. *Please let us have silent reading, please, please.* At long last, it's her turn to read *Forever*. She's the last girl in the class to read it, except Jennifer Robertson. Jennifer's mum said she's not to read any of that 'Judy Blume trash'. Cathy hasn't asked her mum. She looks up at Mrs Henderson and squeezes her crossed fingers even tighter.

'But until the visitor arrives,' Mrs Henderson says, 'I'd like everyone to take out their library book and begin reading in silence.'

Cathy jumps out of her seat and races to the library corner. She knows exactly where to find the book. Linda walks up to her and whispers in her ear, 'It's your turn.'

Cathy tries to act casual, but she's been waiting to read this book since the start of Primary Seven. She scans the shelf but can't see it anywhere.

'Hurry up, girls.' Mrs Henderson is standing behind them.

Cathy looks across at the girl who had it last, but she's already in her seat reading *Last Term at Malory Towers*.

'It's not here,' she whispers to Linda.

Linda looks at her. 'Of course it's here. It has to be. It's your turn.'

'I'm telling you, it's not.'

Mrs Henderson steps between them. 'What are you two girls whispering about?'

'Sorry, Miss,' says Linda, turning on her charm. 'Cathy was looking for a book.'

Mrs Henderson turns to look at Cathy. 'Open your eyes, girl. There must be over a hundred books here.'

'She's after a particular book, Miss.'

Mrs Henderson looks over her half-moon glasses at Cathy. 'Miss Turner and I had a good tidy last week and cleared out all books that we felt were,' she pauses, 'inappropriate for young minds. Perhaps if you tell me the title of the book you're looking for…'

Before Linda can say another word Cathy reaches out and grabs the first book her hand touches. *Knitting for Beginners*. 'This is it,' she says.

'I didn't know you were interested in knitting,' says Mrs Henderson. 'Maybe we could start a club for the girls.' She pats Cathy on the head like a puppy. 'What a splendid idea, Catherine. Well done. I'll get on it right away.'

Cathy is still trying to think of something to say when Linda drags her by the elbow back to her seat. 'Sit down,' she says, 'before you come up with any other smart ideas.'

Cathy sits down behind her desk and pretends to look at the knitting pattern for an Aran jumper, but her mind wanders. What will she do if she starts to bleed again? She's folded several sheets of toilet paper and stuffed them inside her pants, but she can't do this every day.

The clock on the classroom wall ticks loudly to mark each passing second, but its hands don't seem to be moving any closer towards home time. Silent reading with Miss Turner never lasts longer than twenty minutes, but today no one tells them to stop reading or to close their books, and the boys are getting restless, transforming their rulers into catapults and pinging shaved pieces of rubber around the room.

Mrs Henderson doesn't seem to notice.

A paper aeroplane lands in Cathy's lap, and the small blue squares tell her it's from a page torn out of a maths jotter. She glances around the room and spots Richard Wilson grinning at her like an idiot. Cathy flicks the paper to the floor without bothering to open it, and Mrs Henderson pounces on it.

'What's this?' she asks.

She peels opens the sheet of paper, and Cathy could die when she sees there's writing inside.

'Billy Weir! Come out to the blackboard this second.'

The room falls silent as everyone watches Billy take the long walk from his seat at the very back of the room and slowly wind his way between individual desks to stand in front of the blackboard. Without being told to, he holds out his hand. He's had the belt often enough to know what's expected. Mrs Henderson stands in front of the class and presents the sheet of squared paper for everyone to see. *Billy loves Cathy* is scrawled in red felt pen inside a giant love heart with an arrow piercing its centre. Cathy can feel everyone staring at her and, out of the corner of her eye, she catches Richard Wilson laughing.

'How many times must we go through this, Mr Weir, before you understand that school is a place for learning, not a place for carrying on? It's time you learned what's good for you.' She holds the leather strap up high for everyone to see. 'Twelve strikes should suffice.' The class collectively take a sharp inhale of breath. Twelve strikes are more than any of them have ever witnessed. Cathy turns round to see if Richard Wilson is going to admit it was actually him who threw the note. He sees her watching him and blows her a kiss.

'One…'

The belt slices downwards through the air, stopping only when it reaches the palm of Billy's hand. Cathy sees him flinch and wills him to stay still. Pulling away only results in more strikes.

'Two… Three… Four…'

The pause between blows seems to last forever and Cathy wishes her head teacher would hurry up and get it over with.

'Five... Six...'

She closes her eyes but the sound alone is somehow worse and she opens them again. Billy is staring at some imaginary spot in the distance and doesn't seem to notice when the belt strikes the palm of his hand. What does he see in his head that's getting him through this?

At last Mrs Henderson reaches twelve and Cathy thinks her head teacher looks disappointed as her victim walks back to his seat with his head held high.

'Catherine Munro, it is clear to me that you are not innocent in all of this. A boy does not have such feelings without some encouragement. Come out to the front of the class.'

Cathy stands and turns to Richard for help but this time he doesn't look at her. Her legs wobble as she walks to the blackboard and she lifts her shaking hands in front of her.

Mrs Henderson smiles. 'One strike should be sufficient for a first offence.'

The leather hits the cut on the palm of her hand, the one she got from the barbed wire, and she clutches her hand, sure the wound has burst open and is bleeding again.

'Let this be a lesson to all of you. The classroom is not a place for cavorting with members of the opposite sex, and I will not tolerate such behaviour in my school.' Mrs Henderson tears up the note and drops it in the bin.

Just then the classroom door opens and the school minister enters the room. Like Pavlov's dogs, the children all react instantly, standing to attention with hands firmly stuck to their sides, and backs poker-straight.

'Good afternoon, Reverend Small,' the children chime.

Cathy's not looking at the Reverend, she's watching Mrs Henderson, and sees her headmistress transform in front of her. The woman who, moments ago, took pleasure from belting her students becomes a gushing, giggling teenager, batting her eyelids like the girls do when they see Cathy's big brother walk in to the room. Jimmy's always been popular with the girls, and it's not fair because Dad just slaps him on the back and congratulates him on his magnetic charm. 'Just like your old man.' He laughs. She can just imagine if she brought a boyfriend home. Her dad would go through the roof.

Reverend Small hasn't given them permission to sit down yet. His long, scrawny neck sticks up above his white collar and his head bobs on top like one of the nodding dogs you see in the back of cars. He turns his head slowly to look at her and she swears he's reading her mind. He gives her a wry smile, but it's the kind of smile you might give someone before biting their head off. Mrs Henderson is still batting her eyelids at him, and, wait... Did he give Mrs Henderson a wink? The room is suddenly very hot and Cathy's hand is pulsing with pain. If they don't get to sit down soon, she thinks she might pass out.

Reverend Small holds his hands out in front of him and they wait. His tongue flickers across his top lip. Cathy is reminded of the snake in the tunnel, and the silhouette of recent nightmares slithers through her mind before slipping away again as quickly as it surfaced.

'Be seated.'

Everyone obeys his command and he grins. He takes a small, black Bible from his pocket and opens it at a page marked with a strip of red ribbon, and begins reading the passage in a slow, monotone voice. Cathy looks around at her classmates. Everyone, including Billy Weir, is pretending to pay attention.

Finally, he closes the Bible and looks up at the class. 'Any questions?'

Cathy's hand shoots up into the air before she can stop herself.

The Reverend looks surprised. Nobody ever asks a question without first being prompted by the head teacher. 'Yes?'

'Can Protestants go to Confession?'

He looks confused by the question, which isn't really a

surprise; after all, Cathy herself didn't know the word until recently so she re-phrases it for him. 'If I committed a sin,' she explains, 'like, you know, if I did something bad, well, should I tell someone about it and then say sorry to God afterwards?'

The Reverend looks down at her. 'And have you committed a sin, Catherine? Or, as you so eloquently put it, have you done something bad?'

Cathy shakes her head. She isn't about to admit her sins to a man who looks more like a tortoise than a messenger of God. 'My friend Thomas says that if we don't say sorry for all the bad things we do then we'll go to hell. His priest made a boy say three Hail Marys for stealing money from his mum's purse to buy an ice-cream.' She covers her mouth. She promised Thomas she wouldn't tell anyone that story. Oh, why can't she keep her big mouth shut?

The minister laughs out loud, but it's not a friendly laugh. Cathy thinks it sounds like the laugh the bad guy makes before he comes to chop off your head, and she's wishing she'd kept quiet. He strides across the classroom and stops directly in front of her desk. He tucks both hands behind his back and sways forwards on to his tiptoes, making himself look at least seven feet tall.

'And which school does your friend Thomas go to?' He spits Thomas's name out, froth foaming at the corners of his mouth. Can a tortoise get rabies? She must remember to ask Jimmy when she gets home.

'St Mary's.'

Reverend Small snorts, and she can see the hairs inside his nose.

'St Mary's?' he repeats, peering down at her. 'I hardly think we need to worry about what *they* think.'

Mrs Henderson flaps into the conversation, waving her hands in the air about her head.

'Right, girls and boys, time to say thank you to the Reverend.'

Cathy hasn't finished. 'But you said there's only one God.'

Reverend Small clasps his hands in front of him. 'That's right.'

'So if the Catholics say their God won't let them into Heaven without confessing all their sins, then why would he let me in?'

'Because you're a Protestant, and all Protestants go to Heaven.'

'Who says?'

'Catherine,' interrupts Mrs Henderson. 'It's rude to talk to the Reverend in this way.'

'But he asked us if we had any questions.'

'Questions about the church,' says the Reverend, 'not questions about *them*.'

Mrs Henderson raises a single, stern finger to her lips telling Cathy to stop talking, just as the bell rings for the end of the day.

The girls are halfway home when Linda realises she's left her violin in class.

'You can get it tomorrow,' Cathy tells her.

'But I'm supposed to be playing in assembly tomorrow and I need to practise.'

'Yeah, but if I'm late home my mum will kill me.'

'Well, I'm going back to get it, and if you walk home by yourself your mum will be madder than if you're late. You know she doesn't like it if you walk home alone.'

Cathy knows she's right. 'Well, only if we're quick.'

'Come on, then,' Linda shouts back over her shoulder, already walking back towards the school.

By the time they reach the school gates, everyone has left, and the only sound is from the empty crisp packets scratching across the tarmac as they're tossed around in the wind.

'Maybe you could come in early tomorrow morning instead,' suggests Cathy.

'Don't be stupid; we're here now.'

Cathy doesn't like it and tries to think of an excuse to leave. 'The doors are probably locked.'

'Well, we can bang on the staffroom window.' Linda

points to a red sports car in the staff car park. ‘Look. Mrs Henderson’s still here.’

‘She’ll give you a row for forgetting to take it home in the first place.’

‘And I’ll be in bigger trouble if I can’t play tomorrow.’

‘I still think we should get out of here. I’ve already been belted today.’

Linda fires her a look that tells her to shut up.

The main door isn’t locked, and the two girls push it open just enough to squeeze through, stopping at the point before the hinge creaks with a loud groan. They both know the best outcome here is to get the violin out of the building without Mrs Henderson ever knowing they were here.

‘What if we bump into her?’ asks Cathy.

‘Don’t be daft; she’ll be in her office.’

Their quiet whispers are magnified in the empty hallway and neither girl speaks again as they make their way along the long corridor towards their classroom. They’ll soon have the violin in their hands and will be making their way out of here. A single pink glove is hanging on a peg outside the school office, and Cathy wonders how it can still be here in June. It feels like it’s been summer forever.

As they reach the open door at the end of the corridor, they stop and listen. Someone’s in their classroom. Cathy leans over Linda’s shoulder to see what’s going on, and has to bite down hard on her bottom lip to stop herself from crying out.

The Reverend Small has her head teacher pinned up against the blackboard. His face is pressed between Mrs Henderson’s enormous bare breasts. Her blouse and bra are lying discarded on the floor, and he’s groaning as she squeezes her tits together, almost suffocating him. Cathy stares at the Reverend as his hand pushes Mrs Henderson’s skirt upwards, and she sees the lacy frills of her head teacher’s red knickers. Red!

Cathy looks at her friend who presses her finger against her lips. There’s no way they’re going to get the violin now. Linda grabs her by the arm and pulls her away from the scene, but before she leaves, Cathy steals one last look at the minister and sees him slide his hand inside the red knickers. She squeezes her eyes shut and wishes she could undo the image.

The two girls spin round and run away, back down the corridor, past empty classrooms on either side, past the single pink glove and towards the main door. They're nearly there when Cathy hears a loud cry come from the classroom behind them and she turns to look, worried they've been spotted. As she turns, her school bag gets caught. Before she can do anything about it, the fire extinguisher on the wall behind her comes crashing to the ground.

'Run,' shouts Linda, but when Cathy tries to run she can't move.

'It's caught,' she shouts, but Linda is already at the door.

'Who's there?' It's the Reverend Small. She pulls again, harder this time, but the strap won't budge from under the weight of the extinguisher. Cathy makes a snap decision. She slips the straps of her school bag from her shoulders and sprints for the main door, leaving her bag behind.

Linda is waiting for her outside the corner shop. 'Are they following you?'

Cathy shakes her head. They wouldn't have chased her with only half their clothes on.

'Did they see you?'

'Don't think so.'

Linda bursts out laughing. 'So that's what she gets up to after school. Who'd have thought it, eh? Reverend Small is shagging Mrs Henderson.'

'It should be illegal.'

Linda stops laughing and looks at her. 'Maybe it is.'

'What d'ya mean?'

'I mean, maybe there's a rule that stops a Reverend from touching a woman's tits. Isn't he supposed to be married to God or something?'

'I think you're getting mixed up with priests.'

Linda looks deflated. 'Maybe.' She shakes a Tic-Tac from the packet in her hand and pops it into her mouth.

'Imagine what everyone will say when they find out.'

'And how are they going to find out?'

'We could make posters and stick them up on lamp posts near the school, but we'll need to be careful they don't find out it was us that saw them together.' She stops and looks at Cathy. 'Are you okay?'

'My bag. I had to leave it behind.'

Linda stares at her. 'You're kidding, right?'

'I couldn't get it out from under the fire extinguisher and I could hear him coming. I had to get out of there.'

'And you left your bag behind?'

'I had to.'

'Does it have your name on it?'

She shakes her head.

'What about inside? Is there anything inside that has your name on it?'

Cathy tries to think. Her gym kit is in her tray in the classroom, so that's okay, and she doesn't think her name is on her pencil case. 'I don't think so.'

'Right, let's come up with a plan.' Linda twirls a long strand of hair between her fingers. 'Now tomorrow, Mrs Henderson is going to try and find out who the bag belongs to.'

'She might be too embarrassed to ask any questions.'

'She's the head teacher,' says Linda, 'so there's nothing suspicious about her asking who a school bag belongs to. Bags are left behind all the time.'

'So, maybe she'll think I left mine behind too.'

Linda raises an eyebrow. 'You said it was trapped beneath the fire extinguisher.'

Good point.

'So when she holds it up in class tomorrow and asks who it belongs to, you mustn't react.'

'But what about my stuff?'

'What about it?'

'I got my pencil case for starting school this year. It's got a secret compartment and everything.'

Linda stares at her with disgust. 'If you claim the bag

then she'll know it was you that was in the building, and you'll be in serious trouble,'

'I'll tell her we came back for your violin.'

Linda grabs her by the hair and yanks her close. 'I was nowhere near that school, do you understand?'

Cathy tries to nod but she can't move.

'Understand?'

'I understand.'

Linda lets go of her and pushes her away. 'This is our plan. When Mrs Henderson holds up your school bag you keep your mouth shut. If someone says it looks like yours you deny it. Got it?'

'I've got it,' she repeats, 'but what if she asks to see my bag?'

'Bring one of your old bags with you tomorrow and then she won't be able to say anything.'

Cathy doubts it's going to be that easy, but she keeps quiet. When she gets home she races upstairs before her mum can see she's not got her school bag. She quickly pulls on her jeans and a t-shirt and straightens her face in front of the mirror before going back downstairs where Mum is in the kitchen peeling potatoes. The windows are open, the radio is turned up loud and she's in a good mood.

'How was your day?' She doesn't even seem to notice Cathy's late.

'Great.' Cathy takes a biscuit from the cupboard. Mum stops what she's doing and Cathy knows she's overplayed her enthusiasm. 'Sorry, just being sarcastic. Miss Turner was off so we had Mrs Henderson instead.'

Mum laughs and goes back to peeling potatoes. 'I bet that was fun.'

A sudden brainwave hits Cathy. She's going to need all of the help she can get for tomorrow.

'The minister came in to school this afternoon and gave us some homework.'

'Oh?'

'We've to find out about praying.'

'What about it?'

'We've to find out which way of praying works best, you know if you need to ask a favour from God.' Her mum looks up from the sink. 'I mean, he didn't quite put it like that but, you know, we've to find out as much as we can.'

'About praying?'

'That's right.'

'Cathy, not everyone believes in God.'

'I know that, but I need to be able to tell him something when he asks me next week.'

'I'm not sure I can tell you anything you don't already know.'

'Have you ever prayed for something?'

'Not for a long time.' Mum stares out of the kitchen window, and Cathy can hear the birds singing as they flit from tree to tree. She watches her mum and wonders what she's thinking about.

'What sorts of things did you ask for?'

'Silly, childish things, I guess.'

'Like?'

'I don't know, how am I supposed to remember after all this time?' She yelps and lifts her hand out of the water. Blood trickles down her wet finger. 'Now look what you've made me do.'

'Do you remember if it ever worked?'

'I've told you it was just childish nonsense. Now, why don't you leave me alone and let me finish these potatoes?'

Cathy goes up to her room, closes the curtains and takes the shoe box from its hiding place at the back of the wardrobe. She'd love to light a candle to add to the effect, but her mum might smell it and come to see what she's up to, so instead she switches on the bedside lamp. The lamp casts a warm orange circle of light on to the bedside table, and Cathy opens the box and places the Blue Lady in the centre of the spotlight. She lifts the green velvet pouch from the box and carefully lifts out the pendant. The jewels aren't as big as she remembers, and as she looks at it more closely she can see they're fake. But it's still beautiful, and she slips it over her head and tucks it under her t-shirt. The silver cross feels cool against her skin.

She gets down on to her knees in front of the bedside table and clasps her hands tightly. She then bows her head like she's seen Mrs Henderson do in assembly. Now she's ready she's not sure what she's supposed to say. Is it like the letter to Santa? Is she supposed to do the polite bit first, you know, thank him for all of last year's presents and ask how Mrs Claus is, before finally getting round to the nitty-gritty of telling him what present she'd like this year? She decides to play on the safe side and thank God for all of the nice things in the world first. So she thanks Him for the pretty flowers and the butterflies and the bees. Then she thanks Him for stopping the car that almost ran over the dog that lives across the street, and she thanks Him for her mum and dad. She thinks about thanking Him for her big brother Jimmy, but what if God can tell she's lying?

It's time to ask her favour. 'Please, God, I didn't mean to see the minister and Mrs Henderson, and really it was Linda's fault that we went back into the school, I was just trying to be a good friend by going back with her for her violin, so I was wondering if you could help me out.' She looks at the Blue Lady. 'Please, God, don't let me get into trouble tomorrow; don't let Mrs Henderson find my school bag.'

She can hear her mum coming upstairs, and she whispers as quickly as she can. 'Please, make my bag be on the peg tomorrow morning as if nothing happened.' Her mum is on the landing now but Cathy wants to ask God one last favour. 'And if you can keep Mrs Henderson off school for the day that would be amazing.'

'Cathy, here are your clean clothes to put away.' Mum opens the bedroom door.

'Don't you ever knock?'

'What have you got the curtains shut for?'

'I'm about to get changed.'

Her mum looks her up and down. 'But you're already changed.'

She needs to get her mum out of here before she sees the

china statue. 'I'm too hot in these jeans so I thought I'd put on my summer dress.'

Mum beams and walks into the room. 'I'm sure it's in your wardrobe.'

'It's okay, I'll find it.' Cathy stands in front of the bedside table to block the Blue Lady from view.

'I've been thinking about this homework.' Mum takes out a hanger from the wardrobe. 'I'm not sure the school should be asking children your age about praying. That's up to the individual, and if they want to pray they should be going to church, not doing it in school. I'm thinking I should maybe write a note to Mrs Henderson.'

'No,' Cathy shouts and her mum turns to look at her. 'It's fine, Mum, honestly. Please don't draw any attention to me.'

Mum thinks about it for a second. 'Well, just don't tell your dad about it, okay?'

'Okay.'

'Promise?'

'If you pass me my dress.'

Mum laughs and the atmosphere passes. 'What did your last slave die of?'

The First Miracle

Cathy switches off her alarm and slips out of bed. She tiptoes downstairs and slowly opens the door to the cupboard under the stairs, and finds Jimmy's sports bag tucked in the corner. Carrying it upstairs, she closes her bedroom door behind her. Jimmy doesn't have football until Saturday, and by then she'll have her own bag back and he'll never even know she borrowed it.

She empties the bag, stuffing his kit under her bed. All of her school things are in her own bag which is wrapped around a fire extinguisher back at school, but she's worried Mrs Henderson will demand to check inside everyone's bag in an attempt to hunt down the culprit. So she throws in a couple of pencils and a copy of *Black Beauty*.

Her palm no longer hurts after yesterday's belting, but what if Reverend Small wants to deal out his own punishment? She clasps her hands together and tries another prayer.

'Please, don't let him send me straight to hell. I promise never to spy on anyone ever again.'

Time passes excruciatingly slowly and it feels like it's never going to be half past eight, but at last the hand on the kitchen clock moves and her mum shouts at her to get ready. Cathy slips her shoes on and quickly licks her finger and rubs a scuff on the toe before her mum can notice.

Dad appears downstairs. 'I'm heading in to the office so I can give you a lift.'

'I'm meeting Linda halfway.'

'That's okay; I can take you halfway.'

'The walk will do me good; I've got a times tables test this morning and I was going to practise on the way.'

Another white lie. 'Besides it's a beautiful day, and you're always telling me to spend more time outdoors.'

Dad raises an eyebrow. 'Cathy, I'm telling you to get in the car.'

Her stomach churns. Did Mrs Henderson call to tell him about yesterday's belting? Maybe she can persuade Mum to catch a lift into town with them, because whatever Dad wants to talk about, he clearly doesn't want to say it in front of her.

'You look nice, Mum. Are you going shopping today?'

Mum stops and stares at her.

'Dad's about to give me a lift to school, and I thought you might want a lift too.'

'I haven't even done my hair yet.'

'Nonsense, it looks great.'

Mum laughs. 'What are you after?'

Dad walks back into the hallway. 'What's going on?'

'Nothing.'

'Your daughter is up to something.'

Dad looks sideways at Cathy but she doesn't face him. He scoops up the car keys from the hall table. 'Let's go.'

Mum steps forward to give him a kiss and Cathy seizes the opportunity to reach down and grab the handle of Jimmy's bag through her coat. She's practised this already, and if she's careful she can lift the bag and coat at the same time and no one can see what's underneath. She gets it first time and just hopes the coat is long enough to cover the bag.

'Cathy.'

She freezes.

'It's far too hot out there for a coat.'

'But I might need it at lunchtime.'

'Don't be silly. It's boiling out there.'

Cathy looks upwards. *Please, Mary, don't let her see the bag.*

Just then there's a crash in the kitchen, followed by loud swearing. It sounds like Jimmy's broken something.

Cathy leaps on the distraction. 'Have a nice day,' she shouts as she escapes into the early morning sunshine. She climbs into the passenger seat, drops her jacket over the bag and looks up to her bedroom window and mouths *Thank you*.

Dad pulls out of the drive and she fixes her eyes on the road in front of her. Maybe if she doesn't look at him he won't say anything. But they don't even reach the bottom of the hill before he breaks the silence.

'I was speaking to an old neighbour yesterday.'

So this isn't about yesterday's belting.

'He said he'd seen you at the chapel on Sunday.'

She lets go of the cross at her neck.

'He asked if you were planning on taking Communion.' He pulls up outside the shop where Linda is waiting, and turns in his seat so that he's facing her. 'I think it's time you started hanging around with some different friends. Maybe you could invite Linda over for dinner sometime.'

'What do you mean?'

'I mean it's time you stopped seeing Thomas.'

'But he's my best friend.'

'Enough.' He slams both hands on the steering wheel. 'I don't want you to see that boy any more. Am I clear?'

Cathy's hands shake as she throws open the car door. She storms across the pavement towards Linda.

'Can you believe what we saw after school yesterday? Do you think they *did it*?' Linda doesn't wait for her to answer. 'I bet they did. I bet they had sex in our classroom.'

Cathy doesn't understand. Her dad's never angry with her. Why doesn't he want her to see Thomas?

She watches him drive away, and realises Linda's still talking.

'And he's got the nerve to preach to us about good Christian values and tell us how to behave. Well, next time he starts prattling on about going to Hell I'm gonnae stop him and ask him if ministers can get sent there too, and I'll make sure I ask him in front of Mrs Henderson.'

'I thought you didn't want her to know it was us,' says Cathy.

'I've changed my mind.'

'But if she found out we came back into the school building she'd give us ten of the belt.'

'She wouldn't dare.'

'Why not?'

'What do you think our parents would say if we told them what we'd seen?'

Cathy wouldn't dare to tell her mum and dad what they'd seen. She'd rather die first.

Linda gasps loudly and then covers her mouth.

'What is it?' Cathy asks.

Linda stifles a giggle.

'Tell me.'

'What if she's pregnant?'

'What? But how?'

'What do you mean how? Christ, don't you know anything?'

Cathy thinks about telling her you can't get pregnant if you do it standing up, but she stops. What if that's not true?

Linda's marching towards the school singing, '*The Rev and Henderson sitting in a tree. K-i-s-s-i-n-g...*'

Cathy runs to catch up, hoping desperately she'll stop singing before anyone else hears. They arrive at the school gates just in time to hear the morning bell ring.

'Come on,' she says. 'We're in enough trouble as it is. Don't want to draw any more attention to ourselves.'

'Alright. Alright. Keep your knickers on.' Linda laughs at her own joke. Loudly.

By the time they get there, the cloakroom is busy with girls hanging up jackets and chatting about what they did last night. Cathy nudges Linda in the ribs.

'Look.' She points to the spot where the fire extinguisher lay on the floor. 'It's gone.'

'It's back on the wall,' Linda says. 'But where's your bag?'

Cathy knows it's there before she even turns to look.

'It's on my peg,' she whispers. And sure enough, her schoolbag is hanging on the peg beneath her name tag.

'She knew it was you all along.'

Cathy doesn't dare tell Linda the truth. She lifts her hand to the cross beneath her blouse and rubs it gently. It wasn't Mrs Henderson who hung her bag on its peg. It was God.

The girls hang up their jackets and join the line outside the classroom door. Miss Turner waits until the children are quiet, then gestures for them to enter. The class traipse silently into the room, taking up their positions behind their desks until their teacher is ready. She stands in front of the blackboard and greets them with, 'Good morning' and the girls and boys repeat the phrase to her in a tuneless fashion and then sit down in their seats.

'There will be no assembly today…'

Cathy crosses her fingers.

'…as Mrs Henderson isn't in school.'

She coughs and splutters and everyone turns to look at her. She points to her throat, pretending she's got something stuck in it. She can't believe it. God has answered her prayers. She wonders if her head teacher is at home in bed with the school minister, and her cheeks blush as she pictures Reverend Small pushing his hand inside Mrs Henderson's red knickers.

'Instead of assembly, I'll take the boys outside for a game of football.' She's interrupted with loud shouts from the boys.

Linda's hand shoots up but she doesn't wait to be asked to speak. 'What about the girls?'

Cathy hopes they're not going to get sewing. She hates sewing. The home economics teacher always pulls out her stitches and makes her do it again. She wishes the girls would get to play football too, because at least she knows she's good in goals. She considers having a quick word with God, but decides to save her prayers for more important things.

'I'll speak to the girls once the boys have gone to get changed,' says Miss Turner.

'That's not fair.'

'We never get to do fun stuff.'

'Please, Miss, what are we doing?'

Just then the school nurse walks in to the classroom with a video cassette in her hand, and this grabs the boys' attention.

Miss Turner holds up her hand to quieten the class. 'Boys, you can go and get changed.'

But the boys don't move. They want to know what's going on. Miss Turner leans closer to speak to the girls but before she can say anything the school nurse makes an announcement to the whole class.

'There is no need to be embarrassed by menstruation. It's part of the miracle of creation.'

Cathy hears the word *miracle* and wishes she could tell everyone about the real-life miracle that happened here today.

'So, if the girls will stand and follow me through to the medical room, I've got a video that will teach you about periods and puberty.'

Without a word, the girls stand and silently follow the nurse out of the classroom, leaving the boys whispering and giggling behind cupped hands.

The medical room is a small windowless room at the back of the school, normally used for nit inspections. Today, the TV trolley has been wheeled into the room and is set up beside the sick bed. The girls are asked to sit cross-legged on the cold linoleum, and they do as they're told without argument, even Linda. No one fidgets or whispers as the nurse takes out the cassette and slides it into the video player.

Cathy thinks about her school bag hanging on the peg, exactly the way she'd pictured it in her head when she'd asked for God's help. Thomas is wrong. God does listen, and she wishes she'd tried praying sooner; maybe she could have saved the stallion. The video is ready to play, and the school nurse switches the lights off. But surely millions of people around the world pray to God at the same time, so why did He listen to her? What makes her so special?

But she already knows the answer. It's the Blue Lady.

The video starts and a diagram of a woman's body

appears on the screen. It zooms in below the stomach and starts labelling parts of the body she's never heard of before. Fallopian tubes. Cervix. Ovary. She goes back to thinking about this morning's miracle and a terrible thought enters her head. She'd asked God for Mrs Henderson to be off today, but what if her head teacher is sick? Or worse, had an accident? A woman's voice on the television starts talking about the breaking down of the womb wall and images of blood flowing from the vagina fill the screen. Cathy feels faint. What if she's responsible for killing her head teacher?

The room around her starts to dim and the next thing she knows, she's lying on the sick bed and the only person in the room is Miss Turner.

Her teacher runs her fingers gently across Cathy's brow. 'Don't worry; you're not the first girl it happened to.'

'What happened?'

'You were watching the video and you fainted.'

'What's wrong with Mrs Henderson?'

Miss Turner holds out a delicate china cup decorated with roses. 'Here, have a sip of water. You've just woken up and you're confused.'

She's not confused, but she takes the cup to make Miss Turner happy. A red lipstick mark has stained the rim of the white porcelain. Was Mrs Henderson the last person to drink from this cup? She turns the cup to find a clean edge, then takes a small sip and asks once more about her head teacher.

Miss Turner squeezes her hand. 'Why are you worrying about Mrs Henderson?'

Cathy wishes she could tell her teacher about the miracle. 'Linda's been practising really hard on her violin for today's assembly and I was wondering if she'll still get to play.'

'How kind of you to think of your friend. Don't worry, I'll speak to Mrs Henderson and I'm sure Linda can play for the school on Monday.'

'So she's okay then, Mrs Henderson? She's not dying?'

Miss Turner laughs. 'She's fine. She was called away to a meeting.'

'A meeting?' Cathy's so happy she could hug Miss Turner.

'There, now, you suddenly look a whole lot better, I guess that sip of water did you the world of good. Come on, let's get back to class.'

The boys whisper behind their hands when she walks into the classroom, but she doesn't care. Her head teacher is still alive, which means she's not a murderer, and she's still got a chance of making it into Heaven.

After lunch, Miss Turner shows the class a print of a woman and young child walking through a field of poppies. 'I know you missed out on art yesterday, so I thought we could do some painting this afternoon to make up for it.'

Cathy looks at Monet's painting but instead of poppies all she can see is splatters of blood. None of the girls mentioned the video over lunch. Either they already knew everything, or maybe, like Cathy, they're now more confused than before.

The desks are covered with newspapers, and a paint palette is placed in the centre of each table along with a plastic cup of water.

'Can you hand out the paint brushes please, Cathy? I have to go and get some more paper from the art cupboard.' Cathy wishes Miss Turner would stop being so kind. Every time her name is mentioned the boys all snigger.

She moves between the tables, giving out brushes and trying to ignore the awkward looks. She walks back to her seat to begin painting, aware everyone's watching her. How long is it going to take before they move on to their next victim?

She sits down and knows straight away something is wrong. Her seat is wet. She stands up and checks the back of her skirt with her hand. It's wet and it's sticky. She must be bleeding again.

Cathy's got her period.

She brings her hand round and holds it up. It's wet and it's sticky and it's red. Red. The colour of poppies, the colour of paint, the colour of blood.

Cathy's got her period.
Cathy's got her period.

The boys at her table are laughing and pointing at her as they continue chanting, and she looks more closely at her hands and sees that it's not blood. It's red paint.

She knocks her chair over and runs from the room, tears already tumbling down her cheeks.

'Why did you let this happen to me, God?' she shouts. 'I don't understand. How could you help me this morning, and then let this happen this afternoon? It doesn't make any sense. Don't you care about me?'

She throws open the door to the girls' toilets and yanks down her pleated school skirt. She turns the taps on and holds her skirt under the running water and watches her hands turn bright pink as she rubs liquid soap into the material. Standing in her blouse, pants and socks, she waits until the water is almost running clear and then blasts her skirt with lukewarm air from the hand dryer.

By the time she returns to class, the art lesson is over and everyone is busy packing up for home time.

'Still feeling a little dizzy?' Miss Turner asks, and Cathy nods, relieved her teacher doesn't know about the incident with the red paint. Any more sympathy right now would probably kill her.

Miss Turner doesn't ask any more questions and Cathy makes herself busy by helping to tidy up. Linda comes up to her but her best friend can't look her in the eye.

'Are you okay if I walk home with Richard today?' She doesn't mention the paint.

When the bell finally rings for the end of the day Cathy takes her time gathering all of her things and putting them into her schoolbag. She wants everyone to be gone by the time she leaves so she doesn't have to talk to anyone, but as she pulls on her jacket she's aware of a group of boys waiting in the cloakroom. She picks up both school bags and heads out into the playground.

'Hey, Cathy, don't be embarrassed. It's part of God's miracle of creation.' The boys laugh, and she looks around for Miss Turner. 'There's no one to save you now.'

She pretends she's not listening and heads for the school gate, but they continue following her. One of the boys grabs Jimmy's sports bag from her shoulder and throws it over her head to another boy in the gang. The game continues and they toss the bag between them as they chant.

Cathy's got her period.
Cathy's got her period.

She hates them. Hates them all. Thomas would never laugh at a girl like this. Catholic boys have more manners.

'Shut up,' she shouts. 'Shut up the lot of you.'

The bag lands at her feet and the chanting gets louder and faster.

Cathy's got her period.
Cathy's got her period.

She picks up the bag and runs the whole way home.

Matinee

It's Saturday morning, and the queue's already halfway up the street by the time she arrives. Thomas must have got here really early because he waves to her from the front of the line. She keeps her head down and crosses the street to meet him. She's got a packet of Bazooka bubble gum in her pocket, but she's secretly hoping he'll buy a box of Smarties for sharing.

'Great spot in the queue,' she says.

'We don't want to be late.'

Cathy looks at her watch. 'We're half an hour early.'

'Yeah, but I want to get the best seats. I've been waiting to see this film for ages.'

She hasn't told Thomas her dad has forbidden her from seeing him, and she tucks herself in between him and the whitewashed walls of the cinema where she can't be seen.

The doors open and they step out of the sweltering heat into the dark entrance of the cinema. She blinks and waits for her eyes to adjust before looking around at the posters on the walls. A giant poster for *The Empire Strikes Back* hangs by the ticket box, and Cathy thinks Carrie Fisher is beautiful. She's been trying to grow her own hair long enough for plaits, but her mum keeps insisting she gets it cut so she doesn't catch head lice.

They hand over the right money for their matinee tickets and head upstairs to the small cinema. She's disappointed he doesn't buy a box of sweets.

'How was school this week?'

He looks at her. They never talk about school.

'Fine,' he answers cautiously. 'Why do you ask?'

'Just being polite and making conversation,' she says.

'It was okay I guess.' Thomas pulls out a white poke of sweets from his pocket. He digs his hand into the bag of sweets and rummages around until he pulls out a bright orange gobstopper.

'We had the minister in class this week.' She thinks about telling Thomas about finding Mrs Henderson and the minster kissing, but decides not to. She doesn't want Thomas to think that's how Protestant ministers behave. 'He told us about praying, and I wondered if you pray the same way we do.'

Thomas laughs. 'You make it sound like I live on another planet.'

'No, I don't. I was just wondering if maybe Catholics prayed differently.'

'But you saw us praying in the chapel.'

'That's different.'

'Well, I don't know,' says Thomas. 'Tell me how you pray.'

She slips out of her seat and on to the floor and the cinema seat springs back upright. She stays down on her knees and turns round to face him. 'Like this,' she says, and clasps her hands in the praying position. 'Dear God, please keep my family safe and make sure we have enough food.'

Thomas kneels beside her. 'And please can I have enough gobstoppers to last the film.'

She nudges him with her elbow. 'Do it properly,' she says.

'And Lord save me from my crazy friend Catherine Munro.'

'And make my friend Thomas O'Donnell choke on his gobstopper.'

'Oi,' Thomas says. 'That's not funny.'

'Well, stop spoiling it.'

Thomas climbs back into his seat and offers her a sweet from the paper bag. 'Why are you so interested in praying, anyway? Every time I see you lately, you're asking me about the chapel or Mass or something.'

'I'm curious. Has God ever answered one of your

prayers?'

'What do you mean?'

'Has He ever helped you out?'

'I guess so.'

She sits back in her seat and looks at him. 'And have you ever had to pay Him for His help?'

Thomas laughs. 'You really are crazy. How could I pay God for helping me out?'

'I don't know. Like, maybe, He helps you in one way and then makes something bad happen to balance it out.'

Thomas looks at her.

'What is it?' she asks.

'I was wondering…'

'What?'

'Don't get mad at me.'

'What is it?'

'Did you take the statue of the Virgin Mary from my house?'

'Thomas O'Donnell, how dare you accuse me of stealing?'

'I didn't accuse you; I just asked.'

'Yeah, well, it's the same thing. I thought we were friends.'

'We are.'

'Well, friends don't go accusing each other of stealing.'

He looks at his feet, embarrassed.

She reaches into his bag of sweets and hands him another gobstopper. 'Here,' she says and he smiles at her.

'Sorry,' he says before stuffing the big red sweet in his mouth. He bites down on the gobstopper and it breaks in two with a loud crack. 'I should never have doubted you.'

'Forget about it,' she says, and knows she'll have to confess to the Blue Lady tonight for lying to her friend. Confession's not as easy as it sounds.

Thomas takes her hand. It's warm and sticky after being in the bag of gobstoppers.

'*Cathy and Thomas sitting in a tree.*

K-i-s-s-i-n-g...'

She's been so busy talking she didn't notice the gang of boys come up the steps and into the row behind them.

'First comes love, then comes marriage...'

She pulls her hand away from his and sits up straight.

'...Then comes Cathy with a baby carriage...'

'Shut up,' snaps Thomas.

'Sticking up for your girlfriend, are you?'

Just then the curtains pull back. The Pearl & Dean music blares out into the audience, and Cathy can't hear what they're saying anymore.

Like the start of every other matinee, the big screen fills with the image of pigeons settling in Trafalgar Square, and all the kids around her start clapping. The pigeons fly away and a short film from the Children's Film Foundation begins. These films are never any good and always feature some snobby kid with an English accent.

Her gobstopper has finished, but there's no way she's going to reach across and ask Thomas for one now that *they* are sitting behind them. Instead, she leans over to the right, as far away from him as she can get. Kids are still pouring in to the picture house, but it doesn't matter because no one's paying any attention to the short film on the screen. Everybody's waiting for today's main feature, *The Cat From Outer Space.* The place is filling up fast and she keeps an eye on the aisle, hoping Linda doesn't appear. She can't bear to imagine the ribbing she'll get if Linda sees that she's here with a boy. There are still a few seats left and she desperately hopes someone she doesn't know will hurry up and fill the two seats next to them.

But too late. Linda's arrived and she spots them straightaway, waves and runs up the stairs towards them.

'You've saved us a seat, thanks.'

It's then that Cathy sees who Linda's with. Richard Wilson, the most sought-after boy in the whole school. She looks over her shoulder waiting for the gang of boys in the row behind to start singing and teasing Linda and Richard, but there's not a sound. It seems the best-looking couple in the school are untouchable. Typical.

Linda nudges her in the ribs and gives her a wink. 'You're a dark horse,' she says.

Cathy wishes the film would hurry up and start.

The place is finally full and the curtains pull back another inch to let everyone know the main feature is about to begin. The place erupts and everyone's stamping their feet and cheering. She's been waiting to see this film for ages, but now that she's here, with Thomas on one side and Linda on the other, she can't concentrate. She thinks about what Thomas said. Does he really know she's got the Blue Lady? She'll need to be more careful about keeping her hidden.

She flips open the box of Bazooka and shakes out a piece of bubble gum. She offers one to Thomas and then turns to share with Linda and Richard, but, oh God, they're kissing. She looks away quickly before anyone sees that she's watching.

There's a sharp kick on the back of her chair and one of the boys from behind leans forward and shouts in her ear, 'Not joining in, eh? Not kissing Thomas O'Donnell? What's wrong? Don't want to be seen kissing a good little Catholic boy?'

The boy on the other side leans forward. 'Better watch your back, Fenian lover.'

She looks to see if Linda heard any of this, but her friend is glued to Richard at the lips, and their heads are thrashing from side to side as they kiss and it all looks like too much effort. Richard doesn't seem to know what to do with his hand and it's constantly on the move. Leg. Knee. Shoulder. Leg again. Cathy wishes they'd come up for air soon so she can speak to her friend. Surely, the boys won't try anything if they see that she and Thomas are here with the school's best-looking couple.

At last, they stop kissing and Cathy jumps in and offers Linda a piece of bubble gum.

'Don't be stupid,' Linda says. 'How can I kiss with that disgusting stuff in my mouth?'

Cathy apologises and wishes she could tell her friend what just happened, but now doesn't seem the right time.

She's still worrying about what to do when the film finishes, but she needn't worry because as soon as the credits come up at the end, the boys get up and leave.

Linda and Richard make their excuses and disappear, too, leaving Cathy and Thomas alone.

'Fancy sharing a bag of chips from Aldos?' he asks.

The day is too hot for a bag of chips, but she says yes anyway and they cross the road and join the queue. It's even hotter once they get inside the chip shop, and the fan by the till only works to whip up the smell of cooking fat.

'I'm sorry about those boys,' she says.

'That's okay. You can see why they'd maybe think we're boyfriend and girlfriend.'

Cathy wonders what he'd say if he knew they'd called him a Fenian. 'You can?'

'Well, you're a girl and I'm a boy, so…'

'Yeah, I guess.'

Thomas orders a bag of chips and turns back to her. 'So, have you got a proper boyfriend?'

Before she can answer the chips are wrapped in newspaper and handed over and they start walking home together. He doesn't ask again.

They get nearer to home, and Cathy knows she'll be in big trouble if her dad sees them together, but there's something she needs to ask him.

'You know the story about Mary appearing before the girl in the cave? Well, I was wondering if there are any other stories about miracles you could tell me about.'

He holds up his left hand and points to the palm. 'Some people say they've seen the statue of Jesus on the crucifix bleeding at the same points on his body where he was nailed to the cross.'

She thinks of the bleeding statue in the chapel. 'Have *you* ever seen a statue bleeding?'

'Don't be stupid. Statues don't really bleed.'

'But if people say they've seen them…'

'Yeah. And pigs fly.'

She wants to ask another question but she doesn't know how to put it. 'Has anyone ever said their statue has spoken to them?'

Thomas looks at her suspiciously. 'Why do you ask that?'

'If they can bleed, then what's so weird about them talking?'

'I've never heard of a talking statue.'

She's disappointed.

'But I watched a TV programme once about how dead people's souls could talk through objects. It was all a bit weird.'

Cathy's suddenly interested again. 'You mean like people in Heaven?' She thinks of her mum's family who all died before she was born. Is it possible they're looking down on her from above, talking to her through a statue?

The Second Miracle

It's the last week of term, and Cathy's last few days of primary school before she starts at the academy after the summer. The boys are all gathered around a game of Subbuteo in the corner, while the girls are busy helping Miss Turner strip the walls and tidy the classroom in preparation for next year's Primary Sevens.

'How are you feeling about going up to the big school?' Miss Turner asks the girls.

'Can't wait for all the different subjects,' says Paula.

'And there's going to be so many more boys,' says Linda.

Cathy rolls her eyes. Is she the only one who's feeling nervous? Miss Turner has tried to reassure them that the stories of first years having their dinner money stolen, getting sent in the wrong direction, or (even worse) getting their heads flushed down the toilet aren't true, but Jimmy's told her everything.

There's a loud crashing sound from the back of the room and everyone turns to look.

'Miss, come quick. Richard's knocked Monty's cage over.'

'He's dead.'

'Monty's dead.'

Monty is the class's pet mouse, and everyone adores him. Cathy runs across the room, but Miss Turner holds out her arms to stop anyone from getting too close.

The cage is lying on its side and Cathy stares at the white mouse lying lifeless against the wire bars. The class collectively holds its breath as Miss Turner reaches in and cups the tiny creature between her two hands. She lifts the mouse up and leans over and whispers into her cupped hands and Cathy's sure her teacher is praying. She reaches for the cross tucked beneath her school blouse and clutches it firmly. Everyone is staring at their teacher and no one notices Cathy close her eyes. No one notices their classmate at the back of the room as she says a prayer of her own.

'Please, God,' she whispers. 'You've got to hear me. I know you're busy and Thomas says you can't always come and help us, but I'm begging you, just this once, please help us. Nobody meant to kill Monty; it was an accident. Please, please, help Miss Turner bring him back to life. Please.'

She opens her eyes and sees Miss Turner is now rubbing the creature with the tip of her finger. She steps closer, holding her breath. No one is moving, and Cathy doesn't remember a time when her classmates have ever been so quiet.

'Miss Turner,' she whispers, but her teacher is not listening.

Cathy pushes her way inside the circle that's gathered around her teacher. She sees now her teacher is crying. She tries again.

'Miss Turner…' This time her teacher turns to look at her. She's still crying, and Cathy clutches her pendant more tightly and looks down at the little white mouse lying in the palm of her teacher's hand.

'The poor little thing didn't stand a chance. I think the shock killed him,' says Miss Turner.

One of the girls behind her bursts into tears, but Cathy doesn't look up. She focuses on the little white mouse and rubs the cross one last time.

'Miss!' shouts one of the boys. 'Miss, his tail's moving!'

Cathy sees that the boy's right.

'He's moving, he's moving!'

The classroom explodes with shouts of joy.

'He's alive!'

'Monty's alive!'

Cathy looks at her teacher's face and this time sees tears of joy running down her face, and even over the shouts of excitement she hears Miss Turner's words as she holds the little mouse close to her chest. 'It's a miracle.'

She can't stop grinning for the rest of the day. She saved a creature's life. And yet in the back of her mind, a tiny, nagging voice tells her she's going to have to pay for having her prayer answered.

The bell rings and she runs the whole way home, desperate to catch Thomas on his way home from school and tell him about the miracle. She didn't tell him about the bag on her peg because she wasn't sure he'd believe her, but this time she's got proof. She saw that mouse come back to life before her very own eyes. Her Blue Lady has special powers, just like the Mary at Lourdes. She supposes the priest will want to come out and visit the statue, and she's going to have to confess to stealing the Blue Lady from Mrs O'Donnell, but she can't keep the miracles a secret any longer.

She reaches the lamp post but decides to keep going. What if he's ahead of her and almost home? She races round the corner and stops. A white van is parked outside Thomas's house, and a man is hammering a large sign into the lawn. Her stomach does a somersault as she stares at the words on the sign:

For Sale.

She watches the man give the wooden sign a shake. Satisfied it isn't budging, he gets back into his van and drives away. Cathy tears up the street, punching the *For Sale* sign as she runs past it and up to her best friend's front door. She bangs her knuckles against the wooden door repeatedly, not caring who answers it.

The door is opened by Mr O'Donnell. Cathy realises she's never actually spoken to Thomas's dad before, although she sees him cutting the grass every Wednesday and Sunday evening throughout the summer. Unlike Mrs O'Donnell, he's always polite and lifts a hand to wave when she passes by.

'Is Thomas in?'

Mr O'Donnell seems flustered. Is he scared of his wife, too?

'Please, Mr O'Donnell,' she pleads. 'I only want to speak to him. I promise I'll only be a minute.'

'He's not home from school yet.'

She's not sure whether to believe him or not. 'Your house is for sale.'

Mr O'Donnell nods.

'Are you moving?'

'That's usually what people do when they sell their house.'

'Is it because of me?'

Mr O'Donnell looks at her. 'What do you mean?'

'Are you moving away from this street because of me? Because of the things I've done?'

Mr O'Donnell laughs, but it's a gentle laugh and he reminds her of Thomas. 'Of course not,' he says. 'Why ever would you think that?'

Cathy thinks of the Blue Lady hiding in her wardrobe, but keeps quiet.

'Will you tell him I called and that I need to speak to him?'

'I'm not sure that's a good idea, are you?'

'Please, Mr O'Donnell. It's important.'

'I'm sorry, but I think it's best if you stop seeing each other.'

The door closes and she's left standing on the doorstep. Alone.

The Parade

It's two weeks into the summer holidays and Cathy's been stuck inside every day, watching the rain bounce off the paving slabs in the garden. But, finally, the forecast is for sunshine, so last night she'd tied a note around the handlebars of Thomas's bike telling him to meet her at the lamp post at eleven o'clock this morning and to bring his swimming bag. She hasn't seen him since before the *For Sale* sign went up in his front garden, and she has so many questions. Where are they moving to? When? Why didn't he tell her?

She keeps replaying the morning of the matinee over and over again in her head. Her skin tingles every time she remembers the touch of his hand, and she wishes she could relive the whole morning. This time she'd be ready with the right things to say. This time she'd keep hold of his hand when he reached out, and, this time, they would kiss. She's decided to tell him how she feels, and once they're officially going out together, he won't be able to move away.

'That's me going swimming,' she shouts from the front door. She's told her mum she's meeting some girls from school.

'Wait a minute.'

Cathy waits but she already knows what her mum's going to say. *Don't speak to strangers. Don't get into a strange car. And don't go outside with wet hair.* Her mum has this weird idea that if Cathy doesn't dry her hair properly she'll catch pneumonia.

Mum comes running through from the kitchen, drying her hands on a tea towel. She tucks the towel into her belt and places both hands on Cathy's shoulders. Her hands are still wet, and Cathy wonders if you can catch pneumonia from wet shoulders, but doesn't dare ask.

'Now, remember,' Mum starts. Cathy rolls her eyes and waits for the usual speech. 'I don't want you going anywhere near the centre of town today.'

She's suddenly paying attention.

'The streets will be busy with people coming to watch the bands, but if you go straight to the swimming baths then you'll not need to see anything.'

Cathy's curious. 'What time does the walk start?'

'It leaves the community centre at twelve and goes straight through town and down to the new supermarket car park. So, you should be fine.'

'But we usually get a quarter of midget gems from RS McColl's after we've been swimming.'

'Well, not today. Promise me you'll not go anywhere near that parade.'

Cathy crosses her fingers behind her back. 'I promise,' she says.

The sound of drums practising from somewhere in town fills the air and a small shiver of excitement tickles her spine. Linda went to the parade last year and said people were dancing in the street. It all sounds harmless enough to Cathy.

She arrives at the lamp post but Thomas isn't there. What if he never got her note? Maybe he doesn't want to see her. She picks up some stones and starts throwing them at the grit box.

Just then Thomas comes running up behind her out of breath.

'You're late.'

'I know, I know, but I had to persuade my mum to let me come. She's worried that it's not safe today.'

'Not safe?' Cathy laughs. 'Why ever not?'

He points into the air. 'Can't you hear it? There's going to be an Orange Walk through the centre of town. She only let me come because the swimming baths are on this side of town.'

Cathy remembers the promise she made to her mum and blushes. She desperately wants to see the parade so she can brag to the girls in class, and she knows they won't believe her unless she can give them some details.

'Come on,' Thomas says. 'At least, the pool will be quiet today. We should have the place to ourselves.'

Thomas is right; the swimming pool is deserted when they arrive. Cathy grabs her green band and races through to the girls' changing room. She strips down to her costume as quickly as she can, leaving her clothes and towel behind in the changing cubicle. She sticks her head under the shower and wets her fringe to trick the pool attendant into thinking she's showered, and then she steps through the trough with the freezing cold water that stinks of disinfectant. There are no verrucas in this pool.

She appears from the girls' side, sure that she's beaten Thomas, but he's already in the water. She pushes the green band further up her arm and past her elbow so that it doesn't fall off in the pool. She'll need her deposit back to get a sweet from the vending machine when they come out.

The sun shining through the windows in the roof sparkles across the surface of the water and breaks into a thousand diamonds as she jumps in. The water's freezing, but she knows once she gets moving she'll soon warm up. Thomas is already swimming back towards her, and she watches his skinny body slice through the water and thinks of the poor dead minnows. He sees her face.

'What's up?'

'I was just thinking about the minnows. They'd have loved a big pool like this to swim in.'

'Don't be daft; the chlorine would have killed them.' He touches the wall at the shallow end of the pool and pushes off and starts swimming towards the deep end again. She joins him but she knows she won't be able to keep up for long. He's too strong a swimmer for her.

Their band colour is called too soon and they drag themselves out of the water. 'Bet you I'm ready first,'

Thomas shouts as he disappears into the boys' showers, and Cathy realises her mother was so busy warning her to stay away from the Orange Walk that she forgot to tell her to dry her hair. Just as well, she thinks, and scrapes her fingers through her wet hair. Her jeans and t-shirt stick to her damp skin and she slips her feet into her jelly sandals and rushes out of the changing rooms. She's first, and when Thomas appears he complains that she's cheating because he has his trainers to tie.

The sun is still shining and it's tempting them outside. 'I thought you were going to get something from the vending machine?' Thomas asks.

'Didn't have what I wanted.'

Thomas looks at her.

'Come on,' she says. 'Aren't you a teensy bit curious? About the Walk, I mean.'

'My mum will kill me if she finds out.'

'*If* she finds out,' repeats Cathy. 'Do you think she'll be there?'

'What! At the parade? Of course she won't.'

'Exactly,' says Cathy, 'and my mum and dad won't be anywhere near it either. They've forbidden me from going.'

'Forbidden you? Why?'

She shrugs her shoulders. 'No idea.' She counts the change in her hand. She's got enough for an ice pole and a ten pence mixture from McColl's. 'Have you ever seen one?'

'What, an Orange Walk? No, but I heard one once when it went by the chapel.'

'What did you hear?'

'It was during Mass and we were sitting in one of the front pews. Mum always likes to get a seat near the front, says it makes her feel closer to God. Anyway, everyone was about to take Communion when we heard the bands outside. The drums were so loud it sounded as though they were banging on the church doors, and I remember Sarah Warrington hid underneath the pew and her mum couldn't get her to come out again.'

'Maybe it was just scary cos you were inside?'
'Maybe.'
She waits a second before plucking up the courage to ask him, 'Do you fancy watching it from the hill?'
'The hill?'
'Down from the school,' she explains. 'Nobody will see us up there but we'll see everything.'
'What if someone catches us watching?'
She knows by 'someone' he means his mum. 'We'll say the vending machine at the baths wasn't working so we went to the shop to get a mixture.'
Thomas mulls this over. 'Imagine what the boys would say if I told them I watched the Orange Walk.'
'Wouldn't they be angry?'
'Angry?' He laughs. 'Nah, they'd be impressed.'
'Come on, then,' she says, and pulls him by the hand. 'Let's get some sweets for watching the parade.'
The streets are lined with people dressed for the occasion in their best clothes. Little girls are wearing summer dresses, white cardigans and sandals, and the boys are waving plastic Union Jacks on sticks. It looks just like the gala day, and Cathy doesn't understand why her mum is making such a fuss.
'This way's quickest.' Thomas hooks his arm through hers and together they turn into Livery Street, but the pavements are even busier along here and they have to squeeze their way through the mob of people. A large crowd has gathered outside the chapel, and Cathy stops and looks up at the tall sandstone building. She's never noticed the carvings on the outside of the building before, as she's always been too preoccupied with trying to catch a glimpse through the enormous double doors. She points to a thin strip of green metal that runs up the side of the building all the way from the ground to the very top of the steeple.
'What's that?'
Thomas explains how the lightning rod attracts particles of static electricity during a thunderstorm so that when there's a bolt of lightning, it strikes the metal rod. 'And the

rod takes the electricity all the way down to the ground, which stops the building from being struck.'

She's impressed he knows so much about science and wishes her brother could hear him. Jimmy thinks all Catholics are stupid.

'Have you ever seen it?' she asks him. 'During a storm, have you ever seen the lightning go down the rod and into the ground? Does it glow?'

'I think it probably happens too fast for us to see it.'

'How do you know for sure?'

He shrugs his shoulders.

'Next time there's a storm we should come and see.'

He laughs. 'Cathy Munro, I'm going to miss you.'

Her stomach plunges. What does he mean by he's going to miss her?

Thomas sees a gap in the crowd and pulls her through to the pavement's edge. 'This is perfect,' he says. 'We'll see it all from here.'

'Oi!' Two men push their way through the crowd. 'This is our spot. Now get lost.'

'Leave the kids alone. They want to see the bands, too.' Cathy looks up and sees Sandra, the model from down the road, appear beside them. She puts her hands on Cathy's shoulder. 'Isn't that right?'

'Actually, we were going to watch the parade from the hill,' says Thomas.

One of the men puts his arm around Sandra's waist and pulls her towards him. He kisses her forcefully on the lips, and Sandra seems to have forgotten she's still got her hand on Cathy's shoulder.

'At the Green Tree?' asks the other man.

'No chance,' says his friend, pulling free from Sandra and opening one of his cans. Lager sprays everywhere and he throws his mouth over the opening, not wanting to waste a drop, but he's too late and most of it is now on Thomas's t-shirt. 'We've just come from there and it's mobbed. The bands are starting to make their way down the hill and there's not a hope in hell you'll get through the crowds.'

‘Well, that settles it, then,’ says Sandra. ‘You’ll have to stay here and watch it with us. Isn’t that right, Rab?’

Rab ignores her and crushes the empty lager can and tosses it to the ground before opening another.

Sandra leans forward and takes a bottle out of a carrier bag. Cathy watches as she pours some vodka into a pint glass and then tops it up with Barr’s Cola.

‘Fucking classy,’ Rab says.

‘Don’t swear in front of the kids.’

‘Fuck off. I never asked them to stand here.’

Sandra turns to Cathy. ‘So, I’m guessing this is your boyfriend.’ She winks, and Cathy blushes. ‘Aren’t you going to introduce him?’

Cathy can feel her cheeks burning. ‘This is Thomas. Thomas O’Donnell.’

Rab spits out a mouthful of lager. ‘Thomas O’Donnell?’

Thomas stares at the ground.

‘Tell me, Thomas O’Donnell, what school do you go to? With a name like that I’m guessing you go to St Mary’s, am I right?’

The first of the bands arrives at the end of the street, and the crowd erupts and everyone pushes forward, trying to get a better view.

‘You’ve gone awfy quiet son,’ says Rab. ‘Everything okay?’

The music gets louder as the band starts marching along the street, and everyone’s cheering and the children are waving their flags.

‘They’re nearly here,’ shouts Sandra, and she grabs Rab’s arm to get him to turn and watch. But he’s not finished with Thomas and shouts above the noise to be heard. ‘Come to enjoy the bands, have you, Thomas O’Donnell?’

Thomas grabs Cathy’s hand and spins round looking for a way out through the crowd, but they’re hemmed in on all sides.

She squeezes his hand. ‘What did you mean when you said you’re going to miss me?’

‘The house is sold. We’re moving to England.’

His hand is pulled out of hers.

'What do you think you're doing?' Rab yanks Thomas by his t-shirt. 'Think you can just fuck off? No chance.'

'What's going on?' shouts Sandra.

'This wee Fenian thought he could come down the street wi' the rest of us and watch the fucking bands, eh? Well, I'm about to teach him a fucking lesson.' He shoves Thomas forwards on to the road. 'There,' he yells. 'Now you can get the best fucking view.'

The band stops right in front of them and the drummer bangs harder and harder on the skin of the bass drum, and the crowd is getting louder and louder, clapping along and cheering him on. Cathy looks back over her shoulder at the chapel and hopes there's no one inside today.

Just then she spots a group of teenagers with green and white scarves around their necks making their way along the pavement. Rab spots them too.

'What the fuck!" he shouts. "Place is full o' fucking Tims! Have none of them got the fucking decency to stay away?'

The boys wearing the Celtic scarves push past Cathy and make their way onto the edge of the pavement. The boy at the front pulls a flag out of his pocket and unravels it for the crowd to see. The green, white and gold flag depicts a fist holding a rifle in the air.

Rab roars and grabs the pint glass out of Sandra's hand and smashes it against the stone wall outside the front of the chapel. Cathy just has time to note the vodka and coke trickling down the sandstone before seeing Rab lunge forwards, striking upwards with the jagged edge.

Thomas clutches his face and falls to his knees in the middle of the road, blood pouring through his fingers. His mouth is wide open but his screams are drowned out by the beat of the drum.

One Last Miracle

'Please, God, this time I need your help more than ever.'

The removal van has been parked outside the house since eight o'clock. Cathy squints through the chink in her curtains and watches two men in brown overalls struggle with her next-door-neighbours' dining room table. All morning the men have been going in and out, in and out, and she's watched as Thomas's life has been neatly packed into the back of a van.

She picks up yesterday's jeans and t-shirt from the floor and pulls them on. It's the last day of the summer holidays, and it's rained almost every day. At first, she waited for the police to come and question her, but as the days passed it became clear Thomas hadn't told anyone she'd been at the parade with him.

Every morning and every night, she has knelt by her bed in front of the Blue Lady, holding the small, silver cross in her clasped hands, and said a prayer. In the beginning, she prayed for Thomas.

'Please, make sure he's okay.'

But her prayers soon changed when he was safely home from hospital.

'Please, make the people buying his house change their mind.'

She tried this one every day for a week, but the *Sold* sticker stayed put.

'Please, make his mum and dad change their minds.'

She knows the O'Donnells are only doing this to keep her and Thomas apart, but when this didn't work she even prayed for disaster.

'Please, let England be struck by a hurricane.'

But now moving day is here, and there have been no hurricanes, no wildfires and no plague of locusts. Today is her last chance and she's desperate.

'Please, give me one last miracle. You can make me cry, make me bleed, whatever it takes to keep him here.'

She sits by her bed and waits, hoping for some sort of sign. But nothing happens. The Virgin Mary stands silent at her altar on the bedside table.

'Why isn't He listening to me?' she asks the Blue Lady. 'Doesn't He want us to be together? Is it because I'm not a Catholic?'

The Blue Lady keeps quiet.

There's a knock on her bedroom door, probably Jimmy coming to tease her.

'Go away,' she shouts. He doesn't give up and the knocking continues. She turns and throws a pillow at the door but it meets it with a soft thud. 'I said go away. Go away and leave me alone.'

'It's me, Thomas.'

Thomas. She freezes.

He enters the room without waiting to be asked, and the first thing she sees is the angry, red scar running down his left cheek.

'I came to say goodbye, and I wanted to give you this.' He holds out a small bear clutching a red love heart which says *Miss Me.* Cathy takes the teddy bear and holds it close.

Thomas steps forward and kisses her gently on the lips. This time there's no awkwardness, just a simple kiss.

'When are you leaving?'

He looks at his watch. 'In a few minutes.'

'Oh.'

They pull apart and Cathy places the small bear on the windowsill, doing anything other than looking at the scar on Thomas's face.

He walks across the room to her bedside table and picks up the china figurine.

'You lied to me.'

'I didn't mean to take her.'

'I thought we told each other everything. I've had everyone questioning me: the police, my parents, all wanting to know why I was at the Orange Walk by myself. I kept quiet for you because I thought we were friends.'

'We are.' She looks at the Blue Lady in his hands. This isn't how it's supposed to go.

'Here.' He holds out the Virgin Mary. 'You can keep her.'

She takes the china ornament from him, and sees the glaze of her blue sash is flaking. Has she always been flawed like this? Cathy hadn't noticed before.

She holds the figurine up to the light and looks at her painted face. Is she imagining it? Is her Blue Lady smirking at her? She opens her hands and lets the ornament fall to the floor. It hits the pink carpet, and a crack zig-zags its way up one side. Cathy grabs the shoe box from her bedside table and throws the Blue Lady inside. The glitter has fallen off the walls, and in the dull morning light she sees the miniature shrine for what it really is: an empty cardboard box.

Thomas walks towards the door. 'My mum was right. You're nothing but a thief and a liar. I wish I'd never met you, Cathy Munro.'

Part Two

1985

They started it.

Bad Boys

George Michael looks down at me from the posters above Linda's bed. All of the girls in my year think he's gorgeous, but, secretly, I prefer the man at his side: Andrew Ridgeley, the quiet member of *Wham!*, the one nobody else notices. But I notice. I notice his swept-back hair, gorgeous white smile and dark brown eyes, and it makes me feel all fuzzy inside. He appears in all my daydreams and I know him better than anyone else. I'm the only one who understands how difficult the fame is for him, how hard it is that all the attention goes to George when Andrew is the real talent behind the band. He tells me everything.

'Ooh, I love this song,' squeals Linda, and she reaches over to the hi-fi and turns up the volume. The red lights on the stereo flash in time with the music and she throws the copy of *Just Seventeen* down on the bed in front of me, the pages open at a double-page make-up article.

'They're going out in five minutes,' she whispers.

'And?'

'Shhh, wait till they've gone.'

The bedroom door bursts open and Linda's mum bounces in to the room looking like Krystle Carrington from *Dynasty*. The sequins on her dress shimmer and sparkle, and her red lipstick perfectly matches her handbag and shoes. I wish my mum would wear make-up sometimes.

'You girls okay?'

'How many times do I have to tell you to knock before barging in?'

'I like your perfume,' I say, and I can feel Linda staring at me. She's always bitching about her mum, but I think Mrs White is the most exotic creature I've ever seen. She's like a wild bird caged in a world of drab grey.

The bottle of perfume is whipped out from the handbag

and the lid is off.

'Hold out your hand, Cathy.' Mrs White grabs hold of my arm and flips it over to expose my scrawny white wrist. The perfume bottle is dabbed against my skin. 'Pressure points,' she explains, 'are where your pulse is at its strongest, and with every beat of your heart the scent will gently be released.'

I watch the droplets of perfume run down my arm and imagine the blood pulsing, racing through the veins in my body.

'Now rub them together,' she says, gold bangles jangling and dancing as she shows me how to rub my wrists together.

'Thank you, Mrs White.'

'Please. Call me Sylvia.'

'Thank you, Sylvia,' I whisper.

'It's *Anais Anais*.'

I don't understand.

'The perfume,' Sylvia says. 'It's called *Anais Anais*.' She pronounces it with a foreign accent and she sounds even more exotic than she looks. Linda and her family went on holiday to Spain last year and brought me back a donkey wearing a sombrero. I would do anything to go to Spain. Last summer, our family went to a caravan in Whitby, and all I brought back was a stick of rock.

She spots the magazine on the bed and scoops it up. 'Ooh, are you girls planning on a make-up session? That sounds fun.'

'Aren't you supposed to be away by now?'

Sylvia looks at her daughter with an expression of hurt.

'You don't want to be late for the party.'

Her face softens and she strokes Linda's hair. 'Promise me you'll behave yourselves.' She turns to me. 'And thanks for staying over tonight. Linda was scared about being in the house alone.'

Alone? I look at Linda, but she's pretending to read an article on how to shape your eyebrows.

'And I've left the number by the telephone in case you need to get in touch with us.'

'Mum, will you hurry up and go?'

'Okay, okay. Have fun, girls.' Sylvia White spins on her heels and the sequins on her dress catch the light as she twirls out of the room.

I wait until I hear the front door close. 'You never said your mum and dad wouldn't be here.'

'What's your problem?'

'You should've told me.'

'Calm down,' laughs Linda. 'Would your mum have let you stay if she'd known we were on our own?'

'You know she wouldn't.'

'Well, there you go, then.'

'What do you mean?'

'You and I both know your mum would never have let you stay over if she'd known, and so this way you get to stay the night *and* you haven't told her any lies. And now,' Linda looks excited, 'we can do whatever we like.'

'But what about tomorrow, when my mum asks me what we did?'

Linda turns up the music. 'You tell her that we listened to some music and tried on some make-up.'

'So, is that what we're doing?' I ask, but I know Linda better than that.

'I might have some other plans as well, but your mum doesn't need to know every detail.' She winks at me. 'Does she?' She grabs the make-up bag. 'Now hurry up and get over here. We're meeting them in an hour, and we still need to do your make-up.'

'Meeting who?'

'You'll see.' She kneels in front of me and chooses a pink blusher and a giant powder brush.

'Where are we going?' I ask.

She dabs the brush in the blusher. 'Kirkton Park.'

'Are we meeting the rest of the girls there?'

Linda giggles. 'Okay, okay,' she says as though I've got her hand up her back. 'If you must know, Derek came up to me at break today and asked me to meet him tonight. Can you believe it?'

'And what am I supposed to do?'

'Relax. I told him you were staying over so he said he'd ask a friend along.'

'Did he say who his friend is?' Knowing my luck, it'll be some spotty third-year boy.

'I didn't ask, but you don't mind. Do you?' She clutches my hands. 'Can you believe he asked me out? And I thought he hadn't noticed me.'

I bite my tongue. Derek Ferguson would need to be blind not to have noticed Linda. She's been chasing him around school for weeks.

She sits back on her hunkers and looks at my face with a disapproving frown, then lifts my fringe up and tuts loudly. I don't want to know. She rummages through the make-up bag until she finds what she's looking for, and then sits up with her weapon in her hand. Tweezers. She springs forward and attacks my eyebrow. The stabs are fast and furious and bring tears to my eyes. 'Stay still,' she says, and lunges forward to pluck the other side.

When we leave the house an hour later, I don't recognise the girl who looks back at me from the mirror.

The park is empty when we arrive, and I'm not sure whether to be disappointed or relieved. I push my hands deep inside my pockets and rock back and forth slowly on the swing.

'Maybe we should head back and watch a video. Your dad said he got us a copy of *Footloose* from the video shop.'

'No chance,' says Linda. 'Derek said he'd be here.'

'Maybe he got a better offer.'

This answer doesn't go down well and she throws me a dirty look. 'They'll be here soon,' she says, more to reassure herself than to me.

We don't speak as we wait for the boys to arrive, and I'm wishing I'd never agreed to stay over tonight. What if his friend refused to come when he heard I'd be there?

Then the bushes to our left rustle, and Derek Ferguson

makes his appearance, breaking branches and trampling flowers as he struts on to the tarmacadam like a peacock.

'Alright, girls.' The brown paper bag in his hand chinks as he makes his way towards us. 'Fancy a wee drink?'

'What you got?' Linda asks.

He lets the paper bag fall to the ground and is left holding two bottles of Diamond White.

'Cool.'

Derek grins and looks Linda up and down as he moves close. Great, it looks like I'm on my own. What am I supposed to do now? I look up and see a boy walking along the red ash path towards us. He doesn't say a word when he arrives, and hangs back, scuffing the ground with his toes.

'Let's get blootered,' shouts Derek, lifting the bottles of cider above his head.

'Great idea,' says Linda, laughing.

Derek holds his hand out to his friend. 'Pass me the bottle opener.'

'I didn't bring one.'

'How am I supposed to get it open?'

The boy wanders towards the swings and the smell of his aftershave makes my stomach quiver. He's so close I could reach out and touch him with my toes if I wanted to.

Derek looks like he could kill him. 'You were supposed to bring a fuckin' bottle opener. Now what are we going to do?'

The boy shrugs his shoulders.

'Fuckin' hell, Andrew, I only asked you to do one thing.'

Andrew. Like Andrew Ridgeley. It must be a sign.

I sneak a glance in his direction. His hair is loosely permed and he's wearing skinny, stonewashed jeans and a denim jacket. He's gorgeous.

Linda takes a bottle of Diamond White from Derek and picks at the label. 'We've got a bottle opener in the house,' she says.

'I don't think your dad's gonnae be too happy if all of us traipse back to yours.'

She flashes him a smile. 'My folks are away for the

night.'

Derek can't hide his excitement at this revelation. 'What do you mean, for the night? When will they be back?'

'They'll not be back till tomorrow morning,' says Linda, and Derek's grinning like the Cheshire Cat. Then he actually puts his hand down the front of his trousers and adjusts himself. Nothing like announcing your hard-on to the world.

'What are we waiting for?' he shouts. 'Let's go.'

Linda jumps off the swing and leads the way, and I watch as Derek slips his arm around her waist. No prizes for guessing how this evening is going to end.

I follow, and Andrew stays a few steps behind me as we head towards Linda's house. Am I so repulsive that a boy won't even walk beside me? Derek has now got his hand in Linda's back pocket and he's squeezing her arse. God, this is going to be a long night. I wish I could slip away home, but Linda would never forgive me.

I can sense Andrew at my shoulder and I try to think of something to say. Apart from my old neighbour, Thomas, I've never felt comfortable in a boy's presence and I've never tried to hold a conversation longer than three sentences with a boy before.

Can you pass me the ruler?

Sure.

Thanks.

There you go – three sentences. And two of those are one word long.

'Fuckin' hell,' Derek shouts over his shoulder to Andrew. 'You ever been in a street this posh before?'

Andrew shakes his head and looks embarrassed.

Derek turns full circle, sweeping his arms out in front of him.

'Look at it.' He bursts out laughing. 'Just fuckin' look at it. Look at the gardens wi' the fancy flowers and wishing wells. And the cars.' He stops in front of Linda's neighbour's house. 'An Audi. Who the fuck can afford an Audi? And they've even got a fuckin' garage stuck on to the side of their house.' He laughs again, but this time it doesn't sound friendly. 'They've got a fuckin' Audi and they dinnae even pit it in the garage.' He steps over the flower bed on to the perfectly manicured lawn, and stands in front of the large bay window with his hands outstretched like Christ the Redeemer. The curtains are open and the family are all gathered together watching Saturday night telly. 'Yous dinnae even pit it in the fuckin' garage,' he shouts.

Linda looks scared. 'Get out of there before someone sees you.'

Derek chooses not to hear her. 'Fuckin' show-offs.'

A little girl aged maybe five or six looks up from her space on the floor in front of the TV.

Derek moves closer and peers through the window. 'Have you seen the size of their fuckin' telly?'

The little girl screams and everyone in the room looks up. Derek leaps back over the flower bed and races up the street as the front door is thrown open.

'In here,' shouts Linda, and disappears into the shadowed path at the side of her house. I follow her and wonder what Derek would have to say if he saw Linda's dad's car. The silver Jaguar is his pride and joy, and he spends every Sunday afternoon washing and polishing it. Unlike the neighbours, he does keep his beloved car in the garage. Mrs White's Mini is usually parked in the drive, but they've taken it with them tonight and the driveway is empty.

Footsteps crunch on the gravel behind me and I hold my breath, sure it's Linda's neighbour. I stand still and watch the silhouette step closer. A hand reaches out and grabs me and I squeal. It's Andrew. He puts his hand over my mouth to silence me and leans in close.

'Shhh,' he whispers, 'They're looking for us.' His breath is warm on my cheek. That fuzzy feeling returns, and I can't help but think how nice it'd be if he kissed me just now.

The sound of a door closing can be heard as Linda's neighbour gives up his search and heads back inside to be with his family. Andrew takes his hand away.

'Sorry about that,' he whispers, and I wish I was brave

enough to tell him not to be sorry, that I liked his touch. I wish I was brave enough to lean forward and kiss him while he's still close. But I'm not, and he steps back and stuffs his hands into the pockets of his jeans and stares at the ground. 'Guess I'd better go find Derek,' he says, and I watch him walk away.

I turn to Linda. 'Should we go after them?' I ask, hoping she'll say yes.

'Let them come to us,' she says, and we go inside. We go through to the living room and she puts *Footloose* into the video recorder. I wait until the film starts, and dancing feet fill the screen, before slipping my question into the conversation. 'So is Andrew in Derek's year?'

My subtlety doesn't work and Linda leaps out of her seat. 'I knew it,' she shouts. 'I could tell by the way you looked at him.' This can't be true, because she never took her eyes off Derek the whole time. 'I saw the pair of you round the side of the garage; you couldn't have got any closer if you'd tried.'

'He was getting me to be quiet while your neighbour was out looking for us.'

'You didn't seem to mind being close to him.'

'He was just being nice.' I look out of the window, but the only thing I can see is the blossom tree at the bottom of the garden illuminated by the orange street light. 'Do you think they'll come back?'

'They might for these,' says Linda holding up the two bottles of Diamond White. 'Fancy one?'

'Maybe we should wait and see if they come back first.'

'Suit yourself, but I'm having one.'

We sit in the living room, the moving images on the TV screen providing little distraction. I'm sure Andrew likes me; it was obvious when he leaned in close. Wasn't it?

I suddenly feel reckless. 'Pass me the other bottle.'

Linda flips the lid with an opener in the shape of a naked woman. 'Got it in Spain,' she says. I should have guessed. She hands me the bottle and I tip it straight up and imagine Andrew was here to see me knock it back. He'd be so impressed and probably think I'd been drinking for years. I wish he hadn't run off like that. Maybe I should have asked him to stay.

Both bottles are soon empty, and the warm fuzzy feeling they gave is starting to wear off. 'Has your mum got any more drink in the house?'

Linda leans over and opens the door to the pine sideboard. 'There's a bottle of Babycham in here.' She takes out the bottle and cracks opens the gold seal.

'Shouldn't we use glasses?'

'Nah, it's fine like this. Go on, try some.'

The Babycham is sweet and bubbly and goes down easier than the cider.

'So,' Linda asks, 'how far have you gone with a boy?'

Her question takes me by surprise, and Babycham sprays out of my mouth. I think back to the only boy I've ever kissed, Thomas O'Donnell, and I get a squirming feeling in my stomach. I look at Linda, not knowing how to answer. There's no way I can tell her I've never gone further than a kiss before. 'You tell first,' I say, and take a large gulp of Babycham.

Linda pretends to hesitate but I know she's desperate to tell me everything. 'I let Colin touch my tits round the back of the health centre.' She's watching my face for a reaction. 'And I could feel his dick as he pressed against me.'

'Did you touch it?'

'No, but I could feel him rubbing it against my leg as we kissed, and it was so hard I thought he might come right there and then.'

I take another drink.

'He tried to put his hand inside my knickers, but I didn't let him. Not when there were other folk nearby.' She grabs the bottle out of my hand. 'Don't want everyone thinking I'm a slut.'

'What about Derek?' I ask. The Babycham is making me feel brave. 'Would you let him touch you?'

'Maybe,' says Linda.

I think I might let Andrew touch me if he wanted to. But

I'd make him say he loved me first.

'Shit. We've finished the bottle. My mum will kill me when she finds out. What are we going to do?'

'We'll need to bin the bottle before she finds it.'

'But she'll see it's missing.'

'Maybe we could fill it with some juice or cold tea until we can replace it,' I suggest. 'That's what Jimmy did once when he'd drunk some of my dad's whisky.'

'Did it work?'

'Nah. When Dad poured himself a drink at New Year he went absolutely mental.' I burst out laughing, but Linda doesn't seem to see the funny side. 'Here.' I hold out my hand. 'Give it to me. We'll fill it with cold tea for now until we can swap it over.' I take the bottle and stand to go through to the kitchen, but as I get up my head swims and my stomach flips. I know what's about to happen, but there's nothing I can do to stop it, and I throw up all over the living room carpet.

Secrets

Last night, my sleep was riddled with all sorts of weird dreams. I dreamt I was at the swing park with Linda and Derek. He was touching her tits, and she was laughing and pointing at me, saying over and over, '*Cathy's never been touched by a boy. Cathy's never been touched by a boy.*' Walking home, I pass the lamp post where Thomas and I used to meet.

Thomas. Until last night, I hadn't thought of that name in a long time. After he first moved away, I raced to check the post every morning as it landed with a thud on the rug inside the front door, but there was never anything from him. I didn't expect much, but a letter or a postcard letting me know how he was getting on would have been nice.

'Cathy!' It's Rebecca, the youngest from next door. 'Come and see what I'm making.' Rebecca runs down the garden path and grabs me by the hand. 'Come and see, come and see.' She leads me over to where she's been digging in the flower bed and I bend down to talk to her.

'Hey, Rebecca, what you up to?'

'I'm making mud pies. Look.'

Tiny mounds of soil are scattered across the garden path. I look up to the window which overlooks my own back garden, to the spot where the Blue Lady once stood.

'What's in the window today?' I ask.

Rebecca follows my gaze and grins. 'That's Ben's space rocket. He made it out of Lego.'

The little girl holds out a red plastic spade. 'Can you help me?'

'Sorry, Rebecca. I've got homework to do.' I feel bad telling her a lie, but all I want to do is shut myself away in my bedroom. I leave her playing in the mud and walk up the path to my own house.

I open the front door and step inside, waiting to be bombarded by the buzz and noise of family life, but the house is silent. I dump my bag at the bottom of the stairs and shout out, but no one answers, so I go through to the kitchen and I'm surprised to find my dad sitting at the table with the Sunday papers spread out in front of him. He doesn't look up as I enter the room, so I leave and head upstairs to look for Mum.

I find her down on all fours, scrubbing the bath. Her hair is scraped back and tied in a bright pink scrunchy which matches the colour of her rubber gloves. I think about calling out to her and pointing out her fashion statement, but I stop. She's wearing the same distant look on her face as Dad, so instead I slope through to my bedroom and close the door behind me.

I turn on my stereo and scan the row of tapes on the shelf before selecting the latest charts tape I recorded from the radio last Sunday night. *TOP 40* is written in black felt-tip along the edge of the cardboard insert. The songs splice into one another awkwardly, and a few words from the DJ can be heard at the end of each one.

I lie back on my bed and stare up at the poster of *Wham!* on my bedroom wall. All this time and I've been daydreaming about the wrong Andrew. I can't stop thinking about him. Why didn't he come back to the house again? Isn't he interested?

I turn the music up louder and close my eyes. I'm so busy singing along I don't hear Jimmy barge into the room.

'What the fuck are you doing?' He yanks the volume control and spins it anti-clockwise. 'You'll get Mum in a rage again; is that what you want?'

'What do you mean?'

'It's alright for you. You disappear off to your friend's house and leave me alone with them. They've been at each other's throats ever since you left yesterday afternoon.'

'I've got exams coming up soon and we were studying,' I

say, but he pulls a face.

'Mum got another phone call last night.'

I look at him. The arguments began about the same time as Mum started getting these strange phone calls, but until now neither of us has mentioned them. Last week, I came downstairs and heard her talking on the phone in hushed tones, but when she saw me standing on the bottom step she suddenly announced it was a wrong number and hung up.

'Who do you think it is that keeps calling?'

Jimmy shrugs his shoulders.

'Do you think she's having an affair?'

'Don't be daft. Why would Mum possibly need anyone else? She's got Dad, hasn't she?'

'Who do you think it is, then?'

He shrugs his shoulders again.

'Right, so how are we going to find out who keeps calling her?'

'Why do we want to do that?'

Honestly, sometimes my brother can be so stupid. 'Because once we know who she's speaking to, then we can find out why she and Dad keep arguing.'

Jimmy's looking at me as though I've lost the plot.

'And once we know why they're arguing, then we can help them sort it out.'

'So how do we find out?' he asks.

'We could try picking up the phone upstairs when she's talking to the mystery caller.'

'But you can hear when someone picks it up.'

'Maybe we could pick it up at the exact same time.'

'And how do we manage to do that, genius?'

'Okay, okay. At least I'm trying to come up with some ideas.'

We sit together perched on the end of my bed and I can't remember the last time I felt this close to my brother. He's not showing off in front of his pals. It's just him and me, and it feels good.

'Got it!' he says. 'Whenever the phone rings and we're at home, we try and get to the phone first, and when they ask to speak to Mum we simply ask who's calling.'

'I've tried that, but whoever was on the line hung up as soon as they heard my voice.'

Jimmy looks disappointed.

'How about if the phone rings we try and sneak to a spot where we can hear what she's saying?' I say.

'And?'

'And we each have a notebook.'

'We can't go around spying on her.'

'Not spying,' I say. 'But do you remember when we used to be detectives?'

Jimmy laughs out loud. 'And we used to go around with a piece of chalk in our pocket and mark each kerb we passed so we could make our way back home again after trailing someone we thought was up to no good.'

'Well, this time instead of a piece of chalk in our pocket we keep a little notebook and pencil, and we write down everything she says.'

For a few seconds he doesn't say anything, and then he takes hold of my hand.

'Cathy, that worked when we were little kids. But things have changed. We're adults now.' He looks at me. 'Well, nearly. What age are you, sixteen?'

I look away. I know where this conversation is going.

'Things can't be fixed with a piece of chalk, or with a notebook and pen. Whatever's going on with Mum and Dad, there's nothing we can do to help.'

I try to interrupt but he keeps talking.

'Suppose we do find out who's calling, or why they're arguing, what do we do then? This is something they need to sort out on their own, and if we interfere we'll only make things worse.'

'But you agreed with me. You said we should run to the phone before they can get to it and ask who's calling.'

Jimmy squeezes my hand. 'Yeah, well, I wasn't thinking straight, was I?'

'But if we don't help…' I don't need to finish my sentence.

'Listen, Cathy. I hate the yelling and shouting as much as you do, but the awkward silences afterwards are just as bad. It's like walking around on eggshells all the time.' He looks at me. 'I think I'd rather they separated than have to live like this.'

I look at my brother but can't think of anything to say. Surely he's overreacting.

Like a Virgin

Linda won't shut up and keeps going on and on about how gorgeous Derek is, so I make the excuse of going to get some music from Jimmy's room just so I can escape from her. I sit for a minute before choosing the new Madonna album and then I get up and pull the bedroom door shut behind me, waiting for the faint click that tells me it's closed properly. He'll kill me if he finds out I've been in there.

I walk back across the landing preparing to go back in and face her, but as I reach the doorway I stop. She's sitting cross-legged on top of my bed with the shoebox lying open in front of her. The lid is on the bedroom floor and the contents have been tipped carelessly across my bed. I bite down on my bottom lip and barely manage to suppress my horror as I see glitter sprinkled over my bedcovers.

'What are you doing with a statue of the Virgin Mary?' Linda asks.

I stare at the cassette box in my hand, pretending to study the running order as my brain runs through countless possible excuses.

The box isn't mine. It belongs to my mother.

That doesn't explain why my name is scribbled all over the lid in felt tip pen.

A friend asked me to look after it for her.

Still doesn't explain the name.

I'm aware Linda's watching me closely, waiting for me to answer. The tape in my hand is shaking as I press the eject button and the tape deck lurches slowly towards me. 'I've no idea,' I blurt out as I slip the cassette in.

'What?'

'I've no idea how it got there.'

She puts the Blue Lady face down on the bed on top of George Michael's dazzling white smile. 'I think she's creepy. I mean what the fuck is she doing under your bed?'

'I've told you I didn't know she was there.'

She reaches forward and picks up a small, brown bear clutching a red heart with the words *Miss Me* across it. 'And this?'

'A neighbour gave it to me when he moved away.'

'He?'

The opening bars to *Material Girl* burst out of the speakers.

Linda isn't giving up so easily. 'A boy gave you this?'

Even though I know all of the words off by heart I still pull the lyrics out of the plastic case. 'Did you see her on *Top of the Pops* last week?' I ask.

Linda gets up and presses the stop button and my tuneless voice fills the room.

'I'm right, aren't I?' She waves the teddy in front of my face, and I wish she'd put it back in the shoe box. Not that I care about it. I haven't seen Thomas once since he moved away, and he's barely crossed my mind for ages. Still, it's my bear and I wish she would put it back. Carefully.

I step forward to take the bear, but this is the worst thing I can do. Linda sees the opportunity for a game and seizes it. She jumps onto the bed and waves it above her head.

'You want it back?' she teases. 'Just tell me who gave it to you, and then I'll give it back.'

'I told you it was a neighbour. I can't even remember his name.'

'His, his, his,' she squeals. 'I was right; I said it was a boy.'

Downstairs, the front door opens. Shit! Jimmy's home and he'll kill me if he finds out I've taken his new Madonna album. I forget about Linda and the bear, and slam the eject button and snatch the tape. But I grab it a second too soon, and the spool of ribbon gets caught in the machine.

'Help me, it's stuck.' I try to free the trapped cassette, but the reel of magnetic tape starts to unravel and curl, and I can hear Jimmy coming up the stairs.

'Shit…shit…shit.'

The ribbon coils and twists like a snake between my fingers, and an old childhood nightmare threatens to surface. Linda senses the urgency and leaps down from the bed to come to my rescue.

'Where the fuck is it?' Jimmy bursts into the room and Linda yanks the cassette sharply. She slides it into her pocket before he can see it and I drop the empty case to the floor, kicking it under the bed with my foot. 'Cost me nearly a tenner out of my fucking wages, so you'd better not have lent it to any of your fucking pals.' He flashes a look at Linda.

Jimmy started working in the bank a few months ago, and since he got his first pay packet he's never stopped going on about it. I tried asking at the corner shop about a paper round, but Mr Tucker mumbled something about girls not being strong enough to carry the bags, and when I handed him my application form he didn't even bother to look at it. I'd gone to the effort of putting on a dress, but maybe I should have worn a pair of jeans and tied my hair back. People are always telling me I look like a boy when my hair is tied back.

'I'm going out, and that tape had better be back in my fucking room by the time I get back. Or I'm telling Mum you and Linda have been drinking her Martini.'

'That's a lie,' Linda shouts.

Jimmy grins. 'Yeah, well who do you think she's gonnae believe, eh?'

Linda walks over to where he's standing and, although she doesn't even come up to his shoulders, she looks him directly in the eye and for a brief second I could swear they're the same height. 'You do that,' she says, 'and I swear I'll make sure your mum finds out you shagged Jilly Cochrane round the back of the health centre, and that she had to go and get the Morning After Pill.'

The colour drains from my brother's face, and without

another word he turns and walks out of the room.

'Quick, where is it?' I hold out my hand and Linda drops it into my palm, the two snapped ends of brown tape dangling freely. 'What am I going to do now? There's no way I'll ever be able to save up enough money to replace it.'

Linda tilts her head to one side and smiles. 'There's only one thing you can do.'

The Woolworths store is in the very centre of the precinct, lodged between a hairdresser's salon and a shoe repair shop, and I often spend a Saturday afternoon in the record department, browsing the collection of singles and LPs. At weekends the shop is crowded with teenagers, but it's five o'clock on a Tuesday afternoon and the record aisle is deserted. I shove my hands into my pockets and look around me. The woman behind the till is filing her nails and flicking through a magazine, and the only other shoppers are an old couple choosing paint from a colour chart.

Linda reaches in and takes a fizzy cola bottle from the pick & mix.

'Quick,' she whispers, 'while everyone's looking the other way.' This is all her idea, but I know she's right. If I don't get Jimmy's tape back to him straightaway I'll be in big trouble. My mum might not believe the story about the Martini, but I know he won't stop there; he'll make my life a misery.

'Maybe we should wait till Saturday.'

'Are you mad?'

'It's busier on a Saturday and it'll be easier to take it without being noticed.'

'They've got undercover store detectives on a Saturday. Everyone knows that.' She looks at me as if I'm stupid. 'So if you want that tape, it's got to be now.'

The next few seconds unravel in slow motion, frame by frame: the fly landing on the strap of Linda's bag, the flicker of the fluorescent strip bulb above her head, the clumsy, awkward movement as the cassette won't go into my pocket first time and the weight of the store manager's hand as it grips my shoulder. I look up into his round face and see Linda disappear through the automatic doors in the background.

The manager keeps a tight hold of my jacket and pushes me in front of him, through a swing door and up a flight of concrete steps and into a room marked *Office*. The small room has one grimy window, and the magnolia paint on the walls is peeling, revealing the grey plaster beneath. The only décor in the room is a sports car calendar which hasn't been changed since February. He sits down behind the desk and clasps his hands behind his head, revealing enormous round sweat stains on his crumpled shirt.

There's a grey bucket seat on my side of the desk, but he doesn't ask me to sit and so I stay standing, swaying back and forth on the balls of my feet. Why did I listen to Linda? Now I'm in real trouble; a million times worse than Jimmy finding out I snapped his tape. The manager lowers one arm and his hand hovers over the beige telephone, which sits on the desk beside a tea-stained mug and a copy of *Viz*. Is he going to call the police? I look to the window for fresh air, but a wire grid covers it on the inside.

He picks up the receiver and asks for my telephone number, dialling the numbers one at a time until I hear the phone ring on the other end of the line. I can just make out my dad's voice as he answers and the room spins as I listen to the manager give his account of catching me in the act of shoplifting. He hangs up but doesn't speak to me, so I stand, waiting for whatever's going to happen next. The store manager stares at me, tapping his pen on the formica table as announcements for half-price sales are mumbled over the tannoy. Who do they think is listening?

My legs are shaking but I don't dare ask to sit. Is no one coming for me? Will I be here until closing time? I try to see the time on my watch, but I can't make it out without being too obvious.

The office door opens and in walks my dad. I try to catch his eye, let him know I'm sorry, but he doesn't even look at me. He apologises to the manager, promises I won't be back in his store, and shakes his hand before leaving. I follow him down the stairs, past the pick & mix aisle and out through the automatic doors. The air outside is heavy with the threat of a thunderstorm, and we rush up the narrow lane towards the car park. He doesn't say a word the whole way home in the car, and I'm hoping this silent treatment will continue when I get into the house.

It doesn't.

'What the fuck did you think you were doing?'

The force of the f-word is as real as if he'd curled his fist and struck a blow to my stomach. I struggle to stay standing. The kitchen falls into darkness as the first spots of rain hit the patio flagstones, and I remember the time I was sick in bed with the measles and he took time off work to look after me. I can almost reach out and touch the crinkled orange cellophane wrapped around the bottle of Lucozade, and I close my eyes and imagine the sweet taste of the amber liquid as he held my chin to help me sip from a glass.

Now here he is, standing in front of me, but I don't recognise the look in his eyes. I want to tell him it was Linda who snapped the tape in the first place and that it was her idea to shoplift and I was only trying to do the right thing by Jimmy. The words are swimming around inside my head, jostling to be said first.

And then I hear her. The Blue Lady is talking to me again.

Ask for his forgiveness. If you tell him you're sorry, everything will be okay again.

But before I can speak, Mum storms into the room.

'This is all that girl Linda's fault.' She points her finger at Dad. 'I told you we shouldn't let her hang about with her, but oh no, you knew best. If you'd listened to me none of this would have happened.'

'You're her mother,' Dad shouts. 'If anyone should have told her to stay away from Linda it should have been you.'

'Stop it,' I shout. 'This isn't Linda's fault. If you'd both stop fighting all the time you'd know what was going on around here. If anyone's to blame it's you for neglecting us.' I regret this as soon as I see the look on my dad's face. Now he's the one who looks like he's been punched in the stomach and I'm the one who did the hitting.

Upstairs, in the safety of my bedroom, I pick up the delicate china figurine and trace the fine line running up one side. The crack is sharp and cuts my finger.

'I suppose you'd tell me shop lifting is a sin and I should go to Confession.' I place her back on my bedside table, sucking hard on my finger to stop the bleeding. 'Well, there's a lot I should confess to since we last spoke.' I remember the day I hid her away; it was the day Thomas moved out of the street. I can still see the shape of his silhouette in the back of the car as they drove away.

'I started the academy after I hid you away, and made lots of friends.' I pause. Is that true? Do I have lots of friends? Real friends? 'And I'm still best friends with Linda, that's the girl who found you. She's loud and bossy, but she's okay, really. I've not had any proper boyfriends yet but I'm working on it. His name's Andrew and he's gorgeous. We're taking it slow because what we feel for each other is real so there's no rush, although I'm hoping next time I see him we're going to kiss.' I've been dreaming about the kiss for days, now, and can barely think of anything else.

Raised voices can be heard from downstairs.

'And there's them. They're always shouting: at each other, at Jimmy and at me. Nothing is ever good enough for them. *Tidy your room. Do your homework. Wash the dishes*. If I try and help out they just tell me I should have done it differently. They hate my friends and they never ask what I think about stuff.' I reach out and stroke the cold, smooth china. Did they always argue like this? I can't remember. 'I sometimes think they hate me, too.'

My bedroom door opens and Jimmy comes into the room. I pick up my pillow and throw it at him. 'Get out.'

He holds his hands up in defence. 'Whoa, don't you think

there's enough shouting in this house at the minute?' He picks the pillow up from the floor and hands it back to me. I take it and pull it in to my chest. He sits down on the edge of the bed. 'Is it true you were caught shoplifting?'

I can see the Blue Lady out of the corner of my eye. 'Your Madonna tape got caught in the machine and I wanted to replace it before you found out.'

'For fuck's sake, I told you not to borrow it.'

'I'll get you another one as soon as I've saved up enough money.'

'Why didn't you do that in the first place?'

'You'd have killed me if I'd told you it was snapped.'

He looks hurt and I feel bad. Then he puts his arm around my shoulders. I can't remember him ever doing that before.

'I'm sorry,' he says. 'I guess I'm not a very good big brother.'

I nudge him in the ribs. 'You're alright, I suppose.'

We laugh, and things feel good between us again.

'Hey,' he says. 'Guess who I saw standing in the queue at the post office yesterday?'

'Who?'

'You're supposed to guess.'

I stare at him. 'Was it somebody famous?'

'In the post office queue? Don't be daft.'

'Well, how am I supposed to know?'

'You're no fun.'

'Are you going to tell me or not?'

'Okay, okay. Keep your knickers on. It was your old boyfriend.'

My stomach lurches. 'Who?'

Jimmy laughs. 'How many old boyfriends do you have, eh? Something you're not telling me?'

'Jimmy,' I shout. 'Who was it?'

He sees I'm being serious. 'It was our old neighbour, Thomas O'Donnell.'

I stare at him. It can't be true. Has the Blue Lady somehow worked her magic? Maybe another miracle? 'Thomas? Thomas O'Donnell? Are you sure it was him?'

‘Of course I’m sure.’

‘Did you speak to him?’

‘Well, I wasn’t going to ignore him, was I?’

I can’t believe it. Why wasn’t I the one to see him?

‘What did he say?’ I ask. ‘Was he back visiting a friend or what?’

‘Looks like someone’s still got a wee soft spot for their old boyfriend.’

‘He wasn’t my boyfriend.’

‘He was your friend, wasn’t he? And he’s a boy, isn’t he?’ Jimmy’s clearly enjoying teasing me. I grab his hand and push his thumb backwards until he squeals with pain. ‘Alright, alright. I’ll tell you everything.’

I let go of his hand.

‘Jesus Christ, that was sore.’

‘I’m waiting.’

‘I hardly spoke to the boy. We said hi, obviously, and he told me they’ve bought a house in town.’

‘Where?’

‘I don’t know.’

‘Did he say anything else?’

‘I think that was it.’

‘That’s all he said?’

‘We were standing in the queue at the post office, for Christ’s sake. It wasn’t exactly a dinner date.’

‘Did he ask about me?’

Jimmy shakes his head. ‘But honestly, Sis, we only had a minute until he was served. We hardly had time to say hello.’

I can’t believe it. Thomas has moved back.

I wait until Jimmy leaves the room and then I reach under my bed for the cardboard box. I lift out the teddy bear and place him on the bedside table beside the Blue Lady. Maybe Linda finding her was a sign.

The School Goth

The classroom is silent when I open the door. I slip into my seat in the back row, take out my maths textbook, and hope Mr Rathbone hasn't noticed my absence. The lesson started five minutes ago, and he hates it when students are late.

Linda leans over. 'Page 31.'

I flick through the book as fast as I can until I find the right page, and then I begin to write today's date in my jotter. Maths is most definitely not my strong suit, and thankfully I only need a pass to get into Art College.

'Catherine Munro. Step out to the front of the class.'

'You're in for it now,' whispers Linda.

I push my chair back and stand up.

'Now!' roars Mr Rathbone.

I walk out to the front of the room and stop in front of the blackboard.

'You're late.' He doesn't bother asking why I'm late, or if everything's okay. He never does. I can feel the eyes of my classmates upon me, and I look to Linda for help but she's staring at an imaginary spot on the floor.

'Take a seat at the front of the class.'

I look to the front row where there's only one vacant seat, and it's next to Billy Weir. Great! Billy Weir is a total freak, and my life at school has just got a million times harder. I skulk to the back of the room, slip my school bag over my shoulder and pick up my books. Paula and Rachel grin at me as I walk past them, and my cheeks burn as I slide into the seat beside Billy. I contemplate crawling under my desk and hiding until the end of the lesson, but instead I open my textbook and try not to stare at the row of piercings running up the edge of his earlobe or the collection of black leather bracelets on his skinny wrist. He wears more jewellery than most of the girls do. Paula and Rachel poke me from behind with a ruler. I turn round and they blow me a kiss.

Out of the corner of my eye, I see Billy scribble something along the top of his page and I wonder what he's up to. He slides the jotter to my side of the desk and I read the three words he's written for me.

They're only jealous!

I look up at him, and he flashes me a small smile before turning back to face the front of the class.

When the bell rings I'm the first to leave and I race along the corridor to double art, relieved no one from maths is in this class. The time passes slowly and I'm glad when it's eventually break. It's stopped raining and everyone heads outside to the quad, so I make my way to the library where I can get some peace and quiet and postpone the inevitable ridicule.

I try hiding in the horror section, but Linda soon finds me.

'Where have you been? I've been looking everywhere for you.'

'I had a project to finish for art.' She doesn't take art, so I should get away with this.

'Oh my God, I can't believe he put you beside Billy Weir. I'm sure you could make a complaint; I mean there should be a law against it. Did you see his make-up this morning? I think he was wearing black eye liner.'

I hadn't noticed, but I don't argue.

'Everyone's saying he's suicidal. I even heard some of the sixth years have started taking bets on him doing it before the summer holidays.' She grabs my arm. 'Do you think it's genetic? You know, killing yourself?'

'I don't think we've covered that in biology, yet.'

My sarcasm is lost on her and she's getting excited. 'Maybe you could get him to tell you.'

'What are you talking about? Tell me what?'

'About his mum. You could get him to tell you how she did it, how she killed herself.'

Billy Weir's mum committed suicide when we were at primary school, but nobody knows for sure what happened.

'And how am I going to do that?'

'I don't mean just ask him out of the blue, you'd have to work up to it.' She rummages around in her school bag and pulls out a copy of *Smash Hits*. 'Here,' she hands over the magazine. 'You could happen to be looking through this and then you could start talking about music and stuff. He'd love that.'

'In maths?'

'Well, obviously not when Rathbone's in class, maybe before the lesson begins.'

'Forget it. Besides, I don't think he's exactly into Duran Duran or Spandau Ballet.'

'Okay, well maybe you'll have to find another way to get him talking. But imagine if you got Billy Weir to tell you what actually happened. Think how popular you'd be, everyone would want to know the details.'

'Forget it.'

'Cathy, it's Billy Weir we're talking about here. He's always been weird; don't you remember him in primary school? He used to stand and take the belt from Mrs Henderson without flinching. Besides, he doesn't care what people think about him.'

I take the magazine and stuff it into my bag. 'I'll think about it.'

A group of sixth years swagger into the library and I spot Derek amongst them. I scan the rest of the group for Andrew, but he's not there. Derek makes his way over and slips his hand around Linda's waist from behind.

'Alright, gorgeous,' he says. He kisses her on the back of the neck. I look over to the librarian's desk, but Mrs Fowler is busy sorting through a pile of books. 'I was wondering if you're both free on Friday night.'

'Sure, shall we meet in the park?' Linda's playing it cool.

Derek lets go of her waist. 'I was thinking we could meet in the West Port. Say, eight o'clock?'

'Meet you there,' she says, and they kiss. She doesn't

even ask me if I can make it on Friday night.

As Derek leaves, he stops and looks at me. 'Hey Cathy, what's this I hear about you and the School Goth? You trying to make Andrew jealous?' He laughs as he walks away and I panic. What if Andrew hears the stories about me and Billy? Will he think I'm not interested in him?

'Oh my God, this is a proper date,' squeals Linda. 'And it's in the West Port.'

'But I'm grounded.'

'Well, you'll have to come up with some excuse for getting out. Tell them we're studying or something. There's no way you can miss out on going to the West Port.'

'But what if we don't get served?'

'What? Of course we will, we'll just need to wear the right clothes and lots of make-up.'

I feel sick. I'll never pass for being eighteen.

'Anyway,' she says, 'why were you late this morning?'

I concentrate on arranging the books in my bag. I don't want to explain about Mum and Dad's fight at the breakfast table. They were still arguing when I slipped out of the house and I doubt they even noticed I was gone.

'Missed the bus,' I say, and before I have to explain further Sarah rushes over and interrupts us.

'Have you heard what Rachel's been saying?' Sarah flaps her arms like a canary tied to a perch. 'She's being a right bitch and telling everyone you and that weirdo, Billy, are a couple. I told her to keep her mouth shut or else, but you know what she's like.'

Everyone knows what Rachel's like. She's only happy when she's making someone else's life a misery, and for now that someone seems to be me.

'Lisa told me she heard Rachel say to Scott that you're after a shag and that the only boy you can get is Billy Weir.'

This is so unfair. I never asked for any of this to happen. I look up and see Billy over by the doorway. He smiles at me and raises a hand to wave, but I look away before anyone notices. Things are bad enough that I have to sit beside him in class.

Lace Gloves and Crucifixes

It's Friday night at last, and I'm going to meet Linda on the half seven bus. I've told Mum and Dad I'm going to her house to study, and my plan is to get changed at the bus stop because there's no way they'd believe me if I leave the house dressed in my new skirt and top. I look at my watch. It's after half six already.

I set the magazine out on my bed and lay out the assortment of eye shadows, lipsticks and make-up brushes I've been given over the past few years for Christmas and birthdays. I don't have any foundation, so instead I start with a layer of pink blusher across both cheekbones. The blusher glitters in the light and I feel a stir of excitement at the transformation about to take place. Andrew won't be able to take his eyes off me. Next, I choose a baby-blue eye shadow and sweep it across my eyelids. Some of the blue powder drops onto my cheeks and when I try to wipe it off with a square of toilet paper it smudges with the pink blusher. Why doesn't the magazine warn you about this? I apply more blusher to try and cover the mess, but I'm beginning to look like the Miss World doll I had when I was little.

I coat my lips in pink lip gloss and finish the look with electric blue mascara. I don't have the fancy lash curler it shows in the magazine, but I reckon the wand in the mascara tube will do fine.

Downstairs, they're shouting again. Damn it. I blinked, and now I've got streaks of electric blue along the top of my brow. I lick a cotton bud and dab it gently but the mascara runs into the baby blue eye shadow. This is a disaster and I'm going to get thrown out of the pub in front of everyone.

In front of Andrew. I grab a face cloth and scrub until all traces of blue are gone and I'm ready to start again. I check my watch. I've got just under ten minutes until I have to leave. No time for mascara.

The bus stop is empty when I arrive, and I reach into my bag and pull out a bright yellow rah-rah skirt and a black string vest. I pull the skirt over the top of my skinny jeans and wriggle the jeans downwards, hopping from one foot to the other as I struggle to pull them off over my boots. The vest top is easier and I slip it on over my lime green t-shirt before finishing the outfit with a couple of over-sized crucifixes and a pair of black lace gloves. The small silver cross is already around my neck; I've been wearing it ever since Jimmy met Thomas in the queue at the post office. I take out a compact mirror and add some more kohl liner and lip gloss for effect. Done. And this time it's perfect.

I stand and look at the graffiti on the walls of the bus shelter while I wait for the bus to arrive. Most of the names have been here for ages, but I see two new names drawn inside a love heart.

SADIE + THOMAS 4EVER

Could it be my Thomas? If so, who the fuck is Sadie?

I check to see if Sadie has left any other tags, and that's when I spot it:

CATHY MUNRO SUCKS BILLY WEIRS DICK

I'm going to kill Rachel Jones when I see her. There are still a couple of minutes until the bus gets here, and I pull a black marker pen out from the front of my bag. It's about time somebody taught that bitch a lesson. I score out my name and search for a space. Every inch of the shelter is covered, but I find a faded Morrissey lyric and write over the top of it:

RACHEL JONES LICKS PUSSY

I stand back to admire my art work. Maybe next time I should try red, make it stand out a bit more. And maybe next time I'll be able to write *CATHY LVS ANDY.*

I put the pen away just as the bus comes round the corner. I step forward and raise my hand until it stops in front of me.

'A half to Bathgate, please.' I drop three shiny five-pence coins into the slot and stare down the aisle of the bus, aware the driver is looking me up and down. Maybe I should have held back on the eyeliner until I got into town.

In the end, he doesn't question my age, and the ticket churns out of the machine. I pull the stub free with one hand and tug the rah-rah skirt down with the other. It hadn't felt this tight when I tried it on in the changing room in Top Shop. The bus lurches forward and I just manage to grab hold of the handrail before I'm thrown sideways. I throw the driver a dirty look and go looking for a seat.

Upstairs, a gang of boys lie sprawled out across the back seat and I quickly scan the rest of the top deck. There's only them and me, but I know I can't lose face and go back downstairs.

'A'right, sexy,' calls out a boy with ginger hair, but I ignore him and sit down at the front of the bus. I take out my Sony Walkman, and Andrew Ridgeley starts strumming his guitar in my ear. I lean back and imagine he's playing to me from the empty seat beside me. Wolf-whistles and shouts can be heard above the music, but I'm not worried because Linda will be getting on at the Gulf station in a couple of minutes. She'll sort them out.

A crushed fag packet hits me on the shoulder and lands on the floor in front of me. I pick it up and turn to throw it back at them but freeze. The boy with ginger hair has slipped into the seat beside me, the one I imagine Andrew Ridgeley is in.

'You go to Bathgate Academy, right?' He stubs his half-smoked cigarette out on the arm-rest. 'Fancy coming out with us tonight? Let some Catholic boys show you a good time.'

The blue and orange Gulf sign appears in the large front window of the bus. I stand up.

'What's wrong? Are we not good enough for you?'

I push my way past him and out into the aisle, waiting for the bus to slow down.

'From what I heard, you girls aren't that fussy.'

The petrol station sign goes by in a blur. Why aren't we stopping? I spin round and look for Linda, but there's no one waiting at the bus stop. I rush to the top of the stairs, clinging on to the handrail as the bus goes round a corner.

'You running away, Proddy bitch?'

I run down the stairs two at a time, nearly breaking my ankle as I hit the bottom.

'You'll get what's coming to you,' he shouts after me.

'Whoa!' An old man puts his hand out to stop me from falling. 'Everything okay?'

I look upstairs and nod.

The bus pulls up at the stop in town and I get off first and hide around the corner before the boys can see me.

Where's Linda?

She's nowhere to be seen, but I've got no intention of hanging around the precinct waiting for her. Derek and Andrew are supposed to be meeting us in the West Port at eight o'clock, and I'll die if I bump into them on my own. I run across the road and head towards the toilets of the Balbairdie Restaurant. The toilets are on the side of the building and you can get to them without having to go through the dining area.

There are only two small cubicles, but thankfully one of them is free, and I squeeze inside the small space and shut the door behind me.

Proddy bitch, Proddy bitch, Proddy bitch.

I press the heels of my hands against my ears but can't shut out the words. The woman next to me flushes the toilet and I listen to the hand dryer and wait for her to hurry up and leave. The dryer shuts off, and I peek through the gap between the wall and the cubicle door and watch as she backcombs her hair, applying enough hairspray to make a small hole in the ozone layer. When she's finally gone I come out and check myself in the mirror.

'Cathy?' The outer door is thrown open and Linda appears. 'Cathy, thank God you're here, I thought you'd bottled it.' She walks up to the mirror and pulls a lip gloss out of her back pocket.

'You weren't on the bus.'

'I couldn't make up my mind about which earrings to wear so I missed the first bus. Sorry. But what do you think?' She lifts up her hair and shows off a pair of big yellow hoop earrings. My yellow hoop earrings. I must have left them at her house. 'Aren't they perfect with this top?' She sees me in the mirror and spins round on her heels. 'I thought you were going to wear your new mascara.'

'I did, it's just…'

Linda interrupts. 'Never mind, there's nothing we can do about it now.' She turns back to the mirror. 'I just hope we still get served.'

'Linda, I'm not sure I'm feeling up to this.'

'What? Don't you dare back out on me now. There's no way I'm turning up on my own.' She pouts in the mirror, blows herself a kiss and struts out of the room.

We stop outside the West Port and Linda peers through the small diamond-shaped window panes.

'They're here. Oh my God, how do I look? Have I got enough blusher on?' She doesn't wait for me to answer. 'Come on, there's an empty table on the other side of the bar. But whatever you do, don't let them know we've seen them. Don't make eye contact.'

'But haven't we arranged to meet them here?'

Linda sighs. 'Don't you know anything? It's important that they're the ones who come over to speak to us. We can't give them the impression we're too keen.' She looks at her watch. 'It's just after eight. We should probably wait another five minutes. But what if someone takes that table?'

I'm confused. When I agreed to coming along tonight I hadn't realised things would be so complicated.

'Fuck it; let's get this over with.' Linda pushes open the

door to the bar and I follow.

Loud music is coming from the juke box in the corner and the air is heavy with the smell of Silk Cut. I stifle a cough and follow my best friend to a table. We sit down, and Linda turns to me with a ridiculously oversized smile.

'What would you like to drink?'

'No idea.'

'Oh, for God's sake.'

'Well, what are you having?'

She grabs her bag and stands up. 'I'll get us both a half pint of Snakebite.'

I watch her wiggle up to the bar, scared to look around the room in case Derek and Andrew see me. A young man is already being served and I watch as he hands over his money, clenches a packet of crisps between his teeth and somehow also manages to lift three glasses. The young man turns around and I see it's Billy Weir, dressed in a pair of skin-tight black jeans and a *Jesus and Mary Chain* t-shirt, and wearing black eye liner and mascara. He sees me and smiles, and the bag of crisps falls out of his mouth. He puts the three glasses down on the nearest table and I reach forward and hand the packet of Ready Salted up to him.

'Thanks, Cathy.' This time he tucks the packet of crisps into his pocket.

I look at the fluorescent blue liquid in the glasses on the table. 'What's that?'

'Blue Lagoon. It's like drinking sweets. You should try one.'

'I might.'

Billy picks up the three glasses. 'Catch you later.'

I sit back down and see Derek is now up at the bar beside Linda and they're both laughing about something. I look round and see Andrew watching from the other side of the room. Fuck this. I get up out of my seat and walk across to his table.

'Hey, didn't see you there,' I say. 'What time did you get here?'

Laughter erupts at another table and I look up to see Billy

balancing a pile of beer mats on the edge of the table. His friends are cheering him on to flip them in one go.

'I can do that,' I tell Andrew.

'What?'

I nod my head towards the table of boys. 'I can flip beer mats.'

'As many as that?'

'My dad taught me the year we went on holiday to Whitby. We were staying in a caravan and it rained the whole time. And I mean the whole time. There was a bar on the campsite and sometimes we would go along at night for a lemonade.' I blush. 'I was still wee at the time. Anyway, we would sneak all the beer mats out and take them back to the caravan with us, and my dad showed me how to pile them up and flip them.'

I can't believe I'm telling this boy, who I fancy madly, about flipping beer mats in a caravan.

'I love being in a caravan when the rain's chucking it down outside,' he says.

And there, just like that, it no longer feels awkward, and we're still chatting away about caravan holidays when Derek and Linda return from the bar.

'What are you both laughing about?' Linda asks.

Andrew holds up a beer mat. 'Fancy giving it a go?'

Derek looks at him. 'What are you on about?'

'How many of these can you flip?'

'I can flip ten,' I boast. 'Easily.'

'No way.' Derek takes the beer mat and places it on the edge of the table. He checks its position from several angles and then taps it upwards with the back of his fingers. The beer mat falls to the floor and his cheeks flush red. 'It's been a while.'

Linda knocks back her drink and bangs the empty glass down on the table. 'Anyone ready for another?'

I gather all of the beer mats into a pile in front of me. 'I'll have a Blue Lagoon, please.' Out of the corner of my eye I see Andrew watching me. Is he impressed? I hope so.

Linda stares at me. 'A Blue Lagoon?'

'Any good?' asks Derek.

'Tastes like sweets,' I say.

Derek stands up. 'Four Blue Lagoons it is, then.'

'We're going to the loo,' says Linda and she grabs me by the hand and drags me to the ladies. 'Oh my God, have you seen the way Derek is looking at me, he can barely keep his hands off me.'

'What do you mean?'

'Haven't you noticed? He keeps brushing up against me when we're sitting together.'

This probably has something to do with the fact we're all squeezed around a small table, but I know better than to say anything.

'And when we were up at the bar his hand brushed against my tit when we both reached out for a drink, and I know it was deliberate.' She studies herself in the mirror and fixes her hair. 'I think I'm in love.'

I've heard this a million times before. It's the same every time Linda fancies a boy. It's always true love.

'Do you think Andrew likes me?' I ask.

'Of course he does.'

'How do you know?'

'You can tell by the way he keeps looking at you.'

'Then why hasn't he made a move?'

'It's obvious.'

'Is it?'

'Yeah.'

I wait, but Linda doesn't say anymore.

'How's it obvious?' I ask.

She looks back at me from the mirror. 'Don't worry about it; some boys are just slower than others. Andrew's obviously interested and wants to go out with you, but he's one of the quiet types.' She laughs. 'None of the quiet ones are ever interested in me.'

'But what if he's only here to keep Derek company?'

'Don't be daft; he's just shy. But perhaps when we go back out it'd be better if you sit quiet and show him you're not just one of the lads.'

'What do you mean?'

'I mean flipping beer mats. It's not very ladylike, is it? Now, turn your head upside down; your hair has gone flat.'

The evening comes to an end too soon and before I know it our glasses are being collected and it's closing time. I'm not sure the 'sitting quiet' idea worked, because Andrew hardly said another word to me all night.

'Are you getting the bus home?' I ask Linda.

'I was hoping Derek might walk me home,' she says, wrapping her arms around his waist.

'Can someone walk me to the bus stop?' I say, louder than necessary, trying to catch Andrew's eye. But he's too busy counting the change in his pocket.

'We'll walk you,' says Derek. 'We'll be passing that way anyway and can wait until your bus arrives.'

Andrew closes his fist around his loose change and grins. 'Enough for a bag of chips for the walk home.'

My heart sinks as he shouts goodnight and heads off up the hill, and I'm left alone with Derek and Linda who insist on waiting with me at the bus stop. I try to ignore the fact Derek's got his hands inside Linda's top, but it's made more difficult by the fact that all of the men at the bus stop have noticed and can't keep their eyes off them. At last, the number sixteen pulls up at the kerb and I say goodbye. But they don't hear me.

The doors open. Any queuing system that was in place at the bus stop is forgotten, and I'm pushed roughly aside by a group of drunken men who are concentrating on not dropping their kebabs. The man in front tries to chat me up and I wonder if he's aware of the vomit splattered down the front of his *Motörhead* t-shirt. I hold my breath as I force myself past him and head upstairs.

I sit down and lean my head against the window, feeling the revs of the engine rattle through the glass as the bus prepares to go. Gazing out into the darkness, I see Derek and Linda kissing in a shop doorway and I wish it was Andrew kissing me.

'Look, boys, it's our Proddy friend from earlier this

evening.'

I jump up to move but the boy with the red hair slips into the seat beside me, blocking my exit. He smiles and blows out his cigarette smoke in my face. Slowly.

'Thought I saw you coming out of the pub with your boyfriend. Where is he now, eh? Nice boy like that letting you make your own way home?' He makes a show of looking around the bus. 'You should try going out with a good Catholic boy, someone who knows how to look after a lady properly, eh?'

I turn away from him and stare out of the bus window. Street lights pass by in a blur, and the sound of drunken singing rises up from below as everyone downstairs joins in with the chorus of *Bat Out Of Hell*.

It's a Rule

'Did you have a good night?' Billy asks.

'When?'

'On Friday night. I saw you in the pub, remember.'

I look around the classroom and check no one is watching us talking, but everyone's too busy laughing with their friends to notice us.

'Oh yeah, of course.'

'Hadn't realised you and Andrew were going out together. How long have you been seeing him?'

My stomach flips. It must have looked like we were a couple; even Billy Weir noticed us.

'My best friend Linda is going out with his friend Derek. That's why we were together. Well, when I say together you know I mean out together. Not exactly out together, I mean we're not going out or anything.'

'Why not?

'He hasn't asked me yet.'

'So why don't you ask him?'

'Don't you know anything? Girls aren't meant to ask boys out.'

'Says who?'

'Says everyone. It's a rule.'

Mr Rathbone walks into the room and slams a pile of books down on his desk. The class falls silent.

Billy leans close. 'Sounds like a stupid rule to me,' he whispers. 'Besides, from what I heard, Andrew is really keen on you.'

Our maths teacher stands at the front of the room and barks the instructions for today's lesson. I look at Billy, desperate to ask him more, but he's feigning attention. We open our textbooks and turn to the page given while Mr Rathbone goes on about something to do with quadratic equations, but I've given up listening. What did Billy mean? How does he know Andrew fancies me? Did Andrew tell him?

Finally, our maths teacher stops talking, and we're told to complete page twenty-four in our jotter.

'Who told you Andrew's keen?' I whisper, careful that Mr Rathbone doesn't hear.

Billy grins and gives me a wink.

I turn to the first problem but the words might just as well be in Latin for all I understand, and my mind drifts back to what Billy said.

Andrew is really keen on you.

Could it be true? Maybe Linda was right. Maybe he's shy. I think about what Billy said. Would I dare be brave enough to make the first move?

Billy nudges me and I see Mr Rathbone has started walking up and down between the desks, his hands clasped tightly together behind his back. I panic. The page in my jotter is blank and he's nearly at our row.

Billy pushes his jotter over to where I can see it and I start copying down his working as quickly as I can. Mr Rathbone approaches my desk and I bite down on my pencil, pretending to be concentrating on the next part of the problem.

'Good start, Catherine,' he says and moves on.

I look at Billy and mouth, *Thank you.*

The class lets out a collective sigh as our teacher returns to his desk and picks up his pen to start the crossword in today's newspaper. He won't pay us any attention now until the bell rings for the end of class.

'Talking of Friday night,' I say, 'who was that you were in the pub with?'

'Just a bunch of friends.'

'I didn't recognise any of them.'

'They don't go to this school.' He looks at me. 'Come on,' he says, 'everyone knows I don't have any friends in this school.' He waves his hand around the room. 'Look at them,' he says. 'They're all a bunch of self-important dickheads. Why would I want to be friends with them?'

And that's when it hits me. All along, I'd assumed Billy didn't have any friends because no one wanted to be friends with him. It never occurred to me it might be the other way round.

He goes back to working on a problem from the text book and I nudge him with my elbow.

'Am I like them?' I ask him. 'Am I a self-important dickhead?'

He laughs. 'Nah, you're alright.'

'Does that mean we can be friends?'

He smiles at me. 'I thought we already were.'

Ouija

Linda stands by the window and watches Jimmy disappear down the hill.

'Right, let's have some fun.'

'I thought we were going to revise.'

'Fuck that! It's Saturday night.'

'But I promised Mum we'd be studying.'

'That's okay,' says Linda. 'We can tell her we studied for the whole night.'

'What if she wants proof?'

'Proof?'

'Yeah, like some notes or past paper answers or something.'

'Jesus, Cathy, your folks are a nightmare. You do have rights, you know. There was this girl on the TV whose parents were so strict she ended up going to court and getting a divorce from them.'

'A divorce from her parents?'

'Yeah, my mum was telling me all about it after I told her how mean your mum was being.'

'You told her about my mum?'

'Yeah, about you being grounded and stuff. And my mum says they're breaching your rights. She says you can come and live with us for a few days if that'll help.'

There's a loud banging at the back door and we both jump.

'That'll be Jimmy,' I say.

'But he's only just left.'

'Yeah, well maybe he's had a change of heart and decided to stay in after all.'

'I can't believe they think you need a babysitter. You're

sixteen, for Christ's sake. Old enough to get married or have your own kid.'

The banging starts again and we look at each other.

'Did you tell anyone my mum and dad are out?'

Linda doesn't answer. We tiptoe through to the kitchen and she turns off the light.

'Do you think whoever's out there will be able to see us?' she asks.

The handle of the back door rattles and we clutch each other tightly as someone taps on the kitchen window.

'For fuck's sake, let us in before someone thinks we're breaking in and phones the police.'

Linda opens the back door and Derek and Andrew slip into the house, both looking back over their shoulders.

'Been standing out there for ages waiting for your brother to go out.'

'What are you doing here?'

'Well, that's a nice welcome.' Derek grins. 'Linda said your folks were going out for the night and so we thought you girls might fancy a little company. We worked out which house backs on to yours, sneaked into their garden and then pushed our way through the hedge at the back – and, ta-da, we're here.' He stops and looks around him. 'What the fuck did you switch the light off for?'

'We weren't sure who you were,' says Linda.

'Who the fuck else would be banging on your back door at this time of night? The fuckin' Pope?'

Linda pretends to look put out. 'It could've been anybody. Another Jack the Ripper or something.'

Derek laughs out loud. 'Don't worry. Andrew and I will save you.' He winks at Andrew. I grab Linda and drag her through to the hallway.

'Why did you tell them my mum and dad were going out?'

'I thought you'd be pleased.'

'Pleased? They'll kill me if they find out I've had boys round. I'm still grounded from the Woolies incident, remember? And the only reason you're allowed round is because they think we're studying.'

'You alright, girls? Fancy a drink?' Derek follows us through to the hall and holds up a bottle of Babycham. 'I nicked it from my mum's cupboard. She'll never notice it's missing.'

My stomach turns at the sight of it, but I know I can't say no.

Derek opens the bottle and takes a drink before wiping his mouth and passing it to Linda. Linda knocks back a mouthful and hands the bottle to me, but when I lift it to my mouth the smell hits me, and I remember being sick on her living room carpet. I put it back down.

'What's wrong with you?' asks Derek.

I raise the bottle to my lips and take a sip under his watchful gaze before handing the bottle to Andrew. Our fingers lightly touch.

'Fuckin' hell, this place is posh.' Derek opens the door to the dining room. 'You've even got two tables. Who the fuck needs two tables?'

'That's the dining room,' I say, pulling the door shut so he can't go in. 'We only use it at Christmas time.'

Derek has the bottle back in his hands and he drains the last of it as he goes into the living room.

'Got any more?' he asks, opening the sideboard cupboard.

'You can't take anything from there,' I say. 'They'll know if something's missing.'

'They'll never notice if I take a wee sip.' He laughs and takes out a bottle of Martini. 'Want some?'

Nobody answers him as he unscrews the cap and drinks straight from the bottle. He keeps the bottle in his hand and makes himself comfortable on the sofa. He takes another drink and picks up a note pad from the floor.

'I've got an idea,' he says. 'How about we make an Ouija board?'

'No chance,' says Andrew.

'You a pussy?' Derek laughs. 'Scared of fuckin' spirits, eh?'

‘My mum said she tried the Ouija board when she was a girl.’ Linda sits down beside him on the sofa. ‘Said there was this boy in her street who used to run séances. You know, to contact the dead. Anyway, one time she was there and suddenly all the flames on the candles grew really long and actually scorched the ceiling. She never went back after that, but she remembers the boy never returned to school. The story is he’d disturbed some angry spirits during the séance and they’d possessed him. Neighbours said they heard all sorts of weird stuff going on, like plates and glasses flying out of cupboards and the radio blaring at all times of the day and night. Last my mum heard of him they called the priest in to do an exorcism.’

‘Did it work?’ I ask.

‘Don’t know. The boy moved away after that and she never saw him again. She said the house was sold to a new couple and nobody heard of any bother again.’

‘So what do you think?’ Derek asks. ‘Do you fancy giving it a go?’

‘What do we have to do?’ asks Linda.

Derek hands her the pad. ‘Rip up the paper into little squares and write the letters of the alphabet on them, the numbers zero to nine, and the words Yes and No.’ He turns to me, ‘And we’ll need a glass. And any candles if you’ve got them.’

‘Candles?’ I say, thinking of the scorch marks on the ceiling. ‘Isn’t that taking it a step too far?’

Derek laughs. ‘Adds to the atmosphere.’

Linda picks up the pad and starts to tear the paper into little squares. ‘Where should we do this?’ she asks.

‘What do you mean?’

‘I was thinking we should go up to your room in case Jimmy comes back.’

‘I don’t want to burn candles in my bedroom. My mum and dad might smell them when they get back.’

‘Then how about the dining room?’ says Derek. ‘It’s got the table we need and we can open a window to get rid of the smell of candles, and you said yourself it’s only ever used at Christmas time.'

'Perfect,' says Linda. 'Let's bring everything through.'

It's cold in the dining room with the window open, but I daren't say anything. They already think I'm a wimp. I sit down in the seat next to Andrew and the smell of his aftershave makes my stomach flutter.

'You done this before?' he asks me, but I can't answer. My brain is screaming at me to speak to him but my tongue is super-glued to the roof of my mouth.

Derek barges into the room. 'Right folks, let's get this show started.' He spreads the pieces of paper out in a circle, arranging the numbers first, then the letters in alphabetical order and finally placing the word *Yes* at the top and *No* at the bottom. He catches me watching. 'So there's no doubting what the spirits tell us,' he says, and strikes a match to light the candles. He then switches off the light in the room and sits down between Linda and me and clutches our hands. Tightly.

'Spirits of the dead, can you hear us?'

Andrew looks across the table at his friend. 'Aren't you supposed to put a finger on the glass?'

I stifle a laugh and feel relieved when Derek's sweaty hand lets go. I wipe the palm of my hand discreetly on my leggings and place the index finger of my right hand on the edge of the upside-down glass in the centre of the table. Linda shoots Andrew a dirty look; she was clearly enjoying holding Derek's hand. Andrew ignores her.

'Is anyone there?' Derek asks. Nothing happens. He asks again, but still the glass stays firmly in the centre of the table.

'I guess there's no one there,' Linda says, and I hear the tremble in her voice. She's actually scared. 'Maybe we should watch a film instead.'

'Shhh,' says Derek. 'There needs to be silence before we ask the questions, or the spirits might get confused.' He looks at Andrew. 'I think it might be easier for them if only one of us talks, okay?'

Andrew doesn't argue. I watch Derek close his eyes and I

wait for his questions to start.

'Dear spirits who have passed to the other side, are you there?'

The glass beneath our fingers wobbles a little and I look across the table at Linda, but her eyes are squeezed firmly shut.

'Can you hear us?' Derek speaks slowly, carefully pronouncing every word, and his voice sounds an octave lower. 'Can you hear us?' he asks again.

The glass quivers and stutters across the table towards *Yes*. Linda's eyes flick open and her hand rises to cover her gaping mouth.

'Don't break the connection,' shouts Derek, and he grabs hold of her hand. 'It's important we don't let go of the glass.'

'Or what?' asks Linda. She doesn't just look scared any more. She looks terrified.

Derek doesn't answer her question, and I suspect he's making the whole thing up as he goes along. I wriggle in my seat, pretending to get comfy, and manage to slide my finger underneath his. Now I'll know if he's the one pushing the glass. Everyone around the table settles, and Derek asks another question.

'Are you on the other side?'

The glass slides towards *Yes* again, but I can't feel anyone pushing it. I look around the circle as it stops on the *Yes*, but everyone looks scared, even Derek. Whoever is moving the glass is good at acting. We pull the upturned glass back to the centre and Derek asks his next question.

'How did you die?'

I stare in disbelief as the glass starts to move around the circle. Linda reads the letters aloud with a shaking voice. '*F...I...R...E...* Oh my God, she died in a fire. She died in a fire.'

I can't remember the spirit telling us it was a girl.

'Was the fire an accident?' asks Derek.

I feel sick as I watch the glass slowly move towards the word *No*.

'Oh spirit from the other side, tell us, were you murdered?'

The glass almost leaps off the table as it races towards *Yes*.

Linda screams. 'What a horrible way to die. Horrible. What age was she? Ask her what age she was.'

'Oh spirit from the other side, what age were you when you died?'

The glass moves between two numbers on the board.

Linda's hysterical now. 'Sixteen. She was only sixteen.'

I look across the table at her. 'That's the same age as us,' I whisper.

'Spirit, do you know when we will die?' Derek asks.

Yes.

'Tell us spirit, what age will I be when I die?'

The glass slides to the number six and then nine. Sixty-nine.

'What age will Linda be?'

This time the glass moves to the seven and the five.

'Cathy?'

I get the same answer, and Linda smiles across the table at me with relief. Looks like we're going to be friends for a long time.

'Andrew?'

The glass doesn't move and I feel the knot in my stomach return.

'Oh spirit from the other side, do you know what age Andrew will be when he dies?'

The glass moves slowly to the number one and then to the number six.

Linda loses control. 'Sixteen. Oh my God, Andrew's going to die when he's sixteen, like the girl in the fire.'

'Sit down,' shouts Derek. 'Don't break the circle.'

She pushes away from the table, upsetting the circle of letters and knocking the glass over.

'Sixteen,' she screams and points straight at Andrew. 'You're going to die when you're sixteen.'

I reach out and touch his hand. I lean forward so Linda

can't hear. 'What age are you?' I ask.

He turns to face me. Linda is still screaming but I can read the answer on his lips: *Sixteen*. According to the Ouija board, Andrew is going to die sometime before his next birthday.

'You guys are sick,' Linda's shouting. 'Whichever one of you pushed the glass is sick.' She's looking back and forth between the two boys, but neither of them looks guilty.

'We need to smash the glass,' Derek says quietly.

'What?' I ask. 'Smash the glass? Why?'

'To set the spirit free. At the end of a séance you must smash the glass.'

'But that's one of my mum's best glasses. I can't smash it.'

'Do you want the spirit to haunt your house for eternity?'

Linda's crying now, and mascara is running down her cheeks. Derek picks the glass up and lifts it above his head.

'Stop,' I shout. 'You can't smash it in here; it'll go everywhere.'

Without speaking, he walks over to the open window and throws it outside on to the concrete slabs. The sound of smashing glass causes Linda to start screaming all over again, and I watch Derek put his hands around her. Did he do it? Did he push the glass so he could make himself the hero and comfort poor, distraught Linda? I look over at Andrew, who is staring out of the open window as though he expects to see the spirit appear any second.

'I'm taking Linda outside for a bit because she needs some fresh air,' Derek announces. He has one hand around Linda's waist and the bottle of Martini in the other as he leaves the room, and I'm left alone with Andrew.

Together, we pick up the scraps of paper and he holds his small pile of assorted numbers and letters out to me. I take them from him and our hands gently touch. The Babycham has given me some Dutch courage and I let my hand linger, sure he feels the electricity between us, too.

I think of what Billy said to me in class about girls waiting for boys to make the first move being a stupid rule.

Before I can change my mind, I ask him to go out with me.

'Isn't it supposed to be me who asks you?' he says.

'Is that a no?'

'I didn't say that.' He leans forward and we kiss. It's not exactly a scene from *Dynasty*, but it'll do.

We break away and he takes hold of my hand.

'I turn seventeen next week, and if I've only got a few days left to live I want to spend them with you.' He kisses me again and I feel his hand move towards my breasts. Linda and Derek might come back any minute, and I don't want them to see us like this.

'Do you fancy listening to some music?' I ask. I lead the way upstairs and he follows me. He throws himself down into the beanbag on the floor and flicks through my record collection. My heart is racing as I perch on the edge of the bed, confused about what happens next. He holds up the *Wham!* album.

'What d'ya like these poofters for?'

'You're just jealous.'

He laughs and climbs on to the bed beside me. 'So if I've only got a short time left to live, I guess we'd better make the most of our time together.' He presses himself against me and I can taste the alcohol on his lips.

We stop kissing and he looks around my room.

'Have you got anything else to drink?'

'Sure, I'll grab us a couple of cans.' I jump up from the bed and go downstairs to fetch some of Dad's lager. I pause on the bottom step. Shit, I hope I haven't left any underwear lying on my bedroom floor. I hurry through to the kitchen and pull open the fridge door, but it's empty. I grab the key hanging by the back door and after three attempts I manage to open the basement door.

I flick on the light switch and straightaway I spot the empty jam jars on the shelf, now covered with dust. I haven't been down here in years, and I remember the summer Thomas and I caught the minnows in the burn. That was the last year my mum made homemade jam.

The cans of Tennent's are neatly stacked in the corner. I

prise a couple of cans out of the plastic rings and head back up to the kitchen, to find Andrew standing with his coat on, looking seriously pissed off.

'Everything okay?' I ask.

'I've remembered I promised to help a mate out with some stuff.'

'Maybe I could come with you.'

'Don't bother.' He closes the back door behind him and I stand in the middle of the kitchen holding the two cans of lager. What did I do wrong?

I go back upstairs, look around my bedroom, and my eyes fall on the teddy bear holding the red love heart with the words *Miss Me* on it. Suddenly I understand. He's jealous. I jump up and pull open my curtains, but there's no sign of him. Should I go looking for him? Explain to him the bear was given to me by an old neighbour? I wish now I'd confronted him.

Linda comes barging into the room. 'What happened? Andrew just stormed past us without saying a word.'

'I've no idea, I was getting us some beers, and he suddenly said he needed to be somewhere else and left.'

'What did you say to him?'

'I didn't say anything. Maybe he was scared about what the Ouija board said.'

'You must have said something.'

Derek appears behind Linda. 'Are you coming?'

'Give us a minute.'

He wanders into my room and starts looking through my stuff. 'What the fuck have you got that for?' He's staring at the figure of the Blue Lady. 'You never said you were one of them.'

'Who?'

'A Catholic. You never said you were a Catholic.'

'You're Catholic?' Linda asks.

'What the fuck do you go to our school for?' says Derek.

'But I'm not a Catholic. I'm not anything.'

'Then why have you got the fuckin' Virgin Mary by your bed? No wonder Andrew walked out.'

I don't understand. 'What do you mean? Why would he leave because of a statue?'

'Why?' His cruel laugh makes me feel stupid. 'It's the Virgin Mary – that's why! You're lucky he didn't smash her into a hundred pieces.' He picks up the Blue Lady. 'And you've blown any chance of him ever going out with you.'

Linda nudges him. 'Stop exaggerating.'

Derek turns to me. 'You know he plays in a flute band, right?'

I thought it was great when Andrew said he played in a band. The only instrument I ever tried to play was the recorder in primary school, and even then I only learned *Three Blind Mice.*

'So what if he likes music?' I ask.

'Yeah, and when was the last time you heard *The Sash* played on Radio One? Flute bands only ever play in Orange Walks!'

I pick up the brown teddy bear and hold it close to my chest. Why does love have to be so complicated?

Jimmy comes home a couple of hours later and bursts into my room without knocking. 'What the fuck have you been up to?'

'Leave me alone.'

'Get up.' He pulls back the bedcovers. 'And get downstairs and tidy up your mess. They'll be home any minute, and you're supposed to have been studying.'

'Who cares?'

'Me. Things are bad enough around here without you getting into even more trouble. I don't know what you've been up to, or who've you've had round, but I can't be bothered with another fight just because of you. So get downstairs and clear up the fucking mess.'

'No one's been round.'

'Save your lies for Mum and Dad. There's an empty bottle of Martini behind the plant pot in the hall, and someone's been smoking.'

'Now you're the one who's lying,' I say, 'because no

one's been smoking.'

'Then why's the dining room window lying wide open?'

Shit, I must have forgotten to shut the window.

'I can't believe you were stupid enough to let your friends smoke. Mum will be able to smell it from a mile away.'

'Fuck off.'

The front door opens downstairs and we swap a worried glance.

'Looks like you're too late,' he says.

We hold our breath and listen to them go into the kitchen.

'I've told you already, I don't want to talk about it.' Mum sounds like she's been crying. Before we can hear anymore, the phone rings and I run to answer it. This time if someone hangs up I'm going to confront Mum and ask her what's going on. I snatch the handset and hold it to my ear.

'Cathy, thank God it's you who answered. Can you meet me at the park?' It's Linda, and it sounds important.

'It's almost midnight. Can't you tell me over the phone?'

'I need to see you.'

'When?'

'As soon as you can get away.'

I stretch the cable as far as it can reach and look into the kitchen. They're still arguing.

'I'll be there in about five minutes.'

'Be as quick as you can,' she says and hangs up.

I grab my jacket and head for the door.

'Where the fuck do you think you're going?' Jimmy's leaning over the banister.

'Shhh, they'll hear you.'

'Are you trying to get yourself into more trouble?'

'I'll only be gone for five minutes. They won't even notice.' I hand him the empty Martini bottle. 'Here, hide this for me until I get back.' Before he can stop me, I open the door and run down the path, knowing he'll never tell on me.

I've never been in the park when it's dark before, and I'm

wishing I'd never agreed to come. But what if it's not really Linda who's waiting to meet me? What if it's Andrew? Right now he could be waiting by the swings to say sorry for the way he behaved and to tell me he can't stop thinking about me and can I possibly forgive him.

I'm disappointed to see Linda's alone at the park when I arrive.

'That was quick.'

'I came straight away but I can't stay long. They'll kill me if they find out I've gone.'

Linda gently rocks the swing back and forth.

'So, what's up?'

'I thought it could wait until I saw you tomorrow, but I can't keep it to myself any longer. I'm bursting to tell you.'

I sit down on the swing beside her, clinging on to the possibility this is still about Andrew. He's too embarrassed to ask me out so he's asked Linda to do it for him. Should I say yes straight away, or should I make him wait a few days? Show him how much he hurt me? I try to keep my face straight as I prepare for what she's about to say.

'Go on,' I say.

She twists the swing round to face me and grabs hold of my wrists.

'Well,' she says, and I wish she would hurry up. 'Well…'

'Spit it out.'

'I'm no longer a virgin.'

I stare at her, not sure if I heard her correctly.

She leaps out of the swing and jumps up and down on the tarmac, squealing like a little girl on Christmas morning. 'I did it, Cathy. I'm no longer a virgin.'

I stare at my best friend, not sure what to say. Are you supposed to congratulate someone when they tell you this? Can you buy a card for the occasion?

'Can you believe it? I'm now officially a woman.'

My head is reeling. So Andrew didn't arrange this. He's still not interested in me. Nobody's interested in me. The furthest I've ever got is kissing a boy, and on both occasions the boy walked out on me. Linda starts talking again, and I know I’m going to have to listen to the whole story, because that’s what friends do.

But inside, I’m screaming.

They Started It

I slip into the seat next to Billy and take out my jotter. In a strange way, I'm beginning to look forward to these maths lessons.

'Rathbone still not letting you back into your usual seat?' he asks.

I don't know what to say, because I haven't even thought about asking for my old seat back. I change the subject.

'How was your weekend?'

'Quiet,' he says. 'What about you?'

I think about telling him about the Ouija board, but what if he laughs at me for believing in that stuff?

'Linda stayed over on Saturday night,' I say.

'Has she still got her face stuck to her new boyfriend?'

'Something like that.'

'Don't worry; she'll soon need you again once he's dumped her for someone else.'

'She seems to think this is the real thing this time.'

'Don't all girls think that?'

I shrug my shoulders.

'Let me guess. He's told her he loves her and that she's the only one for him. Has he bought her a present yet?'

'She hasn't mentioned anything.'

'Okay, so here's my next question, but you don't have to tell me if you don't want to.'

I watch him, waiting for the next question.

'Has she slept with him yet?'

I blush as I picture her jumping up and down at the swing park telling me she'd lost her virginity.

'Thought so.' Now it's his turn to change the subject. 'Have you heard about the fight that's going to be in the

park?'
'Today?'
'Lunchtime.'
'You going?'
'Might wander past the tennis courts to see what's happening.'
'Who started it this time?' I ask.
'Think they did. I heard some of their fourth years threw a bottle at one of our buses on the way home yesterday.'
'Usual stuff, then.'
'Usual stuff,' he agrees.
'Any of the teachers got wind of it yet?' More often than not these lunchtime fights are stopped before they even begin.
'Don't think so,' he says, 'but I'll make sure I've got a good excuse for being there in case they turn up.'
I doubt any of the teachers would ever think Billy Weir organised the fight.
'Is it going to be a big crowd?' I ask.
'Sounds like it.'
Mr Rathbone takes a walk around the desks, and we pretend to be working on a problem from the text book until he's gone past.
'So, what's happening with you and Andrew?' Billy asks me. 'Any news yet?'
I haven't told anyone about what happened.
'Not sure he's my type.'
'Oh.'
'Turns out he's a self-important dickhead.'
Billy laughs. 'Best stay clear of him, then.'
I try to laugh along, but he sees right through me. 'Sorry, Cathy,' he says. 'I genuinely thought he was one of the good guys.'
'Me too,' I say. 'Me too.'

By lunchtime the whole school is talking about the planned fight. There's a chance Andrew will go along to watch, and I want to show him I'm not bothered by his rejection; I'm doing fine without him, thank you very much. I wait for Linda in the dinner hall.

'Quick,' I say, 'let's grab a sandwich and go.'

'What? Forget it; I'm getting myself a plate of chips and cheese.'

I look at her perfect figure and try not to hate her. 'But we'll miss the action.'

Linda laughs. 'Action? It's just a bunch of boys fighting other boys. Who cares?'

'Derek asked if you were going to be there.'

'Derek? When?'

'I passed him on the way to English,' I lie.

'Why didn't you tell me sooner? Come on, I'm not hungry anyway.'

The school corridors are filled with hushed whispers and an air of anticipation and excitement.

'Let's go this way, it's quicker, and we're less likely to bump into any teachers.' She leads the way down through the PE department and out through a fire exit. We make our way to the gap in the wire fence and climb through into the park that separates the two schools.

We join the swarm of students dressed in black and maroon and head towards the tennis courts, where we're greeted with chants of *Fight! Fight! Fight!* I scan the crowd for Andrew but can't find him. On the other side of the tennis courts is a smaller crowd of students wearing the green ties that mark them out as pupils from St Mary's Academy.

None of the girls from my school have a boyfriend who goes to St Mary's. Fenians. That's what they call them. I roll the word around my mouth like a giant gobstopper. *Fenians.* I look at the faces opposite, but they don't seem very different from the faces on this side of the fence.

A group of girls from St Mary's are gathered to one side, giggling and cooing over the boys. I grip on to Linda's coat. It's Thomas. I'm sure it is. Thomas O'Donnell. He's at the very back of the group of boys.

The crowd is chanting louder now, and both gangs of

boys take a step towards each other. Linda nudges me with her elbow.

'Are you sure he said he'd be here?'

Fight! Fight! Fight!

Jackets are removed slowly and dramatically, and thrown to the ground at either side. Linda nudges me again.

'Are you listening to me?'

Fight! Fight! Fight!

I lose sight of him.

'Did Derek say he'd be here?'

'Yes,' I shout. I wish she'd shut up.

One of the boys from St Mary's breaks from his group and charges forward, head down, straight into the group of boys on this side.

Fight! Fight! Fight!

The crowd forms a circle around the boys, but I stand alone on the outside, desperately searching. I'm sure it was Thomas, but he's disappeared.

I spend my afternoon thinking about him and can't concentrate on any of my lessons. I'm determined to try and see him, so I make up a story about losing my bus money and persuade Linda to walk home. St Mary's gets out fifteen minutes after us, and if I time it right we should be passing their gates when the bell goes.

I run my fingers along the rusted railings that mark the boundary of our town's Catholic secondary school. The iron spikes punctuate the sky like giant exclamation marks, and I look between the metal railings, hoping to see him on the other side.

Linda nudges me in the ribs. Hard. 'You're not listening to a word I'm saying.'

She's right, I'm not. I'm tired of hearing about her and Derek.

'So, he grabbed me as he was making his way towards the science block this afternoon, and guess what? He says he never even spoke to you today.'

'I must have been mistaken.'

'Anyway, guess what he did?'

'Who?'

She rolls her eyes. 'Derek, when I caught him on his way to science.'

I shrug my shoulders. I thought Linda said he'd been the one to grab her, not the other way round.

She undoes her top button so I can see. 'He gave me this chain to show me he loves me. He loves me,' she repeats, as if I should be impressed, and I remember what Billy said about boys giving a girl a present. 'And I'm going to his house tonight and his parents won't be there.'

'That's nice,' I say, but I can tell she's not listening.

'I've been thinking,' she says. 'Now Derek and I are officially going out together, I think I should go on the Pill. The last thing I want is to get pregnant.'

'I thought you said he used a condom.'

'He did, but imagine if it split.' She shudders for effect.

Does that happen? Can a condom split? I look at my watch. It's almost quarter to four, which means *their* bell is going to ring any minute now.

'Come on,' she says. 'We need to get a move on.'

I slow down, staring up at the enormous, grey building merging into the sky above me, but she pulls me forward.

'Let's get home before they get out. There's bound to be trouble after today.'

My heart beats faster as the minute hand on my watch reaches the nine. The bell rings and, moments later, a giant wave of people pours out on to the pavement in front of us. Black trousers, black shirts, black shoes – green ties.

Linda looks scared. 'Quick,' she says, 'let's get out of here.'

She starts running, but I stay put and watch her weave her way through the crowd before she disappears around the corner. I'm alone, but that's okay, the fights are only ever between boys. Nobody's going to hurt a girl. I stand by the wall and watch the exit, desperately willing him to walk through the gate any second now. I've pictured the scene in my head a thousand times this afternoon, and I can almost hear the theme tune.

Just then, a bunch of girls barge into me and yank my bag from my shoulder. It falls to the ground, and one of the girls kicks dirty water over it from the nearby puddle.

'Sorry.' She laughs as they walk away. 'Didn't see you there.'

I button up my jacket, but it still doesn't cover my maroon tie. I need to get out of here. My chest feels like it's going to explode. Shit, I can't remember how to breathe. Clumsily, I pull at the knot until I feel it loosen, and I pull my tie over my head and stuff it into the bottom of my school bag.

The crowd thins out until no one is left in the playground. Is it possible I missed him? Was I too busy watching the girls?

I spot the black shoes ahead of me and freeze. The gang of boys are blocking the pavement. I look around for help, but everyone else has gone and the street is empty.

'Remember me?' The boy with red hair stands in front of me, tossing a stone from one hand to the other. 'Look at you!' He throws the stone into the air and catches it again with his other hand. 'Stinkin' Proddy whore, shouldn't you be home by now?'

'I'm waiting for someone,' I say, and he laughs at my brave words. 'He'll be out in a minute.'

The laughing stops.

'You'd better not be waiting for one of us.' He flicks his wrist and the stone flies through the air and hits me on the cheek. His friends take this as a sign that I'm game, and they bend down to pick up stones from the ground.

'Stinkin' Proddy whore,' they shout, and their stones pelt my body before I can move. I turn and run, their words stinging as hard as the stones hitting the back of my legs.

Stinkin' Proddy whore.

I run and I run, not daring to stop and look back over my shoulder.

Stinkin' Proddy whore.

I run, even when their shouts fade into the distance, and I

keep running until I finally reach home. I throw the front door open and race upstairs to my room, shutting the door behind me and collapsing onto my bed.

The Blue Lady sits on my bedside table watching me, waiting for me to speak. I don't care if anyone sees her. I'm fed up of hiding her.

'I saw Thomas today,' I tell her. 'He was with a bunch of boys at the park at lunchtime but he didn't see me. At least, I don't think he saw me. Do you remember I used to pray to you and ask you for help? Well, I'm asking for your help one last time.' I clutch my hands in prayer like I did when I was a little girl. 'Can you see to it that I bump into Thomas again? He's not like other boys. He didn't stop seeing me just because of his mother. He was braver than that. Stronger. He didn't care if I was Catholic or Protestant.'

I peel off my school uniform and take my jeans out of the middle drawer. Mum throws the door open.

'Don't you ever knock?'

She ignores me and strides into the centre of the room. 'You were late home today.'

I don't answer.

'Where were you?'

'Linda and I decided to walk home.'

'Why?'

'The sun was shining and we felt like walking. What's with all the questions?'

'So, if I pick up the phone and ask Linda's mum if she was late home today, she'll say yes?'

I'm feeling brave. 'Talking about phone calls, who is it that keeps phoning here?'

The colour drains from her face.

'It's a wrong number,' she shouts, raising her finger and aiming it directly at me. 'You'd better not be lying about where you were after school. You're in enough trouble as it is.' And with that she spins round and walks out of the room.

I get up and close the door behind her.

'She's the one who's lying,' I tell the Blue Lady.

'Someone keeps phoning her and she's keeping it a secret from all of us.'

I go to the window and watch Mum drive away. I know I don't have much time, but it shouldn't take long. I stop in my bedroom doorway and look back at the Blue Lady.

'I need to find out the truth.'

Their bedroom is messier than my own; bed covers lie in a crumpled heap at the bottom of the bed, and several days' worth of dirty clothes are strewn across the floor. I don't understand. Mum used to be so house-proud and everything was so neat and organised. Her favourite motto was *A place for everything and everything in its place*. I push aside a pair of jeans and get down on to my knees on a clear space on the carpet. Down on the floor, I lift the valance and look under the bed. Apart from a lost sock and a thousand dust bunnies there's nothing there, but I don't give up. With one hand, I slide the mirrored wardrobe door open and lean forward on both knees for a closer look.

The inside of the wardrobe is in an even worse state than their room, and I can't see anything for the mess. I pull out a bundle of bedding, curtains and sleeping bags – and there, tucked away in a pile of old clothing in the back corner, is the box, exactly as I remember, with the blue ribbon tied round it. I lean over the bedding and curtains and grab it with both hands but it doesn't budge, so I pull and pull until finally the tangle of clothing releases it. It frees with a jolt and I fall backwards into the pile of sleeping bags. I nestle in, surrounded by the warm, familiar smell of childhood holidays spent cooried in, nice and cosy, as the rain and wind battered the thin walls of the caravan. I can almost taste the vinegar from the fish & chips.

I clutch the box close to my chest, unsure of what I'm hoping to find, and I pull one end of the ribbon and watch as the bow slips open and falls to the ground. I lift the lid. The last time I looked in here I'd been a little girl, and hadn't realised what I was holding. Today, things seem much clearer. This is some kind of memory box.

I lift up a pair of white knitted bootees. Does the blue

ribbon mean these bootees belonged to Jimmy? Is this his memory box? If so, do I have one somewhere? Underneath the bootees is a small pile of black-and-white photographs, and suddenly I'm back in the kitchen. It's a hot summer's day and I'm helping to make strawberry jam. Mum appears in the doorway holding a photograph of her own grandmother. I pick up the bootees, and things begin to fall into place. Had my great-grandmother knitted them for Jimmy? Is that why they're so special? I turn them over in my hand and try to imagine my big brother ever having feet small enough to fit into them. I place them on the lid of the box and carefully lay out the faded black-and-white photographs side by side on the carpet.

Is it possible that someone in one of these pictures is the mystery caller? I scan the faces but can barely identify anyone. I think I recognise my mum as a little girl on the beach beside her sister, but even then I'm not sure. These people are like ghosts to me.

The box is almost empty, and I feel a wave of disappointment as I realise I'm not going to find my answer. Some baby clothes are folded at the bottom, and there's an old-fashioned pincushion and sewing kit, but these don't tell me anything about who's been secretly phoning my mother. I get ready to tidy everything away when something catches my eye, and I reach into the bottom of the box and slide it out of its hiding place.

The postcard is yellowed with age, but I can still make out the simple image of a bluebell: my mother's favourite flower. I turn it over in my hand and inspect the stamp and postmark, but the ink has faded. It seems everything is trying to prevent me from finding out what's going on.

My eyes sweep over the words, taking in the extravagant loops, twist and curls. I don't recognise the handwriting, but I imagine it belongs to someone older. I make out my mother's name and our old address on the right hand side, but the card is unsigned, and the message consists of only two words:

Forgive me.

Outside, a car pulls into the drive. She's home already. Without wasting a moment's breath I toss everything back in the box, including the postcard and the blue ribbon, and I throw it into the corner of the wardrobe. Then I throw the sleeping bags, curtains and bedding back on top of the box and slide the wardrobe door back across.

Could the postcard be from the same person that keeps calling? I hope I won't have to wait too long until I find out.

The Third Miracle

The bouncer on the door is too busy admiring the red motorbike that's pulled up outside to even bother looking at our faces, but still I keep my head down as we shuffle forwards into a small hallway and join the queue of people waiting for the cloakroom. Thumping music can be heard coming from the other side of the double doors in front of us, but I don't recognise the song.

The queue takes forever to move and it seems everyone knows everyone else, and there's a lot of squealing and hugging amongst the women and a more reserved back-slapping amongst the men. At last it's my turn, and I try not to stare at the purple hair and eyebrow piercings as I pay my money and hand over my denim jacket to the woman perched on a stool in the small cubby hole that's the cloakroom. I've been practising, and I'm prepared to answer questions about my date of birth, but she doesn't even look up at me; just takes my coat in one hand and struggles to tear two pink raffle tickets from the book with the other. I watch as she forces one of the tickets onto the hook of the coat hanger before handing the other one to me. I fold the small rectangle of pink paper in half and slip it into the front pocket of my handbag and follow Linda into the toilets.

I steal a quick look in the mirror and scrunch my hair with my fingers, taking care not to get tangled in the thick layers of *Insette* hairspray.

'Quick,' says Linda. 'In here.'

I squeeze into the toilet cubicle and we huddle closer to shut the door behind us. She unzips her handbag and takes out a quarter bottle of vodka.

'Jesus, Linda, why didn't you tell me you had that?

'Because you'd have looked guilty as hell and we'd never have got in.'

'But you could have had your bag searched.'

'Well, I didn't, did I?'

'You could have,' I say. 'Why'd you risk it?'

'Cheapest way to get drunk,' she says. 'It's one-twenty for a vodka and coke in this place.'

'Have you brought any coke?'

'Wouldn't fit in my bag.' She unscrews the lid and takes a sip before passing it to me. It doesn't really smell of anything, and I reckon it won't taste too bad, but, fucking hell, I'm wrong. It burns my insides as it makes its way down my throat towards my stomach.

Linda laughs and puts the bottle back in her bag. 'Come on; let's see if we can find anyone.'

By 'anyone' she means Derek, and we leave the toilets and head through to the dance floor. The vodka is already kicking in and the room sways as we push our way past people dancing at the side of the dance floor. Is Andrew in here somewhere? Maybe he's sorry for the way he treated me and is desperately hoping I'll tag along with Linda. He can't stop thinking about me and wants to make it up to me. He'll offer to buy me a drink but I'll lift the glass in my hand and show him I'm fine. Then he'll bring a stack of beer mats out of his pocket.

'Fancy trying to beat me?' he'll ask. 'And if I can flip more beer mats than you, I get to kiss you.'

I'll accept his challenge and soon find out he's been practising. I'll deliberately drop the bundle when I get to four beer mats and he'll bend down to pick them up. He'll stop, and we'll gaze into each other's eyes, and that's when it will happen. He'll lean in and kiss me. I can hear Linda and Derek applauding as we kiss.

A new song starts up, and the crowd push past us to get to the dance floor and knock me out of my fantasy. I look up to see Linda is way ahead of me and I walk faster to catch up, my shoes sticking to the carpet. I try not to let myself think what might be on it, and pray it's only beer and cider.

We find Derek in the corner next to the music, and I feel my heart quicken. Is Andrew with him? I suck my stomach in, push my chest out and try to act casual as I glance over in Derek's direction. Andrew is beside him, but he's not alone. He's got his arms wrapped around the waist of Rachel Jones, and he's laughing as she whispers in his ear. I bet the bitch is going out with him on purpose to get at me. I'll show them I don't care. I turn round to ask Linda to dance but she's already got her tongue down Derek's throat. I'm alone. Rachel sees me and looks me up and down. This is agony.

'Watch it!' A man covered in tattoos is making his way back to his seat with three pint glasses. 'Out of my way,' he growls. I try to step aside, but I'm hemmed in from all sides and lager sloshes over the edge of a glass and soaks my new shoes. He keeps on walking, without bothering to stop to apologise.

Fuck it. I need to get out of here.

I don't bother saying anything to Linda, and I clutch my bag and head for the door. Out in the hallway there's no longer a queue for coats, and I fight back the tears and hand over my ticket. The woman with the piercings has clearly seen it all before, and doesn't comment. She chooses a green jelly baby from the tub on the shelf and bites off its head before passing me my jacket. I mumble thanks but she's already gone back to reading her book. I turn on my heels and take a step towards the door without realising there's someone behind me and I barge straight into them.

'Cathy?'

I stop and look up.

'It's really you. I mean, of course it is, but you've changed. I guess we both have. After all it's been…'

'Five years,' I say.

'Five?'

I nod.

Thomas sees the jacket in my arms. 'You're leaving already?'

Does he look disappointed? A flicker of hope ignites

somewhere deep inside, and I touch the small silver cross around my neck.

'My friend appears to have deserted me.'

We stand across from each other, close enough to touch, yet struggling to find words. He's going to walk away unless I can think of something to say.

'Do you remember the time we caught the minnows?' I ask.

'And we thought we heard someone being murdered in the hay.'

'And you went to rescue them.'

Thomas laughs. 'And I was chased by this guy with no clothes on and he was waving his arms in the air.'

'That wasn't the only thing he was waving in the air,' I say, laughing.

The double doors leading through to the dance floor open and we have to shout to be heard above the music.

'Don't suppose you fancy walking me home?' I can't believe I just said that. *Go you, Cathy.* 'Or maybe you've already promised to leave with someone else?'

He smiles, and I notice the shiny slither of the scar on his left cheek refuses to move, creating a smile that's lop-sided.

'Give me a minute to grab my jacket,' he says and disappears.

I think about going back in and telling Linda, making sure I say it loud enough that Rachel and Andrew hear me too, but then Thomas is back. He pulls on his jacket and smiles at me, and goosebumps ripple across my skin.

'Ready to go?' he asks, and I decide the rest of them can go to hell. They probably won't even notice I'm gone.

We head outside and he pushes his hands deep into his jacket pockets. I'm disappointed. I had hoped he'd slip his hand into mine as we walk home together. I rack my brains for things to say. Then I hit on a great idea.

'Do you fancy a bag of chips?'

It's perfect. If we share a bag we'll have to huddle together, close. And I can brush my fingers against his as I reach in for a chip. My plan is genius.

We turn round and head back towards the chippy, reaching it just as the heavens above us open. We dive inside, laughing and shaking the first drops of water from our hair, and everyone turns and stares at us.

Thomas turns to me. 'What do you fancy?'

I bite my tongue to stop myself from shouting *You, I fancy you!* Instead I say, 'I'm not too hungry, so why don't we share a bag?' I blush and hope my plan's not too obvious.

The door opens and I watch them stagger in. They're drunk. I just hope they're too drunk to notice me. I move closer to Thomas and try to stay out of sight, but I'm not quick enough and they spot me.

'Look, Michael, it's our little friend.'

It turns out Michael is the name of the red-haired boy. He eyes Thomas up, but clearly thinks I'm still game and steps towards us. 'Alright, Thomas?' he says. 'Dating Proddies now, are you?'

I watch Thomas, wondering what he's going to do.

The woman behind the counter interrupts. 'What can I get you both, boys?'

'Smoked sausage, gorgeous,' says Michael.

Thomas leans on the counter. 'A bag of chips please.'

The woman nods, picks up a pair of tongs and opens the glass sliding door to get a smoked sausage.

'Hey!' Thomas says. 'We were here first.'

I wish he'd just leave it, but too late, Michael has heard him.

'What's your fucking problem, wee man? It's only a smoked sausage.'

'My girlfriend and I were waiting to get served before you barged in.'

'Girlfriend?' Michael laughs. He leans close and whispers in my ear. 'I think your boyfriend's a bit fucking tense. You gonnae suck him off, help him out a bit?' He bursts out laughing and I watch a slither of spittle dribble down his chin. He wipes it away with one hand and I see the letters *CFC* tattooed across his wrist in Indian ink. He grabs his crotch and pushes it towards me. 'Then you can finish me off.' He laughs again and turns to the woman behind the counter. 'Is my smoked sausage ready yet, love?'

Thomas moves towards him but I grab his sleeve. 'Just leave it,' I say.

'Did she tell you she's got a fetish for us Catholic boys? Seems to follow us around wherever we go. Gave one of the lads here a wee hand job on the bus last Saturday night.'

'Everything alright here, lads?' The man is about my dad's age, and is dressed in bike leathers with a ponytail reaching down to his waist, Francis Rossi style.

Michael turns to see who's talking, and obviously doesn't like what he sees. 'This has got fuck all to do wi' you, pal, so piss off.'

'As far as I can see you're annoying this young couple right here.'

'Get tae fuck, I was just toying wi' them.' He turns to me. 'Ain't that right, gorgeous?'

I wish our chips would hurry up so we can get out of here.

'Thinking you're the hard man, eh?' The newcomer starts to take off his leather jacket.

'None of that in here,' shouts the woman behind the till. She turns to Thomas. 'Salt and sauce?' But Thomas is too busy watching what's happening.

Michael squares up to the man. 'Hard man? That's funny coming fae a poof wi' a ponytail.'

The woman behind the counter sprinkles salt over the chips and wraps them in brown paper.

'Cut it out,' she shouts, 'or I'm calling the police.' She expertly folds and wraps the bag of chips in a sheet of newspaper while she speaks.

The biker lifts both hands and shoves Michael in the chest. Flyers on the counter go spinning to the floor, and someone in the queue screams as he grabs Michael and slams him against the mirrored wall. I lift the bag of chips and pull Thomas by the arm.

'Quick,' I shout, 'let's get out of here.'

The rain is falling heavier now and we run away from the shop, up the precinct and across the road.

'This way.' Thomas takes hold of my hand. 'Let's shelter in here.'

He clutches the wet, wrought-iron handle and turns it until it finally catches and springs open. I look up and see the same building we stood outside all those years ago during the parade. Memories come flooding back, and I put out my hand to touch the stone wall which marks the boundary to the chapel grounds. The wall isn't as tall as I remember.

I follow Thomas into the grounds and stand inside the doorway, out of the rain. We lean against the painted wooden doors and I unfold the newspaper and peel back the brown paper. The smell of freshly-cooked chips fills the air.

I take a chip and wonder if my plan wasn't so clever now my hand is covered in sauce. Thunder growls in the sky above us and we look up.

'Do you remember the time you told me about how the lightning conductor works?'

'Did I?' Thomas asks.

'It was the day of the parade and we were standing out there on the pavement waiting for the bands to come along, and you explained to me how the strip of metal carries electricity from the sky to the ground.'

The chips are finished and Thomas rolls the empty wrapper into a ball and flicks it over the stone wall.

'Well, then, I guess that means we're safe in here.'

'I guess so,' I say, and dare to move a little closer and breathe him in. Warm beer and Kouros. The combination makes me feel giddy and I can't help myself. I reach up on to my tiptoes and kiss him firmly on the mouth. He responds immediately and we kiss as though we've done this a hundred times before. There's no awkwardness. We fit together perfectly.

He looks at his watch. 'Come on. I'd better get you home before your folks start to wonder where you are.'

I don't say anything. I don't want any talk of my parents

to spoil tonight.

He holds my hand and leads me out of the chapel doorway. 'I don't want them to think I'm not looking after you, or I might not get to see you again.'

I lean into him and inhale his aftershave. Oh my God, he said he wants to see me again.

We walk home, and all too soon we're standing outside my house.

'It's all so much smaller than I remember,' Thomas says. He runs over to the line of conifers in the garden. 'Do you remember we used to measure ourselves against the trees?' He stands tall, but the trees tower above him now. 'I guess I've been away a long time.' He takes me by the hand, spins me round and kisses me passionately, exploring my mouth with his tongue.

'Do you want to come inside? I'm sure my mum and dad will be delighted to see you again.' The words leave my mouth before I can stop myself. What if they've been arguing?

Thomas looks at his watch. 'I'd better not. It's getting really late, and they probably don't want some stranger turning up at this time of night.'

'You're hardly a stranger.'

He grabs hold of my hand and takes a felt pen out of his pocket.

'Hey, what are you doing?'

'Making sure you get back in touch.' He pushes my sleeve up and writes his number on the inside of my arm. 'Now promise me you won't wash that off until you've written it down somewhere safe.'

I won't need to; I'm never going to wash my arm again.

We stand and kiss on the doorstep until I finally pull away and whisper goodnight. The house is in darkness, and I guess Mum and Dad must be in bed. I touch my lips and imagine he's kissing me. I want to remember every moment from tonight; afraid that if I go to sleep I'll wake up and discover it was all a dream. I replay the kiss in the chapel doorway and I look at the writing on my arm. It was definitely real.

I slip out of my high heels and go through to the kitchen for a drink of water and flick on the light in the cooker hood, not wanting to spoil the mood with the stark striplight. I run the cold water and take a glass from the cupboard.

I freeze. There, on the kitchen table, is the blue ribbon.

'I've been waiting for you.'

The glass falls from my hand and shatters across the kitchen floor. Mum steps into the light and holds up the memory box.

'Did you think I'd never notice?' She walks towards me and I want to warn her about the broken glass, but I can't speak. 'Didn't I teach you it's rude to touch things that don't belong to you? Didn't I?'

Shards of glass stand to attention on the linoleum flooring, lit up by the light from the cooker hood, but she hasn't noticed and takes another step closer. I look down and see a droplet of blood ooze out between her toes. The blood looks black in the dim light.

'How dare you? How dare you go through my things? Mine!' She's yelling at me now, and I wonder where Dad is. She picks up the blue ribbon and pushes it in my face. 'This is none of your business.'

'But it's my family too.'

This is clearly the wrong thing to say. She raises her hand and strikes.

Love in the Bandstand

I open my eyes, gasping for breath, clawing at the ribbon tied tightly around my throat. There's nothing there, but I can still picture her coming towards me, holding the blue ribbon between her hands. And this time she wasn't going to stop at a slap, she wanted to strangle me. I slowly move my fingertips upwards to my cheek. Was that a dream too? The painful bruise on my face tells the truth.

I climb out of bed and switch on the small lamp sitting on my bedside table, and it casts a soft, peachy glow across the room. The light helps push my nightmare away and I pick up the china figurine and inspect the fine crack she got on the day Thomas left.

'I guess none of us are perfect.'

It's early Sunday morning and I imagine everyone in his house will be busy getting ready for Mass. I look at the phone number on my arm and can't wait any longer; I need to hear his voice. I tiptoe downstairs and pick up the phone, unwinding the cable and pulling it as far as it will reach until I'm on the other side of the living room door.

Is it possible Mrs O'Donnell might recognise the voice of the Protestant girl who lived next door all those years ago? I'm relieved to hear a man's voice answer the phone.

'Thomas, it's for you. It's a girl.'

I wonder if girls call often. I grip the receiver tightly and listen to the muffled sounds of the phone being passed over.

'Hello.'

'Hi, it's me.' There's silence on the other end of the line. He doesn't know who I am. 'It's me, Cathy.'

'Cathy,' he laughs, 'you're a fast mover. It's only been eight hours since I gave you my number.'

He's been counting the hours.

'I was wondering if you fancy meeting up tonight.' Oh God, he's already called me a fast mover and now I'm asking to see him tonight. He'll think I do this kind of thing all the time.

'Tonight?'

Does he sound unsure? Damn it. I'm acting too keen.

'I'm babysitting my cousin tonight, but I guess we could meet earlier.'

'How about six o'clock?' I hear myself speak and can't believe it's me saying these things.

'That'd be great,' he says.

That'd be great. I bite my lip to stop myself from squealing down the line with excitement.

'Where should we meet?' I ask.

'Why don't we meet at the lamp post at the bottom of your road like we used to do?'

He remembers.

I spend all day deciding what to wear, and go through several costume changes before I decide on my favourite skirt and a short black lacy top. I'm ready early but I force myself to wait until five to six before leaving the house, and by the time I arrive he's already waiting for me. My stomach flips when I see his tall body leaning against the wall.

He grins when he sees me coming, and I catch him looking me up and down.

'Who'd have thought skinny wee Cathy Munro would turn out so beautiful, eh? Do you remember how you used to hang out with all the boys? A proper tomboy you were back then.'

He reaches out and takes my hand and we start walking. We talk and talk and it feels like we've never been apart.

As we get to the park, the heavens open.

'Quick,' he shouts. 'This way.'

I follow him to the edge of the old derelict bandstand building. 'Are you sure it's safe to go inside?'

Thomas jumps up onto the stage. 'Come on,' he urges,

'we'll be out of the rain in here.' He moves to the back of the stage and disappears from sight.

I pull myself up on to the wooden flooring, being careful to avoid standing on any rotten planks.

'Down here.' I follow his voice to the back of the stage. 'There's a room down here hardly anyone knows about.' He holds out his hand and I lean on it and drop down into the small space behind the stage area. I smell his aftershave again and it makes me dizzy.

'I never knew this was here,' I tell him.

'Hardly anyone does,' he whispers. 'No one will find us in here.'

'Have you ever brought a girl down here before?'

'You're my first,' he says and kisses me, and as I close my eyes I can hear the rain batter down on the remains of the bandstand roof. It's cold in here, and he folds me in his arms and holds me close to his chest. I run my fingers across his cheek, carefully tracing the curved line of his scar. He pushes my hand away and kisses me again, harder this time.

We don't stop kissing and I feel him press against me as his hand moves round and cups my left breast, fingertips sweeping over my nipple. His tongue flickers across the roof of my mouth and I tingle all over.

He lifts my skirt and slides his hand inside my pants, and I'm surprised to discover I'm wet. This seems to please him, and he pushes my legs apart and slips his finger inside me and begins to stroke me. I'm not sure what to do and I move my own hand downwards towards him. He pulls my pants down and unbuckles his belt. I see his erect purple cock and remember the day in the hayfield. I think of the girl's screams and feel suddenly scared. Is this going to hurt?

Thomas tucks my hair behind my ears and kisses my neck. He pauses.

'I love you, Cathy Munro.'

I stop breathing. He said it. He said he loves me.

I feel his cock close to me, pressing against me. Has he put a condom on? I'm not sure, and I'm scared to reach down and touch him. He kisses me hard, and I feel him push his way inside and it hurts. Oh God, what if he's not wearing a condom?

'I love you,' he grunts as he pushes inside me. 'I love you…love you…love you…'

And then it's over. He slides himself out of me and leans back against the stone wall. I look down and see his limp penis, droplets of cum dripping from its deflated end.

No condom.

Fuck!

Again I think back to the day Thomas and I saw the couple in the field. I remember he told me that you can't get pregnant if you do it standing up. Christ, I pray that's true.

Thomas pulls up his boxer shorts and jeans and takes out a pack of cigarettes.

I lean against the wall, bewildered and confused, while he drags on his cigarette. Was that it? Wasn't I supposed to feel something more?

When I arrive back home my mum and dad are sitting in front of the television. Neither of them look up to say hello or ask where I've been. Mum's eyes look puffy again, and the hand clutching the glass of wine is shaking.

I look along the hallway and see that the broken pieces of glass have been cleared away from the kitchen floor, but I'm sure I can still see the smear of blood from my mother's foot. Does she remember what happened, or was she so drunk she's forgotten the whole thing? I check for the bruise in the hall mirror to remind myself it really happened.

Upstairs, I sneak into Jimmy's room and spray my wrist with a couple of squirts of his Kouros, and then I rush through to my room and tell the Blue Lady everything.

'He said he loves me.' I gush. 'And he doesn't care what I look like, what I wear or what religion I am. He loves me for being me.' I close my eyes and breathe in the aftershave and I can almost imagine he's right beside me again. I lie back on my bed and imagine his lips on my neck, and I slide my hand downwards and stroke myself gently. I'm soon wet again. He tells me he loves me and I feel breathless. Excited. I rub myself harder. Harder. And harder.

My bedroom door opens and I pull my hand out of my knickers.

'What's been going on with you and Mum?'

I sit up. 'What do you mean?' I sound breathless, but Jimmy doesn't seem to notice.

'You guys haven't said a word to each other all day.'

'It's nothing.' I tug at my ponytail, letting my hair fall loose around my face, covering the bruise.

'Doesn't seem like nothing. Every time one of you walks in the room, the other one leaves.'

'She's mad at me for getting home late last night, that's all.' I don't mention the argument we had last night, I don't mention the broken glass, and I don't tell him our mother struck me.

Invisible

The school bus will be here any minute and I can't wait to tell Linda about last night. I get on and move along the aisle, but Derek's in my seat today. Fucking hell! She's kept me the seat next to her since we started first year, and we've always sat beside each other. I try to catch her eye, but it looks like they're arguing. I can't be bothered getting involved, so I head upstairs to see if I can find a seat up there.

Upstairs is full of all the cool kids, so I take a seat near the back and hope no one will notice me.

'Hey, is anyone sitting here?'

I've never been so pleased to see a friendly face before. I move my bag and Billy sits down beside me.

'You don't normally sit up here,' he says.

'Didn't think you were cool enough to be up here either,' I say. I immediately regret it, but he doesn't seem to notice. He pulls his school bag on to his knee, opens it and takes out a bread roll. He tears it in two and hands half to me.

'Here,' he says.

'What is it?'

'Breakfast.'

'Didn't you have breakfast before you left the house?'

'No time,' he pushes the bread roll towards me. 'Do you want it or not?'

I take it and we eat in silence. We're probably the only ones on the bus not talking or joking about something, and I suddenly feel very aware of his presence beside me. What if the girls in my year spot us sitting together? I'll be the joke of the school.

Billy doesn't seem to notice my awkwardness. He pops

the last piece of bread roll into his mouth then claps his hands together noisily, and brushes any crumbs off his jacket.

'I heard you and Thomas O'Donnell are seeing each other. Is that true?'

I'm relieved. I wasn't sure how to tell Billy my news.

'How are things going?'

'Good. I'm seeing him today after school. We're meeting at the bandstand.' I blush.

'Things are getting pretty serious already, then?'

I remember the pain as he entered my body. 'What's with all the questions?'

He pretends to study his fingernails. 'Just making polite conversation.'

'No, you're not. What's going on? Why the sudden interest?'

'If you say everything's fine then there's nothing to worry about.'

'Why would I have anything to worry about?'

He doesn't answer me so I nip his arm. 'Stop ignoring me and tell me what's going on.'

'I heard he was going out with Sadie Parks, that's all.'

I remember the graffiti on the bus shelter.

SADIE + THOMAS 4EVER.

'Sadie Parks? Who's she?'

'A fourth year from St Mary's.'

'Maybe they used to go out before he and I got together.' I bet whoever Sadie Parks is, she's probably jealous of me.

'Maybe.'

'Who told you they're going out?' I ask.

'Just some of the guys. No one in particular.'

'Right, then it's not true, then, is it?'

'Only, I thought I saw him with a girl last night.'

'He's allowed to have friends of the opposite sex.' I laugh, but I'm not sure what's so funny. Then I remember what Thomas told me yesterday about babysitting his cousin. 'What time was this?' I ask.

'About nine o'clock.'

Panic over. 'He was with his cousin.'

'His cousin?'

'Yeah, he left me to go and babysit his cousin. Maybe he was taking her to the swing park.'

'She looked a bit too old to be in need of a babysitter.'

'Well, maybe they were just hanging out together.'

Why is he being such a prick? Why can't he be happy for me? I stand up as the bus pulls into the school car park, and that's when he spots the bruise on my face. I thought I'd done a good job covering it with foundation, but clearly not good enough because he can't hide his anger.

'Jeez, Cathy. What the fuck happened to you? And don't tell me you walked into a door because I know that's not true.'

'It's nothing,' I say.

We head downstairs and step off the bus, making our way towards the school building.

'I've got to go,' I say, 'or I'll be late for registration.' I walk quickly hoping I might leave him behind, but he stays by my shoulder the whole way.

'Was it Thomas? Did he do this to you?'

'I don't want to talk about it.'

'Fucking hell, Cathy.' He steps in front of me. 'There's no way he can get away with this. He needs taught a lesson.'

'It wasn't Thomas, okay? Just drop it.'

'Drop it? The bastard hit you.'

'I told you to drop it,' I shout. 'Just leave me alone.'

He puts his hand on my shoulder. 'But Cathy…'

'What don't you get? I don't want to talk about it.'

'But we're friends.'

'Friends?' I shrug his hand away. 'You're not my friend. You're just the freak I have to sit next to in maths.'

I storm off and head to the benches to find Linda. She'll understand when I tell her what happened, and she'll probably insist I stay over at hers tonight. She's sitting on the benches with Derek and a bunch of his pals, and they're all laughing about something. I lift my hand to catch her attention and I'm sure she sees me, but she looks away. I watch as Derek puts his arm around her shoulder. Whatever they were arguing about on the bus has clearly been forgotten.

A group of first year boys push past me.

'Watch where you're going,' I shout.

One of the boys turns round, looks me up and down, and then goes back to talking to his friends.

Fuck this. I've had enough of this place.

I push against the crowd of students trying to make their way to registration, and make my way out of the school grounds and head home. Nobody will notice I'm not at school. What would they think if I got hit by a bus and ended up in a coma? I bet Linda would pay attention to me then. I imagine her crying by my bedside, telling me how sorry she is for being such a bitch. She writes to Andrew Ridgeley and he rushes to the hospital with his guitar and all the nurses are jealous because he insists they leave us alone while he plays for me. My eyelids flicker as he starts to play *I'm Your Man,* but before he can start to sing Thomas barges into my hospital room.

I'm still daydreaming about Thomas and Andrew Ridgeley fighting over me when I turn the corner of the street and see a dark green Volvo parked outside the front of my house. Why would someone be parked outside our house when nobody's home?

And then I see Mum's car in the driveway, and I get a sinking feeling deep in the pit of my stomach. Why isn't she at work? Is she sick?

I open the door quietly and step inside. Raised voices are coming from the living room, but I don't recognise the first voice.

'This might be your last chance to sort things out.'

'I tried that twenty years ago. She didn't listen then and she won't listen now.' This voice belongs to my mother, and she sounds upset.

‘You might live to regret it if you don’t see her while you still can.’

‘What do you care about my regrets?’

I creep forward to the door and catch a glimpse of the Volvo’s owner. The woman looks about the same age as my mother, and is wearing a grey pencil skirt with a cream blouse and a set of pearls at her neck. Neither of them has noticed me yet.

‘She wants to see you, Maggie.’

‘If she wants to see me then why isn’t she here?’

‘Don’t be so hard on her.’

Mum laughs, but it’s a harsh, mocking sound. ‘Hard on her? Are you serious? She’s the one who cut me off. Turned her back on me all those years ago. She’s had twenty years to see me, Catherine, twenty years.’

I stare at the woman in the grey skirt. Catherine. This woman shares my name. Could this be Aunt Catherine, my mother’s sister? But that’s impossible; Mum told me she died before I was born.

I step into the room. ‘Catherine?’

Mum spins round. ‘How long have you been there? Why aren’t you in school?’

I turn to the stranger in the room. ‘Are you my Aunt Catherine?’

‘Cathy, you’re not supposed to be here. Go up to your room.’

I don’t move.

‘Do as you’re told.’

‘Or what? Are you going to hit me again?’

My words stop her.

Aunt Catherine steps towards me. ‘I wasn’t sure she’d told you about me.’

‘I’ve seen photographs of you.’

She turns to my mother. ‘I didn’t know you had a daughter.’

‘Why would you?’

‘How old is she?’

I’ve had enough of being invisible. ‘I’m sixteen.’

'You're the same age as Tricia; she's my oldest.'

'I have a cousin?'

Catherine laughs, and, unlike my mother's, it's a gentle laugh. 'You have three cousins on my side and four on your uncle John's.'

I can't take all of this in. Uncle John? Seven cousins? I stare at the woman wearing the pearls.

'My name's Catherine too, but most people call me Cathy.'

Catherine turns to her sister. 'You named her after me?'

'I named her after our grandmother.'

'Oh.' Catherine holds out her hand towards me. 'Pleased to finally meet you.'

I don't understand. How can she be here when she's supposed to be dead?

'Is it you who's been phoning here all the time?' I ask.

She nods. 'I've been trying to speak to your mother, but she's as stubborn now as she was when she was growing up.'

I've never heard any stories about my mother as a child. 'What was she like?'

Catherine smiles. 'You look just like her. You've got the same eyes.'

I think of the photographs in the box.

'And she was strong-willed, stubborn, and hated being told what to do.' She glares across the room at my mum.

'Why have you been phoning?'

Catherine takes hold of my hands. 'Our mother isn't well.'

I look at Mum. 'You told us your family was dead.'

'They might as well be.'

'You told them we were dead?' shrieks Catherine. She lets go of my hands. 'How could you say such a thing?'

'What was I supposed to tell them? That you didn't want to see them? That you thought they were bastards and didn't deserve to be here, on God's earth?'

'I never said any such thing.'

'No? Well, she did. And do you know what she called me

when I last saw her? Do you?' She pauses, but Catherine doesn't answer. 'She called me a whore. My own mother called me a whore.'

'She didn't mean it, she was upset. We all were.'

'And none of you stopped to think how I was feeling?'

'You're the one who walked out.'

'I was pushed out.' Mum walks to the door. 'I think it's time you left.'

'Will you at least think about it?'

'There's nothing to think about.'

'I came here because I hoped somewhere deep down you might still care about the family we once were.'

Mum opens the door. 'I haven't thought about any of you in a very long time. You mean nothing to me.'

I think of the box tucked away inside my mother's wardrobe. *It's not true*, I want to shout out. *She's kept photographs of you. She thinks about you all the time. She cries every time you call.*

But I say nothing.

He Loves Me, He Loves Me Not

I lie on my bedroom floor and suck in my stomach so that I can squeeze into my stonewashed jeans. I'm meeting him in half an hour and I don't want to be late. Things are really serious between us now, and I need to speak to him. I pull open the drawstrings of the green pouch and lift out the silver cross. I've got so many chains and crucifixes around my neck I'm confident Mum will never notice it. I touch it for good luck and head to the bandstand to meet him. He calls it our special place, and says it's more romantic if we're alone together. That suits me fine tonight.

He isn't here when I arrive, so I sit down in a spot of sunshine on the hill and pluck a buttercup from the grass. I remember how when I was little Mum would hold it under my chin and tell me I liked butter. I pull a yellow petal out from the centre. *He loves me.* And another. *He loves me not.* I lie back in the warm sun and close my eyes, and imagine him coming to the house and asking my dad for his daughter's hand in marriage. Dad claps him on the back and pumps his hand up and down in congratulations. Everyone is happy for us, even Jimmy, and we gather round the kitchen table and talk about wedding plans. We plan to get married in the chapel (his mother wants this and we agree that it's important she's happy) and I persuade Dad to wear a kilt.

A shadow falls over me and he lies down beside me on the grass. He doesn't say a word but starts kissing me. My mouth. My neck. He pulls my vest top downwards and starts kissing my breasts.

'Someone will see us,' I say.

He takes hold of my hand and pulls me up on to the stage

and leads me to the deserted room backstage where I lost my virginity. We've made love in here several times now, and each time feels a little nicer. It no longer hurts when he enters me.

He pushes me up against the wall and we kiss as I fumble to undo the button on his jeans. His cock pulses in the palm of my hand as I free it from his boxer shorts.

'Oh God, I love you,' he moans. He's already hard, and I know he won't last long.

'Tell me again,' I say.

'I love you.'

'Say my name.'

'I love you, Cathy.'

I lead his pulsing cock towards me and unbutton my jeans with my other hand. He pushes me against the bare wall and I know I'm going to have bruises tomorrow. I pull my jeans and pants down to my ankles.

'Tell me,' I say as he thrusts deeper inside me.

'I…love…'

But he's come before he can finish saying it, and he takes his limp cock out of me and pulls up his jeans. He leans back against the wall and lights a cigarette, leaving me to pull up my pants and jeans and sort my top. He offers me a drag from his cigarette, although he knows I always say no.

I should have insisted he wore a condom the first time we did it, but I was worried he'd think I was a prude. I guess I was scared he wouldn't want to see me again. The girls in my year call girls who haven't lost their virginity frigid. Frigid. I don't even know what the word means, but I hate it. And I hate the girls who use it.

'I can't stay long,' he tells me. 'My cousin is coming over tonight and my mum wants me to be there when she arrives.' He looks at me and shrugs.

'Maybe I could come with you.'

He laughs. 'Aye. And maybe the Queen will visit the fucking Pope.'

'No need to be like that.'

He stubs out his cigarette with the heel of his shoe.

'Sorry,' he says, kissing me on the neck. 'You know how much I wish you could come to mine. But you remember what my mum's like.'

'You'll have to tell her about us one day,' I whisper, knowing it will have to be sooner rather than later.

'Of course,' he says, flicking his tongue across the nape of my neck.

I make a little groaning sound because I know he likes it when I do this, and he pushes his hand inside my top. 'My mate told me he and his girlfriend did it three times in one night.'

'We need to talk.'

'In a minute,' he says, still fumbling with my bra strap.

'Please,' I ask.

He lets go of me and pulls another cigarette from the pack in his jacket pocket.

'You'd better make it quick,' he says, lighting up and looking at his watch.

I grab the cigarette from his hand, place it between my lips and suck inwards. The nicotine burns the back of my throat and I cough and splutter.

'What the fuck are you doing?' he asks, but I don't look at him. 'Have you been drinking?'

I shake my head. I've been building myself up to telling him ever since I was sure.

'Well, what's the matter with you?'

'I'm pregnant.'

He stares at me. 'What?'

'I'm pregnant.'

'But how can you be? I mean, you're on the Pill, aren't you?'

'On the Pill? What made you think that?'

'I just assumed…'

'Why?'

'I thought all Proddy girls went on the Pill.'

I stare at him. He's still talking but I'm no longer listening. *Proddy girls.*

'Have you told anyone yet? Oh God, please tell me

you've not told that gossiping bitch Linda?'

'I wanted to tell you first. I thought we could decide what to do together.'

'What to do?'

'About the baby.'

'What's it got to do with me?'

'It's your baby.'

'I've only got your word for that.'

'What do you mean?'

'You could be seeing a dozen other boys, for all I know.'

'But I love you. I've loved you ever since we were little.'

He laughs in my face. 'You're kidding, right?'

'We're destined to be together. Didn't you feel it that first night we sheltered in the doorway of the chapel?'

'It was just a bit of fun, you and me. It was never meant to be anything serious.'

I remember something Billy told me, and I confront him. 'Are you seeing someone else?'

'Why d'you ask?'

'A friend said he saw you with another girl.'

'And what? Are you telling me I can't speak to other girls, now?'

'I want you to be honest.'

He doesn't say anything. He doesn't need to.

'Is her name Sadie?'

His face tells me the answer.

'And I'm guessing she's not really your cousin?' I know I have to ask the next question even though I don't want to hear the answer. 'Have you slept with her?'

'She won't let me.'

I stare at him. 'What do you mean?'

'She won't let me go any further than a quick finger-fuck.'

I feel sick.

'Listen, I know this girl in my year who got herself pregnant. Went to a clinic. In Edinburgh. And just like that, it was done. Only needed to take a couple of days off school. Nobody even knew what she was off for. She told people she had the flu.'

How does he know this? Has he got a girl pregnant before? No. He can't have. It must have happened to one of his friends.

'I thought we could get married and bring the baby up together,' I say.

He stares at me. 'You're kidding, right? Once I get the results I want, I'm heading off to Glasgow Uni in September.'

'But it's your baby, too.'

'What the fuck's it got to do with me?'

'We love each other. We've loved each other since primary school. It was fate that brought you back to me.'

'Fate? What are you on about? We moved back here for my dad's job.'

I place my hand on my stomach, desperately feeling for some sort of sign of the baby that's growing inside me. My baby.

'You said you loved me,' I whisper.

But he's not listening. I think of asking him to place his hand beside mine, but I see the look in his eyes. There's no love there. Just anger.

'This would never have happened if you'd been on the Pill. My mum will kill me if she finds out I've got some girl up the duff. It's your problem, and you're the one who's going to have to sort it out.'

He stubs out the cigarette on the cold stone wall and walks away, and I feel his cum trickling down the inside of my thigh as I'm left standing alone in the empty bandstand.

Part Three

1990

Unfold your wings.

Wilting Flowers

Last night's rain has knocked the flowers from the fuchsia bush by the front door, and the red and purple flowers lie scattered across the ramp leading up to the entrance. Cathy bends down and picks up one of the flowers and holds it to her nose, but its scent has gone. She tucks the wilting flower behind her ear and walks through the automatic doors into the reception area, where a thin, stern-looking woman sits poker-straight behind the desk. Cathy smiles and hopes she's not about to be stopped at the first hurdle. Her smile is not returned.

'I'm here to see my grandmother, Helen McLafferty.'

The receptionist picks up the phone and gestures to the seating area, but Cathy stays standing and looks around the small entrance foyer. The usual mix of old magazines lie arranged in a fan shape across a glass coffee table, but she ignores them and wanders back towards the intricately-carved wooden font that stands by the front door. She's not sure if she's supposed to sprinkle herself with the water on the way in or on the way out, or perhaps both, and she's still deciding whether she should anoint herself when a nun appears in front of her.

'I'll show you to Helen's room.'

Cathy follows the nun along a maze of narrow corridors, past embroidered countryside scenes which hang crooked on the beige walls, and bowls of potpourri arranged in an attempt to make the place feel homely. But the dried flowers can't disguise the smell of disinfectant that makes the building feel more like a hospital than a home.

'You'll find her sitting in front of the window watching the birds. That's where she spends all of her time these days. She loves the birds.' The nun waits for Cathy to catch up. ‘Have you been to visit before? I can’t say I remember your face.’

‘I’m her granddaughter.’

‘I thought I’d met all of John and Catherine’s children.’

‘She has another daughter.’

The nun stops and looks at Cathy. ‘Oh. I don’t believe I’ve ever met her.’

‘Her name’s Margaret.’

‘Does she visit often?’

Cathy doesn’t know how to answer. ‘It’s complicated.’

The nun nods. ‘It usually is.’ She stops outside a plain wooden door. ‘I’ll be at the end of the corridor if you need me.’

Cathy half-expects the door to be locked, but the handle turns easily and she peers inside the small room. A single bed is tucked into the corner of the room with floral bedcovers that match the thin curtains at the window, a look that Cathy guesses is repeated in every room along the corridor.

Her grandmother sits in the only chair in the room, which is turned to face the window and the world beyond. Cathy steps into the room, quietly closing the door behind her, and she lets out a loud gasp as she sees the picture above the bed. It’s almost identical to the one that hung in Thomas’s living room all those years ago. He called it *The Sacred Heart*, and it scares her as much now as it did then. The eyes of Jesus bore into her, and she can swear he’s searching for her soul. She blinks to break his stare and looks away.

‘Who’s there?’

The armchair is six steps away at most, but her shoes are suddenly laden with lead. It takes all of her effort to approach her grandmother.

‘Is that you, Father Michael?’

A large sycamore tree blocks any view of the street, its branches scraping against the window pane like long outstretched fingers.

‘I’m Cathy.’

'Catherine?' The old woman twists in her chair and turns to face her, reaching out to her with papery hands. 'What have you done to your hair?'

Cathy runs her fingers through her hair.

'Why aren't you at school?'

The old woman is clearly confused.

'I'm no longer at school. I work in a coffee shop.' She hates working in the coffee shop, but for now it pays the bills and keeps Jenny going in new shoes. That girl couldn't grow any faster if her feet were planted in compost.

'Nonsense,' the old woman snaps. 'Now stop pretending. Tell me, what time is it?'

'It's half past three.'

'Half past three already? Why didn't you wake me sooner? Father Michael is coming over at four. Quick, go and get changed into your best dress.' She tries to push herself up out of her seat but is too frail.

'I think you should sit down,' says Cathy.

'Sit down? I've no time for sitting down, I need to be busy.'

'I'll help you. Tell me what you need.'

Her grandmother eases herself back down into the armchair and smiles. 'That's my girl. Now go and fetch some biscuits and put them on one of our finest china plates.'

Cathy stands up to go and find the kitchen and track down some biscuits.

'And none of those custard creams,' her grandmother shouts after her. 'See if there are any chocolate ones. Only the best will do.'

Cathy leaves the room and goes in search of the nun who showed her to the room, but the corridor is empty. So she follows signs for the dining room, where she finds a young woman in uniform setting the table for that evening's dinner.

'Excuse me,' Cathy interrupts. 'But can I possibly ask for a small plate of biscuits? My grandmother is having a visit from Father Michael this afternoon.'

The young woman laughs kindly. 'You must be visiting Helen; she always thinks the priest is coming for tea, and I'm guessing she told you to get chocolate digestives. *Only the best will do,*' she mimics. 'You do know she's diabetic, right?'

Cathy feels stupid. She knows nothing about her grandmother, nothing at all.

'Don't worry about it. By the time you go back to her room she'll probably be asleep, and when she wakes up she'll have forgotten she sent you in the first place.'

Cathy thanks the young woman and wanders through to the common room and over to the tall window that overlooks the small patio area. Someone's gone to the bother of hanging a couple of bird feeders on the willow tree, and she watches the procession of tiny birds flitting back and forth between them.

'You alright, love?'

She hadn't noticed the old woman sitting in the corner.

'I was thinking about bringing my grandmother through to sit in here. She loves birds, you see, and I think she'd enjoy sitting by the window.'

'I don't think I've ever seen you in here before. Who did you say your grandmother is?'

'Helen. Helen McLafferty.'

The old woman stamps her walking stick on the floor. 'That old cow!' she shouts. 'Huh, you'll never get her through here. Thinks she's better than the rest of us.'

The young woman stops setting the table in the next room and rushes through and places her hand on the older woman's shoulder.

'Shhh, Hilda. You know it does you no good getting upset.' She forces a smile at Cathy and lowers her voice. 'Ignore Hilda,' she says. 'She's always moaning about something or other. Don't pay any heed to what she says.'

Cathy leaves and traces her steps back to her grandmother's room, where she finds her still gazing out of the window. She kneels down beside her.

'Do you know who I am? I'm your granddaughter,

Cathy.'

'Don't be silly, dear; Catherine is my daughter's name.'

'She's my aunt. I'm Margaret's daughter.'

'I had a girl called Margaret once.' Her face falls. 'But something happened. There was an accident.' She turns her head and looks out into the garden. 'Oh, look, is that a swallow? And it's got something in its beak.'

'What do you mean, there was an accident?'

'She must have a nest somewhere nearby with babies in it waiting to be fed.'

'You said there was an accident.'

'Our little girl died.'

'But that's not true. Margaret's still alive.'

'Have you seen the way the babies open their mouths wide to be fed?'

Cathy leans forward and places her hand on the old woman's knee.

'I'm Margaret's daughter.'

'Don't say that,' the old woman shouts. 'I already told you. My Margaret died.'

Cathy gets up and walks over to the window and watches a crisp packet blow against the wire fencing, swirl up and dance and then fall to the ground.

'Who are you? Why are you here?'

'I'm Cathy, your granddaughter.'

'You're a liar, that's who you are! My Catherine's at school just now. Who let you into my house?'

Cathy has an idea. She leans close to her grandmother and slips the silver pendant around her neck out from under her blouse and lifts it up.

'Look, this is my mother's necklace.'

Her grandmother looks at the chain. 'You little thief!' She reaches out and grabs hold of the tiny, silver cross. 'That belongs to my little girl. How dare you steal it? It's hers I tell you, hers.'

'Where is she? What happened to your little girl?'

'She died,' wails the old woman.

But Cathy's not stopping now. 'Tell me what happened.'

The nun appears in the doorway, and Cathy knows it's time to go. She catches a glimpse of the painting above her grandmother's bed as she leaves the room and feels the eyes of Christ follow her. She closes the door behind her.

'I think she thought I was her daughter.'

'Her dementia means she often gets confused between the past and the present.'

'Dementia?'

'I thought you knew.'

Things begin to fall into place in Cathy's mind. 'Tell me, when did she come to stay here?'

'She arrived at the same time as me, which makes it five years this August.'

Five years. That makes sense.

'She said my mum died in an accident.'

'Maybe she was confused.'

Cathy thinks there's more to it than that.

Bubble Wrap

Jenny is already unbuckling herself from the passenger seat when Cathy pulls into the driveway. She's spotted the older girl who lives next door and is waving frantically to her.

'Hey, Rebecca,' she shouts, throwing open the car door at the same time. 'Do you want to come and push me on the swing?'

'Rebecca's probably got her own things to be doing,' Cathy says. She's speaking to herself because Jenny's already on tiptoes, peering over the fence into next door's back garden.

'Hey, Jenny, how are you today?'

Cathy looks at Rebecca and tries to work out what age she must be now. Could she be at high school already?

'Sorry, Rebecca, she spotted you as soon as we drove in.'

'That's okay,' Rebecca says. 'I saw your car coming up the hill and thought I'd come to say goodbye. Are you moving today?'

Cathy hasn't lived here for years, but the old house still feels like home.

'Mum's packing the last of the boxes. The removal van's coming this afternoon.' Her parents have finally got round to buying the house by the sea they always promised themselves.

Jenny has squirmed her way up on to the swing and is now shouting for Rebecca to come and push her. Cathy watches as Rebecca puts one foot on the bottom strap and vaults over the wooden fence. She remembers Thomas used to do the exact same thing.

Thomas. Her stomach curdles at the thought of him. Lately, her thoughts have been haunted by memories from the past, probably stirred up by the house sale.

'If you get bored pushing her, Rebecca, just send her in.'

'You won't get bored, Rebecca, will you?' shouts Jenny from the swing.

'Of course not. Now hold on because I'm coming to push you all the way up to the clouds.'

Cathy leaves the girls playing together and follows the path to the back door. She must have come in and out of this door a thousand times, yet as she puts out her hand and grips the handle she feels like a stranger. She takes a deep breath and tells herself she can do this. She's a grown-up now, whatever that means, and it's time to confront her mother about the past.

She pushes down on the handle and enters the kitchen, and the memory that surfaces takes her by surprise. She'd expected to be faced with echoes of the raging arguments she had when she told her parents she was pregnant, or maybe hear their worried whispers ricochet off the kitchen walls, making their way upstairs to her bedroom where she lay under the covers desperately trying to block it all out. Instead, she remembers the day Dad put up the kitchen wallpaper for the first time, and if she squints in the sunlight she can almost see his silhouette standing at the decorating table, dipping the large brush in the bucket of wallpaper paste. She says 'first time' because he had to peel it off and start again after Jimmy noticed the grapes and plums were all upside down. They'd laughed for months at that one.

She leaves the kitchen and goes through to the living room, where she finds her mum drowning in a pool of bin bags on the floor. Various-sized boxes are stacked on either side of the room, their contents labelled in black pen. Lives neatly folded and packed away. Cathy picks up a Fleetwood Mac album from the top of a pile and turns it over and reads the soundtrack to her childhood. Then she rummages through an open box labelled *Miscellaneous* and picks up an old football trophy of Dad's that used to stand on the mantelpiece beside the carriage clock. The engraved plaque reads,

Player of the Year 1970.

She's never heard the story behind it and she tells herself she'll ask next time she sees him, but knows she probably never will.

The walls where memories once hung are now bare, and she sits down on the floor next to her mother.

'I went to visit Gran yesterday. She's in a nursing home in the west end of Glasgow.'

Mum lifts an old crystal vase and a square of bubble wrap.

'She has dementia.'

'I know.'

'That's what Aunt Catherine meant all those years ago when she said it was your last chance to see her. Your last chance to sort things out. It was because she knew Gran was losing her memory, wasn't it? She wouldn't know who you were for much longer.'

The bubble wrap doesn't reach the whole way round. Mum unravels it, turns the vase and starts again.

'She told me you were dead. Said you died in an accident. Why did she say that?'

Her mum's hands shake as she unravels the bubble wrap for a second time.

'Damn it. Why won't this vase stay put while I wrap it?'

Cathy takes the vase from her mother and places it in the centre of the bubble wrap. She remembers the time she and Jimmy were playing football in the living room with a scrunched-up newspaper, and she was in goals as usual. She'd reached to save the 'ball' but her fingertips brushed against the vase, knocking it off the mantelpiece and chipping its rim on the hearth. They'd never admitted to what happened, and although her mum must have noticed the chip she never mentioned it. Cathy secures the ends of the bubble wrap with sellotape and looks at her mother.

'Why did she tell me you died in an accident?'

'I presume she thought that story was less shameful than the truth.'

'Will you tell me the truth?'

Her mum carefully places the wrapped vase inside a box marked *Living Room* and stares into the box as though she can see the past replaying there.

'I met your father when I was even younger than you are now. We were just seventeen and we fell in love on our first date. I know we were very young, but there's nothing you can do about your feelings. You can't just switch them off.' Mum smiles, and Cathy knows she's remembering the feeling of new love. She thinks of the first time she kissed Thomas in the chapel doorway.

'Anyway, one thing led to another and I discovered I was pregnant. I'd never been so scared in my whole life, but when I told your dad he couldn't have been happier, and right there and then he got down on one knee and proposed to me. It was so romantic.'

Cathy looks at her mum. What would she think if she found out her daughter had let Thomas O'Donnell fuck her under the bandstand on their second date? Where's the romance in that?

'What did you say when Dad proposed?'

'I said yes, of course. We stayed up the whole night discussing our plans for the future. We'd get married and I'd stay at home and look after the baby while he went out to work. It wasn't quite what I'd planned, but I could pick up my studies again once our children started school.'

'You knew you wanted more children?'

Mum puts out her hand and tucks a stray hair behind Cathy's ear, then leans forward and kisses her gently on the forehead.

'Of course we did.'

Cathy is suddenly reminded of the afternoon they spent making jam together. Was that the last time her mother had kissed her? She can't remember.

'So, what happened next?'

A storm gathers across her mum's brow.

'You have to understand my family were strict churchgoers.' She stops and looks at her daughter. 'And in their eyes your dad went to a different church.'

'What do you mean? I didn't think you or Dad ever went to church.'

'My family were Roman Catholic. Your dad's were Protestant. And where we lived you weren't supposed to mix.'

Cathy thinks back to the fights in the park at lunchtime, and the chants and bottles thrown at the buses as they drove past. *Stick to your own kind,* her brother had said. *Stick to your own kind.*

Mum gets up and goes to a packing box marked *Fragile* and brings out the memory box tied with baby blue ribbon. Cathy recognises it straight away. She watches as her mum carefully unties the bow, removes the lid, and lifts out the small collection of photographs. She flicks through the pile, but Cathy knows she's not looking at the pictures. She's remembering.

'Your dad came to the house and asked my father for my hand in marriage. That probably sounds old-fashioned to you, but it was the done thing in those days, and we were sure when he saw how much we loved each other, and how grown-up we were being, he'd give us his blessing.'

She stares at a black-and-white photograph of a young man. Is the man in the picture Cathy's grandfather?

'But it didn't go the way we hoped. He was furious. *How dare you steal my daughter's virginity? How dare you take advantage of my wee girl?* They blamed your dad for everything. After all, I'd been brought up a proper Catholic girl in a good Catholic family, so as far as they were concerned, he'd obviously taken advantage of my innocence. They refused to listen to my side of the story, and tried to send me away until the baby was born and then have it adopted. Your dad's parents were just as angry, and wanted him to have nothing more to do with me. But we were determined. Determined to marry and bring the baby up by ourselves.

'He tried getting a job, but nobody would hire a Protestant man who'd got a Catholic girl pregnant, so we moved through from Glasgow, and he got a job at the new Leyland factory. It paid enough for us to afford the rent on a small flat and have a little money left over, so we booked a date at the registry office.'

Cathy watches her mother's face for any sign of emotion, but finds none.

'Look! I was already seven months pregnant.' She hands Cathy the wedding photograph. 'I had the biggest bouquet of carnations ever to try and hide the bump.'

'Did they come to the wedding?'

'We sent invitations to both families, but the only one who came was my grandmother, and I'm sure she got hell for it. It was to be her first great-grandchild and she was so excited. She came through on the bus twice a week to visit; bringing cooked meals and bags of knitted clothes for the baby. She knitted these bootees. But the rest of the family refused to have anything more to do with me after I married your father. A *mixed marriage* they called it.'

Mum holds the pair of bootees close to her chest.

'The baby was stillborn. The God I'd worshipped every week without fail since I was a little girl let my baby die. Gran told me He had his reasons and I shouldn't question Him. I was furious. How dare she say that? My beautiful baby boy was dead. Was it our fault for daring to be happy? Was God so blind He didn't want me marrying a Protestant? I told her to stay away. Told her I never wanted to see her again.'

The dam bursts and tears run down her cheeks.

'I never saw her again. She died within a month and it was my fault. Not only had she lost her great-grandchild but she'd lost me too.'

Cathy doesn't know what to say.

'I wish she'd lived long enough to meet you and Jimmy. She would have loved you. You're like her in so many ways.' She rummages through the memory box and Cathy knows what she's searching for. She pulls down the neck of her jumper to reveal the tiny silver cross.

'Is this what you're looking for?'

She expects her mum to be angry, but she just smiles and touches the cross.

'I'm sorry I took it.'

'How long have you had it?'

'I found it when I was a little girl.'

Mum pushes away the tears with the heel of her hand. 'My mum gave it to me for my first Holy Communion.' She reaches into the box and lifts out the white Bible, and a photograph falls out from between the pages. She picks it up and hands it to Cathy. 'If you look closely you can see the cross around my neck.'

Unlike the other photographs in the box, this one is in colour. The young girl in the picture is wearing a white dress and veil, and has a blue sash tied around her waist. Cathy can't believe it. Her mother looks like the Blue Lady.

'You're beautiful,' she whispers.

Mum feeds the blue ribbon through her fingers. 'My mother used to have a sewing basket. It was a little picnic hamper and it was always bursting full with scraps of material, pincushions and odd buttons. I used to love searching through the box for shiny treasures. This ribbon comes from the dress in the picture.'

Cathy looks at the photograph of her mother, and sure enough the sash around her waist is the same shade of blue as the ribbon that ties around the box.

'She got it from one of the stalls in the market and bought far too much, but it was a bargain. My mother could never resist a bargain.'

Cathy smiles. Does her mum realise she's just described herself?

'Normally she'd store any offcuts in her basket in case they came in handy, but she let me keep this extra length of ribbon because I loved the feel of it so much.' She holds the length of material up to her face. 'It still takes me straight back to when I was a wee girl.'

Cathy reaches behind and starts to unfasten the chain, but her mum stops her.

'I think she would want you to have it, and maybe you

can pass it on to Jenny one day.'

It feels good to have the cross out in the open.

'You said there were still some things for me to collect.'

'You've left some bits and bobs behind which I've emptied into a couple of boxes. They're upstairs in your room. Why don't you go up and have a look through them? Take some bin bags for anything you don't want to keep, and Dad will take them to the dump later.'

Cathy leaves her mum wrapping the last couple of things in bubble wrap and heads upstairs. Her mum has attempted to remove some of the several hundred *Smash Hits* stickers from her bedroom door before finally giving up, and Cathy runs her fingers across the tacky remains of her teenage years. She nudges the door open and steps back into a previous life.

Grease spots on the wall mark where her *Wham!* posters were once held up with Blu-tack. It's been years since she's thought about her favourite teenage band, and she feels a flutter in her stomach as she remembers the crush she had on Andrew Ridgeley.

Two cardboard boxes stand in the middle of the floor and she looks at the black bin bags in her hand. Can she face going through more childhood memories? Maybe she should ask her mum to drop the boxes off at her flat. But she knows they'll stand in the tiny hallway forever and she'll never get round to sorting through them. Fuck it. There's nothing in either of these boxes that she's looked for since leaving home, so they can go to the tip. Straight to the tip. Do not pass Go. Do not collect two hundred pounds.

She throws the bin bags on top of the smallest box and her eyes fall on the bear tucked down the side. The words *Miss Me* are faded, but she still remembers the day Thomas gave it to her.

She carries the bear through to her brother's old bedroom and gazes out of the window which overlooks the back garden. Jenny kicks her legs and squeals with delight as Rebecca pushes her back and forth on the garden swing. She looks up and gives Cathy a great big wave, and her heart aches with love as it always does when she watches her daughter.

Thomas stopped taking her phone calls after she told him she was pregnant, and when she turned up on his doorstep he denied they'd ever slept together. He told people she'd never got over the childhood crush she had on him, and was jealous of his relationship with Sadie and would say anything to ruin things for them. She never spoke to him again.

She pretended the morning sickness was much worse than it actually was and dropped out of school, promising her mum and dad she'd return for the exams the following year. But by then Jenny was born, and everybody's life was very different with a baby in the family.

She goes back through to her bedroom and takes another look inside the box. If the bear was in here, then *she* should be in here too. She rummages through a collection of old books and soft toys until she sees a glint of blue and white china. She carefully lifts out the figurine and places her in her handbag before throwing the bear back in the cardboard box and closing the bedroom door behind her for the very last time.

'Find anything you want to keep?' asks Mum.

She touches her handbag. 'Nothing special. You can tell Dad to take the boxes to the tip.'

'Here, I nearly forgot, this came for you in the post. Looks important.'

Cathy takes the cream-coloured envelope from her mum and traces her finger over the embossed address on the front. She turns the envelope over and opens the seal on the back, sliding out a card with pink lilies and love hearts on the front.

'Come on, I can't take the suspense any longer.'

'It's a wedding invitation.'

'I guessed that much. But who's it from?'

Cathy opens the invitation and squints to make out the fancy, looped calligraphy. 'It's from Linda. It says she's getting married next month.'

‘How exciting. You’ll need to find a partner.’

Typical. Any excuse for Mum to set her up with someone.

She changes the subject. ‘Is that the last box?’

‘Almost. We just need to decide what to do with the junk in the cellar.’

‘What junk?’

‘There’s some boxes with some screws and nails in them, but I suppose they might be handy for whoever moves in. And of course there’s the jam jars. I was thinking we should leave them, maybe the new owners will make jam.’

‘I’ll take them.’

‘You? What on earth for?’

Cathy can’t think of a reason, but she can’t stand the thought of someone else making jam in their kitchen.

Something Borrowed, Something Blue

She breathes in and stares at her reflection in the mirror. Her mother would say she looks like mutton dressed as lamb.

When she received the wedding invitation she caught the bus in to Edinburgh and took the lift straight to the designer floor in Frasers. By the time she left the store, she'd spent a month's salary on a dress with a matching hat, bag and shoes. She hasn't seen anyone from school in over five years, and she wants to make an impression. Linda was always the fashionable one, even way back when they were at primary school together. She was the first of all the girls in their class to get the new pageboy haircut, and by the time Cathy persuaded her mother to let her get hers done, the style was going out of fashion and she was left looking like a boy. And look at her now. Who ever heard of someone trying to outdo the bride on her wedding day?

She breathes out, watching her stomach round in the mirror. Why should she hide it? This is the same stomach that held her baby for nine months. She should take everything back and spend the money on the weekend away in a caravan that she's been promising Jenny for a long time now.

At first she'd thought about asking one of the guys from work to be her partner, but she stopped herself. So what if Rachel and Paula turn up married or with a partner on their arm? Cathy doesn't need to prove to them that she can get a man. She's doing just fine on her own, thank you very much. But then she'd made the mistake of mentioning the wedding to Jimmy, and he insisted on being her partner. She hadn't had the heart to tell him that the only thing worse than turning up at a friend's wedding alone is turning up with your big brother.

Oh well, too late to back out now. She picks up her sequinned clutch bag and heads downstairs, where she finds Jimmy in the kitchen eating the remains of last night's pizza. She stands in front of him, waiting for a compliment. When none comes she tries a bit harder.

'You look great, Jimmy. The kilt really suits you.'

'Thanks. My mate works in the kilt hire place behind Boots, and as long as I drop it round at his as good as new in the morning no one will be any the wiser. Saved me a wee fortune, I can tell you.'

So much for the compliment.

He checks his watch and puts the pizza box back in the fridge. 'If we're going to make it to this wedding we'd better get a move on. Come on.'

The traffic through the centre of town is at a standstill. Jimmy rolls down his window and leans out of the car to see what's happening ahead, but Cathy can already hear the bands.

'For fuck's sake. I mean, seriously, for fuck's sake.' He slams the steering wheel and throws the gear stick into reverse. 'Now we're going to be late for my wee sister's best pal's wedding.' He pulls the car in to the side of the road and switches off the engine. 'Come on,' he says.

'What are we doing?' Cathy asks.

'We're going to have to walk through the town and hope we don't bump into anyone we know. I look a right fucking prat in this kilt.'

The street is lined with people waving flags and clapping their hands, and Cathy shouts to be heard over the drums.

'Have you ever been to see a walk?'

'No chance. You?'

'Thomas and I came to watch it one year.'

Jimmy chokes on fresh air. 'You took a Fenian to an Orange Walk?'

'Don't use that word.'

'It's just a word.'

'It's a horrible word.'

‘You’re over-thinking it. We’re Proddies and they’re Fenians.’

She hesitates, tempted to tell him his own mother’s a Fenian. Would he still use the word if he knew?

‘And when was the last time you were inside a church?’ she asks.

‘What d’ya mean?’

‘You call yourself a Protestant but you don’t really believe.’

‘Aye, I do.’

‘Really?’

‘You’re asking if I believe in God?’

‘That’s right. So come on, out loud, do you believe in God. Yes or no?’

‘Of course I do.’

‘Then why don’t you go to church? Why don’t you pray?’

‘I don’t need to do any of those things to believe in God.’ He walks ahead, pushing his way through the waiting crowd. She tries to keep up, but her high heels are already killing her.

Jimmy stops and spins round to face her. ‘Do you?’ he asks.

‘What?’

‘Do you believe in God?’

‘Keep walking,’ Cathy says, aware that people are listening. ‘We’re already late.’

‘What’s wrong? Worried about getting struck down by lightning if you say no?’

‘Don’t be daft.’ She pushes her way past him.

‘You still haven’t answered me.’

A baby’s cries can be heard coming from the crowd, and Cathy instinctively turns towards the sound.

‘I stopped believing in any God five years ago.’

By the time they arrive at the hotel her feet are killing her and she’s got a blister on her heel. Jimmy rushes up to an official-looking man waiting outside the function suite.

'Are we too late?'

'You're alright; they've not started yet. Apparently, there's some sort of gala day procession taking place in the centre of town, and the wedding car is stuck in traffic.'

They slip into the room and take a seat at the back. Cathy cranes her neck to see if she can recognise anyone, but all she can see is an assortment of fancy hats and the back of the men's heads. A row of helium balloons in the shape of giant love hearts line the aisle, and pink lilies are placed at the end of each row.

'Do you remember the time we sneaked into the back of the chapel?' Jimmy asks.

'I remember I had to bribe you with my pocket money.'

'And a Mars bar.'

Her cheeks flush, and she hopes he doesn't remember she had to leave because she started her period.

A keyboard begins to play and everyone stands and turns to see the bride enter the room. Cathy tries to catch a glimpse of her friend, but the helium balloons are bobbing about in the heat and obscure her view.

By the time the service is finished everyone in the room is hot and sticky. The women's hairdos have flopped and their make-up is starting to run, whilst the men are clearly dreaming of that first sip of cold lager.

Cathy rushes to the ladies and fills the sink with cold water. She clutches the sink with one hand and peels off the shoe on her left foot with the other, wincing at the pain as the heel of the shoe scrapes against the blister. What made her think wearing new shoes was a good idea? She lifts up her skirt and dips her toe into the cold water. Heaven. She slowly submerges the whole foot, ignoring the other women who come and go, squeezing their way in beside her to sort their make-up in the mirror.

'Cathy? Cathy Munro?

Oh fuck. She spots Rachel Jones in the mirror. Why did it have to be Rachel who found her with her foot stuck in the basin and her skirt tucked into her knickers? She lifts her foot out of the sink, water dripping on the floor.

'It is you. I thought so.' Rachel rushes forward and squeezes Cathy in a bear hug. 'Paula, quick, come out. Cathy Munro is here.' The toilet flushes, and Paula appears in a skimpy red dress. 'Linda never told us you were coming. It's so great to see you. You must join us for a drink.'

Without waiting for a response, Paula hooks her hand under Cathy's elbow and follows Rachel out of the toilets, pulling Cathy along with her, still struggling to squeeze her wet foot back into her shoe.

They head through to the reception area, and Rachel clutches Cathy by the hand and pulls her towards one of the round tables. Cathy looks around the room for Jimmy, but he's nowhere to be seen. Typical, he's probably already propping up the bar.

'Gordon, John, this is the school friend we were telling you about.' Cathy is introduced to Rachel's and Paula's husbands.

'We haven't been all together since sixth year,' Paula says.

'I don't think Cat did sixth year, did you?'

Cathy doesn't ever remember being called Cat before.

'Sorry,' Paula giggles. 'I forgot. It's such a shame you missed it. We all had such a laugh, didn't we, Rach?'

Rachel shuffles closer and places her hand on Cathy's arm as though they've been best friends forever.

'So, how are you? It must be so difficult raising a child on your own.'

'Cathy Munro! You look amazing.'

Linda's timing couldn't be more perfect. Cathy hugs her tight.

Rachel struggles to hide her disappointment at being interrupted just as she was about to find out some juicy gossip she could share around the table between courses later on.

'Look,' says Linda. 'I was searching for something borrowed, you know for good luck, something old, something new etcetera, and I was looking through my jewellery box and found these. Do you remember them?' She tucks her hair behind one ear and shows Cathy her earrings.

'Oh my God. I'd forgotten all about them. I loved those earrings, but I can't believe you decided to wear bright yellow hoops on your wedding day.'

'I couldn't resist. Don't worry, no one will be able to see them in the photographs and I might actually get round to giving you them back this time.' Linda lets her hair fall back into place. 'It's so good to see you after all this time. Tell me, how are you?'

Cathy clears her throat, ready to give the answer she's rehearsed, but as usual her old friend is still talking. Some things never change.

'You probably heard Derek and I split up when I went to uni. I met a guy on my course called Jamie and we were kind of serious for a while but then I discovered he was fucking my roommate. Put that face away, you don't need to worry about me. Jamie had a younger brother, Craig. Anyway, the night I found out that Jamie was shagging Gemma I went round to Craig's flat. You know, a shoulder to cry on and all that.'

Cathy knows what her friend's going to say next.

'And we ended up in bed,' she laughs. 'Jamie was livid when he found out.'

'Doesn't he mind that you're marrying his brother?'

'Don't worry about it; he's fine. I'll introduce you to him later; I don't think he's seeing anyone just now. You'll love him, he's absolutely gorgeous.'

Cathy's only been on a couple of dates since Jenny was born, but as soon as they found out she had a daughter they never got back in touch. Usual story: if you're a single dad raising a child you're a hero, but if you're a single mum you're a slut. Not that it bothers her; her beautiful daughter is the most important person in the world to her, and nothing can change that. She decided early on that she'll never let Jenny meet anyone unless it's serious.

'Cathy?'

She looks at Linda.

'You haven't changed a bit, still daydreaming and not listening to a word anyone says. I was just about to tell you about the moment when Craig proposed to me.'

'Sorry, Linda, please tell me.'

'We were on holiday in Goa a few months ago, and we were both on the back of an elephant when he asked me to marry him.'

'A few months ago? What was the rush?'

'Don't worry, I'm not pregnant. God forbid, I'm not that stupid.' She stops, realising what she's just said. 'Oh Christ, I'm so sorry. That was so thoughtless of me. You must hate me.'

Before Cathy can reply, Jimmy appears beside Linda with a pint glass in one hand and a shot of whisky in the other.

'Linda, I can't believe you're married. I was keeping myself for you.'

Linda giggles and Cathy can't help but smile. Same old Linda, flirting with the boys. 'Then why'd you never ask me out?'

'You were my sister's best friend.'

'And...?'

'Against the rules, I'm afraid.'

Cathy can't bear this much longer. She looks around the room for someone else to talk to before Rachel or Paula pin her down again.

'Cathy Munro?'

She turns around.

'Don't you recognise me?'

Of course she recognises him. Even without the eye make-up and the leather bracelets.

'Let me buy you a drink,' says Billy, ignoring everyone else sitting around the table.

Cathy smiles. Billy Weir clearly hasn't changed and still doesn't care what others think of him. She follows him to the bar.

'Thanks for rescuing me.'

'You looked in desperate need of saving. Are you here on your own?'

'I'm here with my brother, Jimmy, only he's chatting up the bride. So, what are you doing here? Were you one of Linda's best friends in sixth year too?'

'Distant cousin on the groom's side.' He raises his hand to get the barmaid's attention. 'I was hoping you might be here, but I wasn't sure if you and Linda were still friends.'

'We've barely seen each other since leaving school.'

'And yet you still got an invite?'

'She and I go way back to primary school together.'

'Hey, you and I go back to primary school too, you know. Surely that counts for something?'

'I hardly think chasing me in the playground counts.'

'Ouch. It only goes to prove I was a romantic back then, too.'

'There's nothing romantic about Kiss, Cuddle, Torture.'

'Oh, come on, give me a break, I was just a wee boy back then trying my best. Do you remember the day Richard Wilson threw a paper aeroplane at you and we both got belted?'

All those times they sat side by side in maths and he never once mentioned primary school. She'd assumed he didn't remember her.

'I wonder what he's up to now?'

'Last I heard, he moved to America.' He orders their drinks and turns back to look at her. 'So, how are things?'

'A whole lot better now I've bumped into you. You've no idea how much I've been dreading this wedding.'

'Why?'

She sweeps her hands around at the pink flower arrangements, the pink tablecloths and the pink balloons. He laughs.

'So what happened to the Goth look?'

'It's hiding somewhere underneath this fancy suit.' He looks at her and grins. 'Stay here. I'll be back in a minute.'

She watches him leave the bar and hopes he'll be back before Rachel spots she's on her own again. But he's back as quickly as he left and picks up his pint glass.

'Everything okay?' she asks.

'I've swapped a couple of place names.'

'What do you mean?'

'The seating plan. I was supposed to be sitting beside that bunch at the meal.' He signals to Rachel and Paula's table. 'So I've swapped my name with an old aunt who's had so much champagne she'll never remember where she was supposed to be sitting anyway.'

'So, who are you sitting beside now?'

'You.'

'But who did you come with?'

'Me? Nobody. Less complicated that way.'

'Don't you mind coming to a wedding by yourself?'

'Why should I? I like my own company. And besides, now I get to sit beside you. It'll be just like old times, only without Mr Rathbone keeping an eye on us.'

Once the meal and speeches are finished, and after the first dance, the DJ starts playing the usual cheesy pop songs. It's Cathy's turn to order the drinks and she finds Jimmy by the bar, drinking with a man she doesn't recognise. Jimmy introduces her and then quickly excuses himself, leaving her to make polite conversation with a stranger.

'So, how do you know the bride and groom?' she asks.

The man laughs. 'I don't. But I'm staying in the hotel for the night and fancied a wee dance so I thought I'd gatecrash. Nobody'll notice anyhow; they're all too pissed.'

She wishes Jimmy would hurry up. He's been in the toilet for ages and there's only so long you can be polite to a drunk, middle-aged man who can't take his eyes off your tits. 'What brought you through to Bathgate?' she asks.

'I was playing in the band with some of my mates. It's been a brilliant day; one of the biggest crowds of the season so far.' He leans forward, spilling some of his pint on her dress. 'So, tell me gorgeous, have you got a boyfriend?'

She looks over at the table where Billy's sitting. 'He's over there,' she says.

‘Ah well, ye cannae blame a man for trying.’ He drags his eyes away from her chest and back to the pint in front of him. ‘Cannae blame a man for trying.’

Jimmy makes his way back from the toilet, and she grabs hold of him before he can take up his place at the bar again.

‘What took you so long?’

‘I thought you might like some time together.’ He winks at his friend.

She stares at him. ‘Did you deliberately leave me alone with that creep?’

‘I thought you might like him.’

‘He was marching in the parade, for fuck’s sake.’

‘Eh?’ Her brother has clearly had too much to drink.

‘This new pal of yours is an Orangeman.’

‘Leave the man alone, he’s sound.’

She shakes her head.

‘Honest Sis, he’s not like your usual bigot; he’s a good guy once you get to know him. Wait, where are you going?’

‘I’ve changed my mind about getting a drink. I’ll leave you with your *pal*.’

She walks back to her seat and grabs Billy by the hand.

‘Come on,’ she says. ‘Let’s have some fun.’

They make their way to the centre of the dance floor and Cathy can feel the eyes of everyone sitting at Rachel’s table on them, but she doesn’t care. It’s been a long time since she’s danced, and the mix of champagne and loud music soon makes her forget any inhibitions. She kicks off her high heels and moves to the music.

‘Think you’re fuckin’ clever pal, eh?’ The drunk from the bar is standing in the middle of the dance floor between her and Billy.

Billy holds his hands out. ‘Listen, mate, I don’t know what your problem is, but I think you’ve got the wrong person.’

‘Think you can just walk away, eh?’ His words are laced with a toxic mix of alcohol and aggression.

Jimmy rushes across the dance floor. ‘Look, just leave it, guys. We’re all here to have a good time.’

'Look at him dancing wi' her in front of everyone.'

'What are you on about?' asks Jimmy.

'No one else is going to touch her now, not after she carried this Fenian's baby. She's damaged goods.'

'Listen, mate,' says Billy. 'I think you've had enough to drink. Why don't you head on home and sleep it off?'

The drunk lifts his glass and images flood Cathy's mind: the jagged edge of a pint glass, the trail of vodka and coke running down the chapel wall, the blood flowing through Thomas's fingers. She's back outside the chapel and the bass player is grinning at her as he pounds the side of his drum. She holds her hands to her ears, but the beat of the drum only gets louder.

Her screams put him off his throw. The glass misses its target and smashes on the dance floor, spraying Jimmy with lager.

'Wee Fenian bastard thinks he can get a girl pregnant and then fuck off.'

'You stupid cunt,' shouts Jimmy. 'This young lad's called Billy. Sound like a fucking Catholic to you, eh? Now clear off before I call the police.'

The drunk stares at the broken glass, and zig-zags back to the bar.

'Jimmy, what's going on?'

'Oh Jesus, Cathy. We were arguing about whether or not Protestants and Catholics should be allowed to marry, and I told him about you getting pregnant and…' Jimmy's voice trails away.

'You told an Orangeman your sister got herself pregnant by a Catholic?'

'We were just talking, and somehow our stories got mixed up and I guess he thought Billy was Thomas.'

'What the fuck gives you the right to talk about me?' The music's stopped and everyone's listening.

'I'm sorry, Cathy, he seemed like a nice guy and we just got chatting. I never thought he'd do anything like that, I mean, he seemed so…'

'Don't tell me. Nice?'

He looks down at himself. 'Shit! I guess I'm gonnae have to pay to get the kilt dry cleaned now.'

She's ready to scream at her brother, but Billy takes hold of her hand.

'Come on,' he says. 'Let's get out of here.'

They go through to a quiet corner in the lounge bar where no one can see them, and Billy orders a couple of drinks at the bar.

Cathy changes the conversation to something safe.

'So what do you do for a living?' she asks.

'I'm an accountant for a legal firm in Edinburgh.'

'Maybe I should have copied you in maths more often.'

He laughs. 'Sounds more impressive than it actually is. What about you? Are you working?'

'I've got a job managing a coffee shop.'

'A manager? Wow, you definitely win on the impressing score.'

'Afraid not, but at least it pays the bills until I get my results.'

'Your results?'

What's she doing? She hasn't even told her parents any of this yet.

'I went back to school last year. Well, night school. And assuming I've passed my exams I start Art College in September.'

'That's amazing.'

'Hardly.'

'No, I mean it. You always said you wanted to study art and now you're actually going for it. You're following your dreams.'

'I wanted to show my daughter, Jenny, that anything's possible.'

'If you don't mind me asking, why didn't you sit your exams in fifth year? You'd already done all of the work.'

She prepares to repeat the well-versed story about morning sickness, but stops. She looks at him, and for the first time ever she tells the truth.

'I was embarrassed,' she says. 'And scared. I guess I

wasn't brave enough to come back and face everyone.'

'I'm sorry.'

'I'm not. Jenny's the best thing that's ever happened to me, and I wouldn't change her for the world. She's smart and beautiful and…' She stops. 'Sorry, just a typical proud mum, I guess.'

'What about Thomas?'

'He wasn't interested. Refused to take my calls after I told him I was pregnant, and even denied the baby was his.'

Billy spills his pint. 'What? He said the baby wasn't his?'

'It's fine. I realised I was never really in love with him. And I didn't need his help in bringing up Jenny. I could do that fine by myself.'

'Have you got a picture of her?'

She opens her purse and takes out a picture of her and Jenny taken at the beach together.

'Look at that gorgeous smile. She looks just like you. I'd love to meet her.'

Cathy smiles. She'd like Jenny to meet him too.

Strawberry Jam

The bungalow is a stone's throw from the beach, and her parents have settled in straight away. Shelves are already crammed full with the ornaments they've collected over the years. The walls are filled with framed photographs of Jimmy and Cathy growing up, and Jenny's paintings cover the fridge door. Anyone looking in would see a home filled with love and would think their lives had been perfect.

Cathy wonders if perhaps this is as perfect as it gets.

She watches Billy, winding his way down the garden path towards the small, pebble beach with her dad and Jimmy. He's dressed all in black, but no longer wears the black eye liner of his youth. He's yet to tell her the whole story about why his mother took her own life, but she's patient and knows he'll tell her when he's ready. All families, it seems, have their secrets.

Mum walks over to the kitchen window and places her hand on Cathy's shoulder.

'He seems nice.'

'Nice?' interrupts Aunt Catherine. 'He's not just bloody nice, he's drop-dead gorgeous.'

Cathy blushes. They've all been invited to lunch at the new house, and today's the first time she's introduced Billy to the family. She opens another loaf of bread and continues buttering.

'Are you sure we need this much food?'

'I don't want anyone going without.'

Jenny comes running into the kitchen. 'Can I help?'

Mum pulls out a kitchen chair. 'Why don't you climb up here and I'll show you how to prepare these strawberries. We're going to be making jam this afternoon.' In the end,

Cathy's mum decided to take the jam jars herself, and restart a family tradition. 'Does that sound fun?'

It obviously does, because Jenny quickly climbs up onto the chair beside her grandmother and leans forward, ready to listen.

'Okay. The first thing we're going to do is wash the fruit nice and gently under the tap, and then we're going to use our thumbnails to remove these green stalks. Much better than using a knife. If you use a knife you'll lose half the fruit.'

Cathy smiles as she remembers the day she and her mum made strawberry jam. She can almost feel her great-grandmother looking down on them. Maybe there's a Heaven after all?

Aunt Catherine interrupts her thoughts.

'I can't believe how quickly she's growing.'

'She starts school after the summer.'

The two women pick up the tray of sandwiches and go through to the dining room to set the table. 'And you'll be starting college,' says Aunt Catherine. 'You're a great role model for her.'

'Thanks, Aunt Catherine. And thanks for coming today. It's nice having you.'

'And it's nice to be invited. I think I have you to thank for that, am I right?'

'When I was growing up I always dreamed of having a big family around the table. I just wish I could convince Mum to visit Gran, but she still refuses.'

'You've done the best you can.' Aunt Catherine stops by the fireplace and picks up a photograph. Cathy recognises it immediately; it's the black-and-white picture of her mum in her grandmother's arms.

'I remember the day this was taken,' Aunt Catherine says.

'You do?'

'It was the first day of the Glasgow Fair. We were going *doon the watter* for the day, and Granny made a picnic of boiled ham, egg sandwiches and flapjacks.'

Mum appears from the kitchen. 'What are you two

talking about?'

'I was telling Cathy about the day we all went to the beach at Saltcoats, and Granny made a picnic big enough to feed everyone on the bus. Do you remember?'

Mum takes the photograph from her sister. 'Don't be daft, I was only a baby.'

'When was the last time you saw her?'

Silence fills the room until Mum finally answers.

'She came to see me in the hospital, just after…' She can't finish the sentence. 'I was so upset after losing the baby that I couldn't think straight.' She places her hand on her stomach. 'She told me it was God's will. That He'd look after my baby now. And I was furious. I told her to stay away and never come near me again.'

Aunt Catherine steps towards her. 'That's understandable; anyone else would say the same.'

'I don't think she ever got over it.'

'What do you mean?'

'She died within the month. It was my fault.'

'Your fault?'

'I pushed her too far. Broke her heart.'

'But by the time the doctors found out what was wrong with her it was too late, and there was nothing they could do. The cancer killed her within a month.'

'Cancer?' Mum falls down into a chair. 'She never said.'

'She didn't tell anyone.'

'No one?'

'We only found out about it after she died. I don't think she wanted anyone to worry.'

Jenny comes skipping through from the kitchen and stops. 'What's wrong with Granny?'

'She's fine, darling,' Cathy says. 'She's remembering some things that happened a long time ago.'

'Did something get broken?'

Aunt Catherine bends down by the chair and holds her sister close.

'I suppose it kind of did,' Cathy says. 'But it's getting fixed now.'

The front door opens and the men stamp their boots on the mat in the porch to knock the sand off.

'It's perishing out there,' Dad says. 'That wind would cut you in two.'

Mum gets up and goes back through to the kitchen and switches on the kettle. Cathy follows and stands beside her.

'I can't imagine what it must be like to lose a baby.'

'It gets easier,' Mum says. 'And I was so lucky to have your big brother and then you.'

Cathy reaches out and holds her mother's hand. 'I love you.'

Mum smiles. 'And I love you, too. More than you'll ever know.'

Cathy looks through the doorway and watches Jenny helping Aunt Catherine set the table. 'I think I do know,' she whispers.

The kettle clicks off and Mum fills the teapot. 'Lunch is almost ready,' she shouts through, and everyone pulls up a chair at the table. Cathy goes back through and sits next to Billy. He smiles at her and she takes this as a sign that her family haven't managed to scare him away.

Mum appears a few minutes later with the teapot and a plate piled high with fruit scones. Everyone leans in and helps themselves. Jenny gives the sandwiches a miss and goes straight to the scones.

The clatter of teacups, and the buzz of chatter, is music to Cathy's ears, and she sits back and listens. This is how she always imagined it would be.

Blue Satin

There's a play park across the road from the nursing home, and she watches Billy sit across from her daughter on the see-saw.

'Higher, higher,' shouts Jenny, and Cathy laughs. The girl has no fear. She knows Billy will be scared to bounce her much higher, but he'll get there. He and Jenny are quickly becoming friends.

She leaves them playing and walks up the ramp to the entrance. As usual, the receptionist greets her with a stern face.

'You're her second visitor today, so she's likely to be tired.'

This suits Cathy fine. She's already decided this will be her last visit, and she doesn't need to stay long. Just long enough.

She makes her own way along the winding corridors until she arrives at the door to her grandmother's room. The old woman is sitting in the armchair in front of the window, and she looks up and smiles.

'Hello, dear, I didn't hear you come home.' She looks at Cathy's clothes and a cloud passes over her face. 'How was school today?'

'It was fine.' Cathy no longer tries to correct her.

'That's nice, dear.'

They watch out of the window together, neither one speaking for several moments.

'Can you find my hairbrush? I've been looking for it everywhere, but you know how forgetful I am. And my hair, it's such a mess. Father Michael is coming to visit this afternoon and I must look my best.'

Cathy goes over to the small table by her grandmother's bed and lifts the silver-plated hairbrush from its place next to the hand mirror. She imagines the set once had pride of place on a dressing table in her grandmother's bedroom.

'It's here, next to your flowers.' She stands behind the chair and gently brushes her grandmother's hair.

'I don't know what's happened to my hair lately. Do you remember when it used to be so thick? Everyone was jealous of it and wished they had a strong head of hair like mine. Now look at it, there's hardly any left.'

Cathy softly brushes the long wisps of grey hair. Her grandmother pats the arm of her chair.

'Here, come and sit beside me. Come and watch the birds.' Cathy sits on the armrest. 'The adults spend all spring collecting twigs and sticks to build the nest, filling it with fleece and anything soft they can find that will help to keep their eggs warm and safe. They never tire, and if the winds come and destroy their work they don't give up, they just start again. And then, when the chicks finally hatch, they spend every moment of daylight going back and forwards to the nest carrying worms to their young. They're quite possibly the most devoted parents in the world, giving everything up for their young. But do you know what happens next?'

Cathy waits to hear.

'Once a baby bird flies the nest it never returns. The parents' job is done.' The old woman closes her eyes. 'So sad.'

Cathy watches her sleep for a few moments before replacing the hairbrush on the bedside table, and then she reaches into her handbag and lifts out a parcel wrapped in tissue paper. She sits down on the edge of the bed and carefully unwraps the china figurine, then folds up the tissue paper and tucks it back into her handbag. She places the Blue Lady on the bedside table beside the silver-plated mirror and hairbrush.

'Watch over her for me,' she whispers, and leans over and kisses her grandmother gently.

She stands to leave, but something is nagging her, a familiarity she can't quite place. She pauses to look at the crystal vase on the bedside table and runs her finger across the small chip on the rim. The spray of bluebells inside is tied with a length of blue satin ribbon and a card is tucked into the bow. She steps closer to read it, and recognises her mum's handwriting.

I forgive you x

Cathy smiles as she closes the door behind her.

THE END

Printed in Great Britain
by Amazon